THE SINGING
OF THE DEAD

G·K
Hall
&Cº.

Also by Dana Stabenow
in Large Print:

So Sure of Death
Fire and Ice

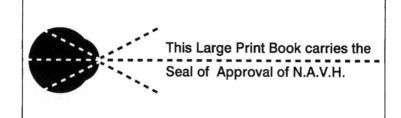

THE SINGING
OF THE DEAD

Dana Stabenow

G.K. Hall & Co. • **Waterville, Maine**

Published in 2001 by arrangement with St. Martin's Press, LLC.

G.K. Hall Large Print Core Series.

The text of this Large Print edition is unabridged.
Other aspects of the book may vary from the original edition.

Set in 16 pt. Plantin by Christina S. Huff.

Printed in the United States on permanent paper.

Library of Congress Cataloging-in-Publication Data

Stabenow, Dana.
    The singing of the dead / Dana Stabenow.
      p. cm.
   ISBN 0-7838-9516-X (lg. print : hc : alk. paper)
   1. Shugak, Kate (Fictitious character) — Fiction. 2. Women
private investigators — Alaska — Fiction. 3. Women in politics
— Fiction. 4. Alaska — Fiction. 5. Large type books.
   I. Title.
PS3569.T1249 S55 2001b
  813'.54—dc21   2001024921

This one is for
Carl Marrs —
high-school heartthrob,
long-time friend,
and
the man who makes things happen.

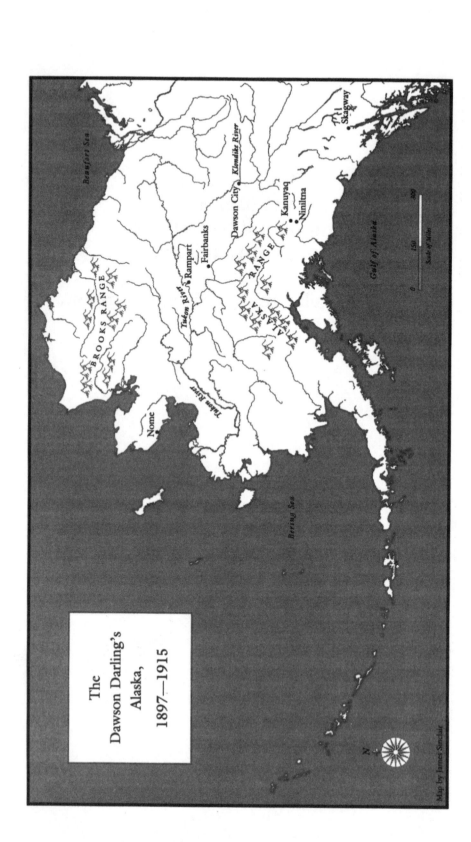

The
Dawson Darling's
Alaska,
1897–1915

Beaufort Sea

BROOKS RANGE

Nome

Yukon River

Rampart
• Fairbanks

Klondike River
Dawson City •

• Kanuyaq
• Niniltna

ALASKA RANGE

Gulf of Alaska

Bering Sea

Skagway •

0   150   300
Scale of Miles

N

Map by James Sinclair

Acknowledgments

My thanks to Angela Fiori of the Alaska State Archives Office in Juneau, who disentombed the documents concerning the inquest into the death of Mrs. William C. Harp, also known as Alice Astor and born Eugenie Antoinette Felicie Roussey, a real-life good-time girl who served as the model for my own protagonist, and whose 1915 murder remains unsolved to this day;

and to Lael Morgan, whose marvelous book, *Good Time Girls of the Alaska-Yukon Gold Rush*, first brought Alice and all of Alaska's early working girls to my attention;

and to Pierre Berton, for writing what remains the best account ever of the Klondike gold rush, *The Klondike Fever.*

The only way I can lose this election is if I'm caught in bed with a dead girl or a live boy.

—Edwin Toms, governor of Louisiana

Birth Announcement
Melun, France
from the *Melun Journal, 13 Juin 1875*

**née à Léon Marc Louis Beauchamp
et femme,
une jeune fille,
Léonie Angélique Josephine Beauchamp**

Dawson City

December 24, 1897

She walked out on stage wrapped in fifty yards of sheer white chiffon, a pair of high-heeled shoes with jeweled buckles, and nothing else.

There was a second of stunned silence in the packed, smoky saloon, before deafening and prolonged approval threatened to raise the roof.

She waited, a faint smile on her face, for the first roar to moderate and pitched her voice to be heard. "Good evening, gentlemen, and welcome to the Double Eagle's Christmas Eve auction." Her voice was husky, with the slight hint of an accent she tried to control. She let her smile broaden, giving it her special up-from-under and through-the-lashes look, part Madonna, part whore, all woman, and added, "I'm the best present you'll ever find under any Christmas tree you ever saw."

This time the stage literally trembled beneath her feet, and she gave a fleeting thought to all the gold dust spilled on the floor this night, now being shaken through the cracks in the floorboards. It wouldn't go to waste. Japanese Jack and Big Ben Bentson

11

would crawl beneath the building the next morning to sweep it up and add it to the night's till. Likely she wouldn't see her percentage, but at the moment she couldn't allow herself to be distracted by that realization.

Big Ben was the owner and Japanese Jack the bartender of the Double Eagle Saloon, doors open around the clock at the corner of Front and York Streets in downtown, boomtown, gold town Dawson City. The Double Eagle was the biggest building in Dawson, the first to add on a second story. It had a long mahogany bar that matched the mahogany wainscoting, eight mahogany gaming tables, a polished brass footrail that matched the brass spittoons, large, elaborate paintings of reclining nudes lit by tiered crystal chandeliers, windows made of stained and beveled glass, and a dozen rooms upstairs with thick carpets, many more mirrors, and furnished with suites in the very latest style. A cleaning staff of a dozen kept the place spotless, although they kept leaving to stake claims in the search for their very own Eldorado.

They were all men, the cleaning staff. Women could do so much better, selling dances for a dollar, a pint of champagne for eighteen dollars, an hour in one of the rooms upstairs for considerably more. Big Ben got fifty cents on the dance dollar, three-quarters of the price of the pint of champagne, and she never told anyone what the split was on the third.

She had been headlining there for the past year, specializing on stage in the Flame Dance that kept two hundred yards of chiffon in the air at one time, and specializing in what one reporter called "the long, juicy waltz" in the clubrooms upstairs. At the end of fourteen months, she had twenty-seven thousand dollars in the bank. She was twenty-two years old, although she admitted to nineteen, and it was her great good fortune that she looked even younger than that. Most laboring men Outside, of any age, were lucky to earn a dollar a day.

She could have kept working for years, especially here, where men outnumbered women six and seven to one, but she had plans, big ones. One more winter, one last contribution to her savings, and she would be ready to move on.

She looked around the room, at the sea of faces upturned to her, and felt that thrill of power she always felt at being the center of so much concentrated male attention. The chiffon began in a spiral of fabric at her ankles and finished up in a graceful swath around her shoulders, the loose end draped over her bare arm. So closely bound together were her feet that she could take only tiny, mincing steps, which was just as well given the height of the heels on her shoes. Big Ben had wanted her to go barefoot, but she knew what the heels did to the line of her legs, displaying their graceful and well-turned length to best advantage, making a man imagine them wrapped around his waist.

One miner had fought his way forward to the edge of the stage. He was ragged, bearded, and smelled as if he hadn't bathed since the river froze over. He looked hungry, and so very hopeless. She gave him a

13

special smile all his own, inviting everything, promising nothing. She was a whore, but she was an honest whore. She gave value for money received, so long as the money was received. That didn't mean she couldn't be kind.

"It's going to be a long, cold, lonely winter, boys," *she said, and there was a shout of agreement. She walked down to center stage and out onto the catwalk thrusting into the room, the little mincing steps causing her breasts to shimmy. The tuft of hair at the vee of her legs was a shadowy patch beneath the chiffon; she put a little extra into the roll of her hips to underline just what was on the auction block that evening.*

"For me, too," *she added, pouting, and they howled like wolves on the scent.*

Again she felt the thrill, a flush of power that began somewhere low in her belly and spread up her torso and down her limbs. A faint film of perspiration broke out over her skin, and a commensurate low, prowling growl rose from the crowd. She performed a three-quarter turn and paused to cast a roguish glance over her right shoulder. "We have a saying here in the north country, boys. I know you've heard it. The odds are good, but the goods are odd." *She winked a violet eye at one man standing in the back, watching her over a glass of Big Ben's watered-down whiskey. He was a regular of hers, a banker who was as conservative with his own money as he was acquisitive of others'. He hadn't liked the idea of his favorite dance partner taking herself out of circulation for the entire winter, but then he wouldn't be bidding this evening, either. She had no doubt that he was ready to take her evening's earnings in deposit, however, just as soon as it had been paid over and Big Ben's commission deducted. She let one hand skim suggestively down her cocked hip, reminding him of what he'd be missing. His eyes narrowed against the smoke of the cigar clenched in his teeth, and she laughed her husky laugh. "I'm sure you'll agree, these goods aren't the least bit odd."*

Big Ben and Japanese Jack had been priming the bidders for the last week with announcements of the auction, including tantalizing hints as to exactly what skills and services the highest bid would bring. The flyers were papered all over town and every claim from Log Cabin to Circle City. The always needy miners of the Klondike had been quivering for days at the prospect of the Dawson Darling dancing the slow, juicy waltz just for them for six exquisite months. No one would notice the dark or the cold with the Dawson Darling waiting in his bed.

"Here I am, gentlemen," she said. "It is generally held that my looks are pleasing and that my figure is good." She waited for the chorus of agreement and was not disappointed. "What are my terms?"

She tossed the end of chiffon over her shoulder, where it trailed behind her like the train of a wedding dress as she walked downstage again. She came to the end of the catwalk and met the fierce blue eyes of a tall blond man standing near the double doors. In a room full of men who wanted her without reservation, the biting intensity of his look gave her pause, but she rallied and held his gaze, a definite challenge in her own. "Terms? Well, I'm willing to sell myself tonight to the highest bidder, to act as his wife in word —" she paused delicately "— and in deed —" there was another roar "— for the next six months, from this night, December 25th, until June 25th."

"Start the bidding!" yelled one man who had yet to look above her chin.

"Yeah, stop talking and start bidding!"

"But," she said, raising one white, well-tended hand without breaking away from the stare of the blue-eyed stranger, "I reserve the right to accept the next lowest bidder if I do not like the highest." Her eyes lingered on the Greek, who looked at her out of cold, acquisitive eyes that held no lust for her personally, only for the money she could make him when he put her to work in one of his cribs.

"You'll like me all right!" someone yelled.

"The man who buys me must provide a decent cabin and a good stock of food. I'll cook for him, and I'll clean for him, and I'll —" she paused "— dance for him," and again, she was forced to wait for the noise to subside.

"But understand this," she said, smile vanishing, and there was something in her expression that caused all comment to pause. "The man who buys me, and lifts a hand to me . . ."

"I'd like to see him try!"

"We'd fix him for you, Darling, never you worry!"

She waited, and then repeated, "The man who buys me, and lifts a hand to me, will have attended his last auction on this earth. Am I understood?"

She looked at the Greek, whose calculating expression didn't change. She waited long enough for her words to sink in, and smiled again to take the sting out of them. "You'll want to know," she said, dropping her voice, "I'm not exactly an iceberg." She turned, contriving so that the top fold of chiffon covering her breasts slipped down to be caught and held, barely, by her nipples.

No one looking at her doubted that she was telling anything but the absolute truth.

Into the dead silence that had fallen, she said softly, "So here I am, boys. Ready and willing." She smiled, making a slow, graceful pirouette, caressing the faces in the crowd with a warm, welcoming gaze. "What are you waiting for?"

Big Ben had a hard time getting them quieted down after that. The bidding opened at one thousand. It was at five thousand thirty seconds later, offered by a squat, dark man with a matted bush of greasy hair and a mouthful of rotted teeth. She repressed a shudder and paraded down the catwalk again. "Now, boys," she said, laughing, "that last bid was only five thousand. Aren't you going any higher than that?" She paused at the edge of the catwalk and put up a hand to the thick auburn hair tucked into a graceful swirl. When the hand came down, it traced an invisible line from throat to breast to waist, to settle again on her hip.

"Sure, girlie," called out an Irishman with a handlebar mustache and a white, wide-brimmed hat, "I was only waiting for the pikers to drop out. Ten thousand, and that's only two days' cleanup on my claim!"

"Twelve!" the squat man growled.

"Thirteen!" yelled a man in spectacles and bib overalls with a watch chain made from gold nuggets hanging from the front pocket.

"Fifteen," the Greek said, his voice as flat as his eyes. There was neither lust nor longing in his tone, only a look that calculated how much she could earn for him when he turned her out. She repressed a shiver, and reminded herself that she had right of first refusal.

"Sixteen," the banker snapped. She met his eyes, startled. He shrugged. She couldn't help it. She laughed. "Sixteen," he repeated, looking faintly irritated at the sound of the word forced out of his own mouth.

"Seventeen," a new voice boomed, and she looked up to lock eyes again with the tall blond man at the door. "Seventeen thousand dollars," he said again. His voice was deep with no trace of an accent. Second-generation Swede, perhaps? He was strong-featured rather than handsome. His face was impassive, but she sensed that he was angry. She didn't know why, but it made her chin come up.

"Seventeen-five!" the squat man snapped. His eyes were little and cruel and calculating.

"Eighteen," the tall man said imperturbably.

The squat man swore in a foreign tongue — Italian? — and said in a rising voice, "Nineteen!"

"Twenty," the Greek said.

Everyone else seemed to have dropped out and were now swiveling their heads among the three bidders. There would be a fight before the evening was

18

over, and they all knew it. Lust and blood lust, thwart one and the other stepped in.

She wasn't going home with the squat man, but she had a good idea of what six months of her exclusive attention was worth, and it was more than twenty thousand dollars. "The last bid stands at twenty thousand, boys," she called out into the silence, and when they turned to look at her, she shook her head once. The single pin, artfully placed, loosened itself, and her hair tumbled down in a thick, gleaming fall to her waist. "I know you can do better than that."

One auburn strand fell forward to curl around her breast. The crowd watched it, mesmerized. Someone gave a little moan. Someone else swore not quite beneath his breath.

"Twenty-five," the man at the door said.

The room fell silent. He drained his mug and said into it, "Oh hell, what's the use of wasting time." He looked up to run a possessive look over the Dawson Darling and said, "Thirty thousand dollars." He smiled, showing strong white teeth. He didn't seem angry anymore.

She couldn't help herself. She had always had a weakness for good teeth. She smiled back.

The Greek said nothing. The banker looked as if he were performing a complicated mental calculation. The squat man saw her smile and screamed, "You crooked, dirty whore!"

He struggled to reach her and was thwarted by the crowd, as protective of her now as they had been avaricious before. With a sudden change of direction, he rushed the man at the door, and this time the crowd parted eagerly before him so that his opponent was grabbed up in a crushing grip immediately. The tall blond man struggled and got one arm free to fend off the hands reaching for his throat.

"I break him! I smash him!" the squat man shouted. His arms quivered, muscles bulging. He lifted the tall man so that his feet dangled a foot above the floor. The tall man went limp. Everyone watching expected to hear the snap of the tall man's spine.

Instead, when the tall man went limp, the squat man's grip slipped, and the tall man smashed him instead, one large-knuckled fist to the squat man's jaw with a force that laid the squat man flat on his back on the floor, out cold. The tall man almost went down with him, then caught his balance and remained on his feet.

There was a roar of approval and a surge toward the tall man, who held up one hand, and such was his presence that they halted. "My name's Sam Halvorsen," he said, looking across the room to where she stood on the catwalk, skin gleaming through white chiffon and auburn curls. "You going to exercise your right to the next lowest bidder, ma'am?"

She could barely speak around the lump in her throat. "No, Sam," she managed to say. "I am not."

The crowd, silent again, parted before him as he walked to the edge of the stage. She didn't have to look down that far and realized he was even taller than she had thought. He held up one hand, and she *placed hers into it, only to give a startled shriek when he yanked on it, jerking her off balance. She fell forward, and he caught her neatly in his arms.*

He grinned at her. "We've only got until June 24th," he said. "Time's a-wasting."

And, carrying her easily, he shouldered his way out of the bar.

1

I'M WATCHING YOU.

"That's all?" Jim Chopin said.

Darlene Shelikof handed over a manila file folder, and Jim leafed through half a dozen similar missives, all on eight-and-a-half-by-eleven-inch sheets of plain white paper folded in thirds.

He held one up to the light and read the watermark out loud. "Esleeck Emco Bond, twenty-five percent cotton content." He lowered his arm. "Available by the ream from Costco at six-seventy-nine a pop, the last time I looked."

"Can't you tell something from the writing?"

He shuffled through the sheets again. "Looks like he — or she — used a black Marksalot."

I KNOW WHERE YOU LIVE.

"The big block printing is an obvious attempt to disguise the handwriting."

ABORTION IS MUDRER.

"I take it Anne's pro-choice?"

"She started the family-planning clinic in Ahtna."

"That does tend to make the nuts fall from the tree." He held the letter closer. "Probably printed with the left hand, or whatever hand is not their hand of choice in writing poison-pen letters. Also, he can't spell."

YOUR HUSBANDS CUTE.

Jim's eyebrows went up. "Is he?"

Darlene smiled. "Not as cute as you are, Jim."

His smile was swift and predatory in return. "Why, Darlene, I didn't know you cared." Even to himself the words sounded formulaic, and tired as well, and he looked back down at the file. Well, hell, he was tired. It had been a long week, what with a rape in Slana, a death by arson in Copper Center, and a suicide by cop in Valdez that he would have missed if he hadn't had to overfly Cordova due to weather and over-night on the Valdez chief of police's couch. He focused on the papers in his hand.

YOUR DAUGHTER WEARS HER SKIRTS TOO

The writer had written in letters so large he or she had run out of room before finishing his or her thought, and had had to add "SHORT" in smaller letters in the lower right-hand corner of the paper.

STAY HOME AND TAKE CARE OF YOUR KIDS.

"Ah, a traditionalist," Jim said.

The seventh letter was more direct. RUN FOR SENATOR AND ILL KILL YOU.

He held it up so she could read it. "This the one that made you bring them all in?"

She nodded. "They've been coming in one at a

time ever since she announced. Then last week, we got two."

"All date-stamped except the first one, and you kept the envelope for that one, too. Smart," Jim said. "We appreciate smart in law enforcement."

She smiled again.

He examined the envelopes, all of them stapled to the backs of the letters. "All postmarked Ahtna. Well, I'll give the post office there a call. You never know, somebody might have noticed something."

"You don't sound very optimistic."

"I'm not. The Ahtna post office handles all the mail that goes into and comes out of the Park. That's, what, three thousand people, a little less? And these are pretty anonymous letters, Darlene."

"What about the handwriting? Isn't there an expert you can send them to, figure out who wrote them?"

"Sure, and I will," he said, stuffing them into an evidence bag. "Today. But unless and until the state crime lab already has a sample of the perp's writing to compare them to, we're SOL as far as identifying the writer."

"What about fingerprints?"

He looked at her. What he wanted to say was, "You've been watching too much television," but what he said instead, patiently, was, "Who opened these?"

"The candidate, the first one." She thought.

24

"The rest were opened by volunteers, I think. Oh."

"Right. And then they got passed up or down the food chain to you, and then your assistant had to file them. There are probably ten sets of fingerprints on every letter, and we can't even be sure that every letter has the same set of ten." He sealed the bag. "Have you fingerprinted your staff?"

An expression of revulsion crossed her face. It was a very nice face otherwise, black eyes set in a broad, flat face with a tiny pug nose and a merry mouth, hair in a permed black frizz standing out around it. She was thick through the body and short, although her erect posture made her seem taller. She carried weight, did Darlene Shelikof, and not necessarily just body weight. Her jeans were faded but clean, the blazer over it a conservative navy blue, the shirt beneath a paler blue and open at the throat. Ivory dangled from her ears and adorned her lapel and both wrists.

She had been leaning forward, just a little, and now she leaned back, just a little, not enough to give the impression she was in anyway relaxed. "What about protection?"

"What about it?"

For the first time she allowed herself to look angry. He admired her control. "How much can you give us?"

"Darlene, you worked for the AG. You know exactly how much protection we can give you."

Her mouth thinned. "The threats are escalating, in delivery and in degree."

"Yes."

"Chances are he — or she — will try to make contact."

"Chances are he — or she — already has."

"What do you mean?"

He shrugged. "How long has Anne been on the campaign trail? She announced in June, didn't she?"

"Yes."

"What day in June?"

"The sixteenth."

"The first of those envelopes is dated June twenty-seventh."

She thought about it. "So he's been following her since the beginning?"

"That'd be my guess. She's been doing the usual things politicians do, going to church in Chitina, walking the bars in Cordova, shaking hands and kissing babies and promising to throw the bums out, like they all do." Darlene looked indignant. He waved away whatever comment she had been about to make about her candidate being all new and improved and completely different. He'd been an Alaska state trooper for going on twenty years; he'd seen a lot of political campaigns whistle-stop through; he had seen every single candidate of every political party (and in Alaska there were about seventeen separate and distinct political parties with more springing up every year), and he had seen every successful candidate as a first order of Juneau business cuddle up with the lobbyist with the most money to spend. Call him a cynic, but he didn't see anything changing just because this candidate was a woman and a Native and homegrown.

Juneau seemed to have that inevitable and invariable effect on elected officials, he reflected. Or maybe it was just political office everywhere, because the nation as a whole seemed to be in about the same shape. Substitute Washington, D.C. for Juneau and what did you get? Bill Clinton for president. Jesus. It wasn't that Clinton was a rounder that bothered him so much, it was that he'd been so awful goddamn inept at it. If you're going to philander, he thought now, for crissake do it with some style.

"So we have to wait until he takes a shot at her before you'll do anything?" Darlene said.

"It's a big step from writing a nasty letter to someone popping off with a thirty-ought-six." He held up a hand to forestall further commentary. "What I will do is put the word out to all the local law enforcement agencies that your candidate's getting hate mail, that it's personal, and, yes, that it is increasing in amount and degree."

She gave an impatient snort. "What's that get us?"

He was starting to get a little annoyed. "Nothing, if you don't call ahead to let the local agencies know when you'll be there."

27

She glared, and he sighed to himself. No point in getting the person who was very probably going to sit at the right hand of the next senator from District 41 mad at him. "I'll e-mail all the troopers in the area, and all the police chiefs. I'll give you a list of names and numbers, and I'll tell them you'll call when you know your candidate will be speaking in their jurisdiction. You need to call every time, Darlene," he said with quiet force. "They can't plan to look out for you if they don't know you're coming. They've got jobs, full-time ones, already." He thought about the suicide by cop in Valdez. "Full-time jobs," he repeated. "You releasing this information to the press?" She hesitated, and he groaned. "Don't tell me you think that this is going to get her the sympathy vote?"

She had the grace to flush.

"All you'll do is get him off," he warned. "That's what he wants, attention, film at eleven."

"Or she," she reminded him.

He looked at her in sudden suspicion. She read his thought before he could speak it out loud. "Fuck you, Chopin," she said, her voice rising.

"Okay," he said, patting the air. "Okay. Sorry. Just a thought, a dumb one, I admit, but —"

"As if I would — as if Anne would — just fuck you, Chopin!" She shot to her feet and marched to the door. Hand on the knob, she turned and said, spitting the words like knives, "Thanks for nothing. If — *when* Anne gets into office, if this

28

asshole doesn't kill her first, we'll remember this when it comes time to look at the budget for the Department of Public Safety. I'd say trooper salaries and step rates for Bush posts are way overdue for review."

"Darlene!"

His voice, cracking like a whip, stopped her halfway out the door. She looked back, very ready to escalate hostilities.

"If you're that worried, if you really think Anne's in danger . . ."

She didn't move. "What?"

"What about hiring security for the campaign?"

"You mean like guards?"

"I mean like one guard." The one he was thinking of wouldn't need any help.

She let go of the handle, and the door hissed closed on its hydraulic hinge. "You suggesting someone in particular?"

He just looked at her and, being a well-trained law enforcement professional of intensive and lengthy experience, was able to pinpoint the exact moment when realization dawned.

Also because she said, "Oh fuck, no."

"She knows the Park," Jim said. "Who she isn't related to she's drinking buddies with." He thought of Amanda and Chick, Bobby and Dinah, Bernie. Old Sam, the quintessential Alaskan old fart, Auntie Vi, the quintessential Alaskan old fartette. Dan O'Brien, the only national-park ranger in Alaska to survive the change of federal administrations and gain the affection if not the actual respect of Park rats. George Perry the air taxi pilot, next to whom Jim had stood on that airstrip south of Denali last September. He banished that memory the next instant, or told himself he had. "If she was a drinking kind of woman, that is."

"Not her."

"She's probably related to Anne, come to that."

Darlene's voice rose. "Not her, Jim."

He was surprised at her vehemence. "Who else?" he said. "She's a teetotaler. She a local. She's a Native. She has a reputation —"

"Oh yeah, she's got a reputation, all right, a well-deserved one."

"Took the words right out of my mouth." Curious, the curse of any good cop, he went fishing. "You sound like you know her."

She opened her mouth, met his eyes, and closed it again. "I knew her," she said at last.

He waited hopefully. No weapon in the cop's arsenal worked better than the expectant silence.

"We went to school together."

He raised his eyebrows. "I didn't know you were from Niniltna."

"In Fairbanks. UAF."

He gave a neutral kind of grunt, and waited again. In the ensuing stony silence, he wondered why the feud. If one person hating a second person who, so far as Jim knew, was indifferent to the first person's existence, could be called a feud. Did Kate crib from Darlene's test? Wear

Darlene's favorite sweater without permission? Steal Darlene's boyfriend? It irritated him that he would like to know, to add to his fund of Kate Shugak lore. Said irritation moved him to say, "Just a suggestion."

"A bad one," she snapped.

"No," he said, suddenly weary. "Just a suggestion."

2

"Sit still," Dinah said, yanking Kate's head around by a fistful of hair.

"Ouch!" Kate, wedged into Katya's high chair, muttered something beneath her breath.

"Stop whining," Dinah said, no sympathy in face or voice. "It wasn't my idea to give you a crew cut."

"It's not a crew cut."

"It might as well be. Why don't you let it grow out again?"

Trooper Chopper Jim Chopin, watching from where he leaned against the wall with his arms folded, saw a shadow pass across Kate's face.

Kate looked up and met his eyes. She felt cold metal slide between her nape and her hair, heard the crunch of shears. Her skin prickled. "I like it short," she said.

Something in her voice kept Dinah from pursuing the subject. "Well, if you're going to keep it this short, you're going to need a trim once a month. If you're going to get a trim once a month, you have to sit still for it." Dinah paused, hand holding scissors the way Van Gogh might have held his brush in a pause between stars, and looked Kate over with a critical frown.

"You look like you're putting the final touches to a masterpiece that's going to sell to Bill Gates," Jim said, echoing Kate's thought in a manner she found more than a little eerie. "It's just a haircut."

Dinah extended the scissors. "You want to give it a try?"

He held up both hands, palms out. "No way. I like living."

"Then put a lid on it."

"Yes, ma'am." Jim shifted, and Kate saw the gleam of a shield. As usual, Jim was immaculately turned out in the blue-and-gold uniform of his service. As usual, he looked like a recruitment poster. Not as usual, his presence sent a definite ripple of unease up her spine. She looked away.

A pillar ran through the center of the house, around which a built-in counter supported a variety of electronic gadgets, including radios, VCRs, tape decks, a turntable, monitors both television and computer, music in vinyl, cassette, and CD format, and boxes of parts and tools. It should have been a mess, but it was very well organized, with hooks on the pillar to hang the tools from and sets of Rubbermaid drawers beneath the counter to store parts in. Lines to the satellite dish and the antennas mounted on the one-hundred-twelve-foot tower outside snaked up the pillar and disappeared through the roof.

At the console in the center of this mess, Bobby flicked a few switches. There was some kind of electronic whine and into the mike Bobby said, "Okay, folks, it's show time. Bobby's all talk, all the time, when it isn't all music all the time, one and only Park Air. Coming to you live once a month, or whenever I feel like broadcasting a little pirate air. Lately, I've been feeling like it a lot. That's right, it's election season again, god help us. In less than two months we elect a new president and reelect our congressman-for-life. And with me tonight is one of the candidates for the office of state senator from District 41. Yes, all you Park rats and ratettes, that's your very own election district. Remember, if you don't vote, you can't bitch, and what's a democracy without bitching?" He adjusted the fuzzy black microphone hanging from the articulated metal arm. "Anne Gordaoff, how the hell are you?"

"I'm fine, Bobby. Thanks for having me on the show."

"Couldn't hardly not, seeing as how you're going up against my boy, Pete Heiman. What's wrong with him? He's been in, what, two terms now? What can you do that he can't do better with the benefit of experience and seniority?"

Anne Gordaoff smiled. "Gee, Bobby, according to you, everybody who isn't one of the good old boys ought to just fold their tents and steal away by dark of night."

Anne Gordaoff's campaign manager stood two feet away, a sheaf of paperwork cradled in one arm, a pencil tucked behind one ear and another in her hand, alert, attentive, following every word of the discussion as if it were being broadcast live on *60 Minutes.*

"Not in this lifetime," Kate said.

"Quit muttering," Dinah said. A judicious snip, one more, and she stood back with the air of Hercules finishing up his twelfth labor. Kate, no less relieved, extricated herself from the high chair and removed the dishcloth from round her neck.

Dinah put the shears away and scooped up her daughter in the same motion, a plump little coffee-with-cream-colored toddler with tight black curls and a broad, merry grin exactly like her father's. Little of Dinah's ethereal blondness had been reproduced in her daughter, if you didn't count the blue, blue eyes. Kate tried to remember what she'd learned about recessive genes in high school biology, and failed. Didn't matter; whatever the ingredients, the result was superb.

"Kate," Jim said.

"Not in this lifetime," she repeated, watching Dinah and Katya blow bubbles at each other, an oasis of tranquility in the crowded, noisy house.

"Her boss needs help. Your kind of help."

"Let her hire a rent-a-cop."

"You know the Park the way a rent-a-cop from Anchorage never would."

"You sleeping with her, Jim? You afraid you're going to lose your latest main squeeze?"

He looked at this short, lithe woman with the golden skin, the eyes like hazel almonds, the neat cap of shining black hair, and the old white scar across her throat, and felt an unfamiliar sensation rise up in his chest. He investigated. Anger. Fury, maybe. Might even have been rage. "No," he said, his voice clipped. "I'm not sleeping with her."

"Sorry," Kate said, not sounding sorry at all. "Given past history, it was a logical assumption."

Darlene must have heard her, or at least the tone of Kate's voice had registered, because she raised her head to look at Kate. Their gazes met and held, identical impassive stares that gave nothing away to curious onlookers, of which there were more than one.

Darlene looked away first. "Not in this lifetime," Kate said for the third time. "Dinah, you got any coffee made?"

"Sure."

The immense A-frame on the bank of Squaw Candy Creek was lit up like a Christmas tree, and cars and trucks spilled over from the yard across the little wooden bridge and down both sides of the creek. Inside, the kitchen table had been extended with sawhorses and a piece of plywood, the whole covered by a series of dis-

36

posable tablecloths in a garish red-and-blue plaid pattern.

Bobby didn't like doors so there were only two: one to the outside and one to the bathroom. Both were wider than normal doors, and the countertops and tables were low to the ground, as was all the furniture, all the better for someone who'd lost both legs below the knee in Vietnam and who now relied on a wheelchair for locomotion. Well, two, actually, a new racing model for when he was sober and a twenty-year-old clunker for when he was hung over.

"How are you, Kate?" Dinah said, keen eyes examining Kate for signs of wear and tear. Katya fussed and Dinah gave her a carrot to gnaw on.

"I'm okay, Dinah," Kate said, a little wearily. "Really, I'm okay." The inspection continued in silence, with the addition of one upwardly mobile eyebrow. "All right," she said. "I miss him, is that what you want to hear? I miss him like hell. I'll always miss him. But almost the last thing he said to me was that life goes on."

"Jack is dead," Jim had said. "You aren't." She did not look over her shoulder to see if he had heard her. "I'm home now." She looked at Dinah and tried to smile. "It would help a great deal if my friends didn't treat me like I'm about to break."

"You were."

"I'm not now."

Dinah, a slender blonde who was about as

37

white as Bobby was black, seemed to make up her mind. "Fine," she said. "Hey, kid."

Johnny appeared at her elbow to regard the spread on the extended table with wide eyes. There was caribou sausage, smoked fish, moose steaks, deer stew, blood stew, mulligan stew, fry bread, zucchini bread, homemade bread, cranberry bread, date nut bread, banana bread, raisin bread, macaroni salad, carrot salad, potato salad, three-bean salad, pickles dill and sweet, olives black and green, cubed cheeses cheddar and jack, chocolate cake, pineapple upside-down cake, apple and cherry and Boston cream pies. And that was just on the table. It didn't include the counters full of chips and dips overflowing into the living room.

"Help yourself," Dinah said, and Johnny said "You bet," and picked up a paper plate and a plastic fork to wade in with the infinite appetite of the fourteen-year old.

"Okay, let's get a little serious," Kate heard Bobby say, and turned to watch.

"All right," Anne Gordaoff said, who never looked anything less than.

"I have a friend, Mary Ellen. She's Native."

Mary Ellen Chignik, Kate thought, a Native rights activist who spent more time in Juneau picketing than the legislature did in session. She lived and breathed confrontation.

"She's this amazing woman, really smart, really informed, knows a lot about Native culture and history."

Knows a lot about Athabascan culture and history, Kate thought.

"We were at the Roadhouse a while back. She was talking about the Black Death, an influenza epidemic that was brought to Alaska by gold miners and reduced the Native population on the Y-K Delta literally by one-third."

"Yes."

"Turns out the Black Death Mary Ellen's talking about hit in 1919. I said, 'Mary Ellen, that was the influenza pandemic that hit the whole planet after World War I. Over twenty-one million people died, not just Alaskans.'" Bobby paused. "She was angry with me. This is a smart woman, well-educated, a leader. But she didn't want to hear that the Black Death hit everywhere, all over the planet. The Black Death was personal. The Black Death was brought to her tribe by Anglos, just one of many instances of white wrongdoing in Alaska. That's the way she was told it, that's the way she sees it, and that's the way she's going to tell it to her children."

After a moment of dead air, Anne said, "What's your question, Bobby?"

"Hell, I don't know," he said, frowning. "I guess, why? Why was that her reaction? And why was she angry when I told her the truth about the Black Death?"

Maybe it was the late hour. Maybe Anne Gordaoff had had a long day and a longer week, and the campaign trail was taking its toll.

Maybe she had been infected with Park Air's no-bullshit policy and made a snap decision to abandon discretion. Whatever the reason, her answer was blunt. "Political correctness sucks."

Everybody blinked, including Bobby. "Excuse me?"

"Family pride is going to kill all of us if we're not careful."

The A-frame's large single room was crowded with Park residents, from Old Sam Dementieff to Billy Mike to Mac Devlin to Aunties Vi and Joy to Dan O'Brian. Even Bernie Koslowski was there, turning the Roadhouse over to the inmates for the evening. Native, white, fisherman, ranger, homesteader, miner, hunter, trapper, they were all listening to Anne Gordaoff. Behind her, Darlene looked, for a change, indecisive, as if she couldn't decide whether to interrupt or let her candidate rip. In the end, it was obvious that Anne was on a tear and there was no stopping her, and Darlene was smart enough not to try.

"For a long time," Anne said, leaning forward and fixing Bobby with an intense gaze, as if she were talking only to him but pitching her voice so that everyone could hear, "for hundreds of years, the Alaska Natives and the Native Americans were subject races, subject to the will of a more powerful nation. Then, along about the Sixties, America woke up to the fact that the Native American population had dropped to less than, what, I think it was something like a

40

hundredth of what it had been before Columbus hauled his ass across the pond, and suddenly everybody's wringing their hands and bemoaning their brown brothers' fate, damning Americans for the closet Nazis they were, and elevating the Native to the status of sainthood." Her mouth pulled into a wry expression. "All of a sudden, the Native way of life is perfect, or was, before the big bad Western Europeans came along and ruined everything."

"And it wasn't," Bobby said.

"What's perfect? I know an Inupiaq elder from Barrow. She was telling me stories about life up there, about whale hunting, and the big dance festival they've got every winter, and the polar bears coming in off the ice so you have to be careful before you go outside so you don't run into one." She paused. "The one thing I remember most vividly is when she told me about the whale hunting, the strikes, the landings, the town getting together to butcher the whale and cut up the maqtaq. It's a delicacy now, she told me, not a staple, and then she looks at me and she says" — Anne's voice slowed and an almost imperceptible rhythm began to shape her words — " 'In olden days,' that woman says, 'we hunt to eat. Now we have stores. We buy food. Some years we get a whale; some years we don't. When we get a whale, that's a good thing for the people. It brings us together; it reminds us of the olden days.'

"And then," Anne said, "and then she

dropped her voice so no one else could hear her say it, and then she told me, 'I lived in olden days. Olden days was not so good. Nowadays is better, because everybody has enough to eat.' "

Bobby, for probably the only time in his life, was at a loss for words.

"If it really was the olden days," Anne said, "and the town didn't get its whale, it became the duty of the eldest and most useless of the tribe to walk out on the ice as far as they could and stay there until they died, of starvation or exposure, whatever came first."

"I thought that was just an old fairy tale," Bobby said.

"Not unless real people die in fairy tales," Anne said. "And, yes, baby girls born to a tribe living on the edge of starvation were put to death as another useless mouth to feed too." With deliberate intent, she looked at Dinah, still holding Katya on her hip. "You know who had to kill them?"

"No." But he did.

"Their mothers."

There was another moment of dead air. "I'm not saying there weren't real wrongs perpetrated against Alaska Natives and Native Americans," Anne said. "Even Disney couldn't pretty up what turned out to be genocide. But what I really hate is the mythology that seems to be growing up around this new awareness of Native life. Nobody talks now about the wars fought between tribes years ago, even though you can see examples of the armor the warriors wore into battle in museums, but you call your friend Mary Ellen the Athabascan an Eskimo one time and see what she says. And we, the Native peoples, a lot of us are buying into it, into the myth. Everything was wonderful then, everything's lousy now, and it's all the Anglos' fault. Baloney. All that attitude does is nourish resentment, perpetuate stereotypes, and fund political campaigns. Turns us into victims. I am not in anyway, shape, or form a victim. Rousseau has a lot to answer for."

"Who?"

"Jean Jacques Rousseau, a French philosopher back in whenever, precolonial days. Inflicted the idea of the natural man or the noble savage on the rest of the world. I had to study him in Humanities at college, and I'll tell you right now I never read such nonsense in my life. There's nothing noble about hunger. Hunger is a stronger force than either fear or sex. It always, always takes priority. In the olden days, like my friend in Barrow knows only too well, the bottom line was you did what you had to for the tribe as a whole to survive, and if that included killing off the elderly when they became less of an asset and more of a liability or killing a baby because you couldn't feed it, that's what you did. It's not about humanity or compassion then, it's about survival. It's easy to idealize that time retrospectively, when you're full."

There was a brief silence. "Don't be shy,

Anne," Bobby said. "Tell us what you really think."

Anne stared at him for a moment, and surprised everyone by bursting out laughing. There was a palpable lessening of tension in the room. "I don't know where all that came from. I must be tired." She looked up when Darlene put a hand on her shoulder and gave her a reassuring smile.

"Okay, folks, you heard it here first. Anne Gordaoff is not a victim," Bobby said into the microphone. "This is Park Air, taking you now to the studios of beautiful downtown Detroit, with some music to raise campaign funds by." He put in a CD and pushed a few buttons, and the Temptations singing "Ain't Too Proud to Beg" rocked out of the quadraphonic speakers in full surround sound.

"Turn it down, Clark!" Dinah yelled, and he did, marginally, and caught sight of Kate, standing stock-still and staring at Anne Gordaoff with an odd expression on her face. "Shugak!" The wheelchair rolled forward like it was jet-propelled, and Kate emerged from her trance in time to sidestep the wheels and save her toes, only to be yanked into Bobby's lap and thoroughly kissed. She disengaged herself with difficulty, after which Mutt reared up to pay Bobby her respects, which left him with a very wet face. "Goddamn!" he bellowed again. "You let the fucking wolf back in the house! I keep telling you no fucking wolves in the house!"

Mutt, paws on the arms of his wheelchair, laughed down at him lupinely, not in the least alarmed at his tone of voice. He gave her an affectionate cuff and rolled over to the wood box, where there was always a Jurassic anklebone or two to keep the wolves at bay. "How the hell are you, Shugak?" Bobby said, dark eyes examining her for nicks and scratches.

"I'm fine," Kate said. "Really."

Easier to convince than his wife, or maybe just wanting it to be true, he accepted this. "Well, join the damn party! Gimmee some beer, woman!"

"Excuse me a minute," Kate said, and threaded through the crowd surrounding Darlene and Anne. She waited for Darlene to notice her, and when she didn't, nudged her ungently in the ribs.

"Hey," Darlene said, turning. "Oh."

"I hear you're looking for my kind of help," Kate said.

The door opened and another group of people jammed into the house. The noise jumped seven or eight decibels, and then a figure moving very fast shot around the pillar and hit the back door at a dead run. The screen door slammed sharply in its wake.

"Johnny!" The voice, high-pitched and furious, bounced off the ceiling. "Get back here!"

"I'll get in touch tomorrow," Kate said, and beneath Darlene's astonished eye hit the floor and was under the counter that encircled the central pillar of electronic equipment. She scrabbled around the pillar, the snake's nest of

45

cables slowing her down.

There was the whisk of rubber tires on wood. "And who might you be, madam?"

"I'm Johnny Morgan's mother, and I just saw him run out the back door. Let me by! Johnny! Come back here right now!"

There was a brief scuffle, followed by an "Oof!" as someone came up against a solid wall of chest.

"Do you have any identification, ma'am?" said Jim Chopin.

There was the shuffle of a lot of feet, and Kate pictured everyone crowding around to watch, forming a barrier between Jane Morgan and the back door. One for Rats, Rats for All, she thought, and grinned in spite of the situation. She shook off a piece of coaxial cable determined to keep her beneath that counter forever and made a break for the door. Bodies parted and closed in behind her. She pushed open the screen door. It squeaked, loudly.

"Who's that? Johnny? Johnny, is that you? Get over here, right now! Johnny?"

"Hey, lady, watch who you're shoving," Old Sam Dementieff growled.

"Relax, jeeze, have a beer," Mac Devlin said. "You busy tonight, honey?"

"Ayah," said Auntie Vi, "never mind these men, they just want to get you drunk and take advantage. Have some iced tea. We have lemon."

"I don't want any beer or any iced tea! I want my son! Now let me through!"

Kate slipped outside, dodged the northwest

leg of the antenna tower, and trotted through the vehicles parked in the yard, over the bridge and down the road to where her truck was parked. Johnny's face gleamed white in the shadows beneath the dashboard.

Kate climbed in and started the engine. "You'll have to talk to her sometime, Johnny."

"Just get us out of here, okay?"

Kate, in the full awareness that she was breaking half a dozen statutes and probably a couple of federal laws while she was at it, put the truck in gear and headed down the road to her homestead.

3

Paula Pawlowski was a writer.

She had been rewriting the first four chapters of her novel for going on eleven years now. When she got them perfect, she was going to send it to Simon and Schuster, whose address she had found in a copy of the 1987 edition of *Writer's Market* on the shelf at the Salvation Army.

She'd recently given some thought to letting Hollywood have first crack. Steven Spielberg was an obvious first choice there, although she worried that he had a dangerous predilection toward the saccharine. He'd found ways to end movies on racism, the Holocaust, and World War II on an upbeat note, which said a lot for his abilities as a filmmaker but not much for the accuracy of his vision. Still, she owed him the right of first refusal for *ET*. Honor among artists, she thought, coining a phrase.

She stretched and rolled her head back, left, forward, right. Microfilm was a wonderful invention, no doubt, but watching it spool past for more than two hours at a time tended to make her muscles cramp up. Not to mention making her seasick.

Seated at a reader in the Fairbanks library, she compared the stack of microfilmed and microfiched issues of the *Anchorage Daily News*, the *Anchorage Times*, the *Fairbanks Daily News-Miner*, the *Alaska Journal of Commerce*, and various public records going back sixty years that she had skimmed through with the stack that she hadn't, and sighed.

Her day job was also that of a writer, of technical reports, grant proposals, position papers for political candidates of any party, and press releases for corporations too small to have their own PR departments. She was a good writer and better still, she was fast, but even so, sometimes there just weren't enough writing jobs to make the payment on the Airstream trailer parked on a weedy five acres that was all her mother had left her when she died of smoke inhalation in another trailer parked on that same lot five years before. The Airstream had a built-in double bed, a tiny kitchen, and an even tinier bathroom, but it had running water, at least in the summertime, and in the Park, where homes, of any kind, from a one-room, two-by-four tarpaper shack to a split-level ranch brought in premium prices, she was lucky and she knew it. True, January's heating bill sometimes hit three hundred dollars, but at least it was better than her friend Lillian, who had moved in with a man she didn't even like that much just for a warm place to stay.

She who moves fastest moves alone, Paula thought to herself, and bent back over the reader. Her job was to look at the incumbent's family history going back as far as there was any in Alaska. "Don't get ridiculous about it," Darlene had said. "Don't go back to the Russians or anything, but take a look, see what pops up. If you spot anything with potential, let me know."

For "anything with potential," read any nasty surprises Anne Gordaoff could attack Peter Heiman on, like a secret abortion, a messy divorce, an unacknowledged child, an indiscreet affair, a lie on a Permanent Fund Dividend application, a too-large and too-obvious quid pro quo from a lobbyist anytime during the past eight years Heiman had been in office.

At the last minute, as Darlene was leaving, the campaign manager had stopped in the doorway of the Airstream and added, "Look up the Gordaoff family history while you're at it, too." She saw Paula's raised eyebrow. "If there's anything to find, you find it first."

Paula had shrugged. "Okay." She'd worked for Darlene Shelikof before, on other campaigns, on political action committees, on lawsuits. She was a good researcher, and she was for hire. One thing about this campaign was that it was extremely well funded. Peter Heiman had tried to hire her, and Darlene had outbid him, which had to be the first time that had happened to an Alaskan Republican since the early days of the pipeline.

Speaking of Peter Heiman — she sighed and bent over the reader once more. Peter Heiman had been elected senator from District 41 eight years before and had been returned to office four years after that with minimal opposition. That was before the legislature and the governor had pissed off everyone in rural Alaska by ignoring, avoiding, bullshitting, and otherwise bypassing the hot-button issue of subsistence to the extent that they had managed to overturn a publicly mandated demand to submit the issue to a general vote. The legislature's passive resistance on the issue of subsistence was what had put sovereignty on the map as an Alaska Native issue; if their own state government couldn't or wouldn't give them preference to hunt and fish, particularly in times of game shortages, they'd sidestep it and appeal to the federal government for the authority to oversee their own lands and waters, and take *that*, Juneau.

The sting was all the sharper since the Native community had put the current governor and half the legislature in office, with endorsements from most of the Native regional corporations and a little matter of two hundred fifty-three votes from the tiny — and closest to the International Date Line — Native community of St. Martha's and therefore the last to be counted after voting day.

Two days later the hottest selling item in St. Martha's was a T-shirt, the front of which read, "ST. MARTHA'S — THE LITTLE TOWN THAT ELECTS GOVERNORS!" Eighteen months later the hottest selling item in St. Martha's was that same T-shirt, the back of which now read, "AND AREN'T WE ASHAMED OF OURSELVES."

All of which only went toward making Anne Gordaoff's chances of attaining office better than even.

But Peter Heiman's credentials were impeccable; he was a card-carrying Alaskan old fart. His grandfather had come north with the U.S. Department of Agriculture right after the Alaska Purchase. ("Seven cents an acre! Did we take the Russians to the cleaners or what?" Peter Heiman was reported to quote his grandfather as saying in a profile in 1986, front page, Metro section, *News*. Paula noted that Peter's grandfather had died in 1943, and Peter hadn't been born until 1947.) The first Peter Heiman had been a farmer, sent to Alaska to oversee operations at five experimental farms (Homer, Anchorage, Fairbanks, Rampart, and Sitka) to see what would grow in Alaska and what would not. He had some success with crab apples, and even more with a gold miner's sister who shot the Lake Bennett rapids in 1898 along with the rest of the stampeders. At least she said she was his sister, and her alleged brother backed her up, but with a lot of those old gals you never knew.

Once she was married, Elizabeth Heiman settled into a life of quiet and what looked to Paula like stiflingly dull respectability.

Peter Heiman's father, the second of that name in Alaska and Elizabeth and Peter's only child, had been, in turn, a gold miner, a big-game guide, a Bush pilot, a Bristol Bay fisherman back when the Bristol Bay fleet fished under sail, had maintained radios for the U.S. Navy on the Aleutian Chain, and when the Japanese invaded, joined the Alaska Scouts, also known as Castner's Cutthroats, although as the second Peter Heiman was fond of saying after the war was over, Lieutenant Castner had disliked the name. They took the islands of Attu and Kiska back from the Japanese, during which action the second Peter Heiman was wounded and for which he was later awarded a Purple Heart by no less than Major General Simon Bolivar Buckner, Jr., Alaska Defense Commander, Himself. There was a grainy black and white photograph (*Alaska* Magazine, "Forty Years After," May/June 1984) with the second Peter Heiman looking gaunt and tired, standing in a line of other soldiers, and trying his best to throw out a negligible chest for General Buckner to pin his decoration on. He had the same narrow face, the same lantern jaw, and the same thick thatch of coarse dark hair as his father did in the sepia photograph of his parent's wedding (*Alaska Life* Magazine, "Centennial Tales," September 1967).

After the war, the second Peter Heiman left Fairbanks for the Park and homesteaded eighty acres of land, established a profitable truck farm, and started a hauling business on the Kanuyaq River Highway, moving freight between the port of Valdez and the interior market town of Ahtna. Eventually he expanded operations to include Fairbanks and Anchorage.

It was to Ahtna he brought his bride in 1946, an Isabella Chapman, daughter of a Fairbanks merchant. They had two sons, a third Peter in 1947 and then Charles in 1949.

Peter was the first of the Peter Heimans to go to college, the University of Alaska. He was a National Merit Scholar (UAF student newspaper *Polar Star*, February 1969), and then he left school to join the U.S. Army and do one tour in Vietnam. He was back in Alaska by Christmas 1972, back in school in 1974, and had his bachelor's degree in May 1975 (list of UAF graduates in May twentieth issue of the *Fairbanks Daily News-Miner*).

Charles followed his brother to Vietnam and didn't come back. Obituary, November 24, 1971, *Ahtna Tribune, Anchorage Times, Fairbanks Daily News-Miner.* Two generations of war heroes and one war tragedy, Paula thought. Bad luck on the parents, and on Peter the Third, too, if he and Charles had been close.

It seemed they had been. The third Peter Heiman went into business with his father's backing, formed a trucking company, and made out like a bandit during the last half of the '70s and the first half of the '80s, back when oil was king. Every other load into Prudhoe Bay was a Heiman Trucking Kenilworth tractor-trailer ("Teamsters in Alaska," CBS *60 Minutes*, 1976). The third Peter had expanded into services, a sort of Kelly Girls for contract employees like plumbers, welders, carpenters, and electricians, so that he was sitting pretty when the bust came in the mid-'80s and the oil companies started looking around for contract employees who worked by the hour and didn't come with all those expensive benefits attached, like health and retirement and investment plans.

In the fullness of time Peter Heiman married, a roustabout he met overnighting at Galbraith Lake on a trip to Prudhoe. She was a big woman, big-haired and big-hipped and big-busted, and she lasted nearly two years (notice of divorce of Peter A. and Shirley F. Heiman, *Ahtna Tribune, Anchorage Times, Anchorage Daily News-Miner, Fairbanks Daily News*, October 1977). The third Peter married again, a flight attendant with Wien Air Alaska he met on a trip to Anchorage to pick up a new rig. Another blonde, shorter, skinnier, and more fertile, Cindy F. Heiman divorced her husband when she caught him in bed with a third blonde in 1980, and when she left she took his son, the fourth Peter, and a good half of the business with her. (A delicious series of articles reporting the very juicy trial in the *Anchorage Daily News*, March and April 1981. The *Times* seemed to have stayed away from the story.) The third Peter then married the third blonde, a Bush pilot called Walkaway Jane after the second time she wrecked a plane and walked away from it, who promptly died in her next crash two months after the wedding.

The third Peter didn't marry again. He tended to his business, buried his father next to his brother when the second Peter died in 1994 (obituary, December 1994, *Ahtna Tribune, Cordova Times, Valdez Star, Valdez Vanguard, Seward Phoenix-Log, Anchorage Daily News,* the *Times* was out of business by then, *Eagle River Star, Frontiersman, Fairbanks Daily News-Miner, Juneau Empire*), buried his mother next to his father when she died in 1995 (obituary, *Ahtna Tribune, Anchorage Daily News,* June 1995), and took over as the heir and sole proprietor of Heiman Transportation and Service Corporation, Inc.

By then he was already a state senator, and from all indications (AP photos of the third Peter dining with the governor in Juneau, conferring with the senior U.S. senator in Washington, D.C., shooting grouse with Alaska's U.S. congressman in Oregon and, of much more interest to Paula Pawlowski, seen in the company of every mover and shaker of any importance in Alaskan politics for the previous ten years, some of whom were still out of jail) a successful one.

She took many notes, followed by a lunch break.

When she got back to the library, the greasy

burger and fries from the Sourdough Cafe sitting uneasily between her chronic heartburn and her incipient ulcer, she went back through a lot of the same spools looking for the name Gordaoff. She was in Fairbanks in the first place because both the Heiman and the Gordaoff families had a lot of history there. Plus, she wasn't paying for it. She wasted a moment speculating as to where all the Gordaoff campaign funds were coming from, decided she didn't care so long as her checks cleared the bank, and got back to work.

The Gordaoff family was no less distinguished than the Heiman family, and with a lineage that went a lot farther back. Anne Gordaoff's grandmother was a feisty little (four feet five, "The Little Lovelies Who Would Be Miss Fairbanks," *Fairbanks Daily News-Miner*, 1910) Athabascan woman, who married an Irish con artist with fingers in every pie south of Livengood, and who when those pies began to burn started drinking and beating his wife. She made Alaskan history by being the first Native woman ever (and the only one for a long time afterward) to sue her husband for divorce, get it, get the kids (there were four, two adopted), and get all the property that hadn't been gambled away. There were a lot of photographs of her, a tiny woman with dark skin and straight black hair piled high on her head. By all accounts Lily Gordaoff MacGregor oversaw her husband's business interests with so attentive an eye and so firm a hand that she became something of a local real estate magnate.

Paula did some more digging and her eyebrows rose a little. Lily Gordaoff MacGregor had been a landlady of some consequence, owning an office building on Cushman, two boarding houses, one in Livengood, one on Wickersham, and — this time Paula's eyebrows rose very high indeed. She grinned down at the Fairbanks tax rolls for 1915. Lily Gordaoff MacGregor had been the owner of record of two houses on Fourth Avenue between Barnett and Cushman Streets in Fairbanks, Alaska, also known as the Fairbanks Line. Men had been lining up at the Fairbanks Line from 1906, when the Fairbanks city fathers created it at the behest of Archdeacon Stuck. The Fairbanks Line was, in fact, the longest-running and certainly one of the most profitable red light districts in Alaska and possibly the entire American West until its closure in 1955.

Paula toyed with the idea of selling this information to Peter Heiman, and then decided against it. When you offer yourself to the highest bidder, you ought to stay bought. She looked down at the tax rolls and grinned again. Any professional worthy of the name would say the same.

In 1919 the influenza epidemic had carried off two of Lily's children, which two were not called by name in that issue of the *Fairbanks Daily News-Miner.* All the June 12th article said, and on the front page, too, was that Lily Gordaoff MacGregor was moving her family to Cordova, where she had relatives, and that she would be sorely missed by all who remained behind.

Quite a tribute for a white-run newspaper of the time to pay to a Native woman. Paula was impressed. She ran the spool backwards, and her attention was caught by a headline datelined Niniltna, a village in the Park that comprised the greater part of Anne Gordaoff's chosen district. She had to rewind to find it again. Someone had been killed, murdered, a woman, in the spring of 1915.

It had nothing to do with Anne Gordaoff, of course, but the circumstances listed in the paper were such that Paula might be able to work them into her novel. The third chapter could use a little spicing up, and what better for spice than a discretionary helping of blood and guts? After all, everyone loves a murder.

She glanced at her watch. Three-forty-five. Her time was bought and paid for until five. She wondered what Anne Gordaoff's stand was on subsidizing the arts.

She decided Anne was for it.

Rampart

January 14, 1899

The man died at five minutes past two o'clock in the morning. The boy was born at three.

They had moved to Rampart from Dawson the previous spring along with fifteen hundred other stampeders. At first it was the same there as it had been in Dawson, a lot of people who would speak to Sam Halvorsen but none who would deign to notice the Dawson Darling, no matter how respectably married she could now claim to be. Sam Halvorsen was the scion of a wealthy and respected Minneapolis family who had made money in lumber, and Rampart, for all its small size and remote location, was like many of the gold towns of the north filled with people of similar backgrounds, people who, if they didn't know Sam's family, had at least heard of it, and displayed their disapproval of his marrying so far out of his class by soundly snubbing his wife.

"What do we care?" he said, tumbling her into the bed of the tiny bedroom at the back of the tiny cabin on the bank of the Yukon River. "I've got you, what the hell do I want with a bunch of snobs hanging

around getting in the way?"

But she thought he did want them, and it worried at her.

She was, in fact, his lawful wife. They had married in March, three months to the day from when he had snatched her from the Double Eagle stage in Dawson.

He had enough of his father in him that the cabin, built of logs and insulated with sod, was solid and as air-tight as anything in the Arctic was at fifty-two below. The post took up most of the space, with a tiny bedroom in one corner, just wide enough for the bed, which was a big one to accommodate the length of Sam's legs. "And yours," he had said before investigating their cumulative length in painstaking detail.

Ah, she loved him, how she loved him. She now thought she had loved him from the first moment she had seen him, standing so tall and so angry next to the door he had just come through, fresh from the claim on Orogrande Creek he had sold the month before, looking for nothing more than a cold beer and an honest game of poker.

Instead he found her, prancing around nearly naked in front of a lot of drooling idiots with more gold than sense, for sale to the highest bidder. "I knew you were my wife," he told her later, "and I sure as hell didn't know what my wife was doing up on that stage."

It was a week before they got out of bed, a month before they'd left his cabin, two months before they realized that her auction had made even wide-open

Dawson City too hot to hold them. They hadn't been able to find a minister to marry them, and had had to fall back on an itinerant preacher headed for Nome, riding a bicycle down the frozen Yukon River. They followed him as far as Rampart, where Sam built their post and she filled it with goods to sell. He put in a few tables next to the Franklin stove they brought in from Outside, where Sam ran a few card games, losing more than he won, but "hell," he'd said when she remonstrated, "I already won the big pot," and kissed her.

That fall, the ax had slipped when Sam was chopping their winter's supply of wood. He'd cut his leg, not badly, and the wound had seemed to heal. It had opened again in November, though, and become infected, until great dark streaks ran up his leg. She had sent for a doctor from Dawson, another from Fairbanks, depleting funds already low from lack of sales due to the stampede for the new gold fields at Nome. No one had been able to help him.

"Take care of that boy, Darling," he said at the last, his voice slurring. "Take him to my folks in Minneapolis. They'll look out for you both."

But she knew, as she sat next to what was now his funeral byre, that the Halvorsens in Minneapolis would have nothing to do with her or her son. The Darling's Rampart neighbors had been faithful correspondents.

She had fifty dollars in scrip, a few silver coins, and two small pokes of dust received in payment from a couple of miners laying in supplies for the winter, and who had pretty much cleaned out hers.

She had her clothes. And she had a new-born baby rooting at her breast for milk that wasn't there.

There was a knock at the door. It was Sam's best friend, Arthur Hudson. "I came as soon as I heard," he said, stepping inside and closing the door.

Arthur had traveled the Chilkoot Trail with Sam in 1897. He'd staked the claim next to Sam's at Orogrande Creek, although he hadn't done as well as Sam. He'd been present at the Double Eagle Saloon on Christmas Eve two years ago; he might even have been one of the bidders. He had stood up for Sam at their wedding, and now he had traveled all the way from Orogrande to Rampart in the dead of an Arctic winter to see how she was.

She was exhausted from nursing Sam and the birth of the baby, and she gladly handed over the details of the business to Arthur. He moved Sam's body to the shed out back, as the ground was too frozen to bury him. He sent for canned milk from Circle City, and by the end of January the boy had begun to thrive. By the end of February Arthur had found a buyer, a trapper backed by the Hudson Bay Company. It wasn't much, he told her, but it would be enough to get her to Minneapolis, and the trapper wouldn't take possession until spring, when she and the baby would both be well enough to travel.

By the end of March, he was in her bed.

He'd wanted her; he'd never made any secret of it. And it was so very cold, alone in the bed she had shared with Sam. She couldn't keep herself warm, let alone the baby. Arthur built a cradle and placed it next to the fireplace, and devoted himself to her.

He was very gentle and very determined.

She responded as best she could. She was grateful, and she wanted to show him that she was, but it was as if something inside her was frozen. It didn't help that the window of the tiny bedroom looked onto the back yard of the post and the shed where the body of her husband lay stiff and cold. Arthur understood, and made up curtains of grain sacks so she wouldn't have to see.

But Sam could see through the curtains. She could feel his eyes upon them as they came together beneath the bedclothes, straining for closeness, for climax, for physical relief, for cessation from worry, for ease of grief. Oh yes, he watched them in the cold and lonely reaches of the night.

Spring came, and warmer temperatures, and the ice in the river began to break with booming cracks that echoed up over the bank like thunder. Daylight lengthened and the temperature warmed, melting the high banks of snow next to the paths shoveled between the post and the outhouse and the wood pile. Tiny brown birds with golden crowns appeared and began to sing a three-note descant from the limbs of budding birch trees, and the light increased every day. She felt as if she were coming out of a long dark tunnel, and was dazed by this assault on her senses. One night she found true, unfeigned pleasure in Arthur's arms, and he smiled down at her as if he had known all along, and had only been waiting. The next day they buried Sam's body next to a hedge of wild rose bushes a half mile from the post.

One morning in late May when there was enough

river to launch a boat, Arthur told her he was going to Dawson for supplies and the news. "I'll be back in a week, maybe two," he said. He smoothed back one of her red-gold curls and added with a smile, "I'll bring back a pretty hat for your pretty hair." She kissed him good-bye, and waved him off from the bank, baby on her hip, as he launched the skiff into the swift, silty waters of the Yukon. He rowed standing up, facing upriver, and just before he vanished around the first bank, he turned to wave one last time.

There were fewer people in Rampart now, as many had left to follow the gold to Nome and Fairbanks, and few of the ones who were left were speaking to her, so she was surprised when, ten days later, there was the sound of footsteps coming down the path to the front door. She had just risen to her feet, baby in her arms, when it opened without permission.

At first she didn't recognize him.

And then she did.

It was the Greek, the one who had bid in the auction at the Double Eagle.

Her first instinct was to run, but there was no place to go, and she was hampered by the baby. Desperate, she looked for a weapon, but Arthur had taken the pistol with him to Dawson.

The Greek watched her with those cold, acquisitive, and now possessive eyes, and laughed as he closed the door behind him.

4

"Why?" Johnny said. His tone indicated that no answer to his question would be acceptable.

Kate debated what to say, and fell back on the truth, or a piece of it. "We need the money."

"For me?"

"Partly."

"You don't need any money for me."

"Yeah," she said. "I do."

He stood in the middle of the floor of Kate's cabin, a one-room building twenty-five feet square with a loft, a wood stove for heating, an oil stove for cooking, an old-fashioned pump handle for water in the sink, a built-in couch covered in faded blue denim that ran around two walls, and shelf after shelf of books and cassette tapes. Kerosene lamps hung from all four corners. One sputtered. Kate took it down and made a business out of checking the fuel level, anything to keep from looking directly at the erect figure of resentment and rebellion that dominated the center of the room.

"She told me the last time I ran off that if I did it again, I could just keep on going and never come back."

God damn Jane Morgan, Kate thought, and said out loud, "Parents lose their temper and say things they don't mean sometimes, just like everybody else. And she did come."

"Yeah, well, she took her time. I been here a month. And don't tell me she didn't know where I am. If she had a brain in her head, she'd know where I was coming. I told her I never wanted to leave Alaska in the first place. I told her I hated Arizona. And Grandma hated having me."

"Johnny —"

"She did," he insisted, and then with a flash of perception older than his age he added, "I don't blame her. She's seventy-three and she weighs almost three hundred pounds. All she does is eat and watch soap operas. I'd be bound to make her get out of her Lay-Z-Boy once in a while. So I left. I told Mom I would. I told her that if I had to I'd hitchhike all the way back."

And he had, and the thought still had the power to make Kate's blood run cold. It was over a thousand miles from the northern border of Washington State to Tok alone. She didn't even know how many it was from Arizona to the border. "You never did tell me how you talked the border guards into letting you into Canada," she said. "Or back into Alaska at the other end."

He dropped his eyes, blue eyes so like his father's. "I didn't ask permission," he muttered, and Kate had visions of him wriggling through patches of dense undergrowth peopled by bears and wolves and moose.

"Anyway, Mom's dumb, but she's not so dumb that she wouldn't know where to start looking."

"She's your mother, Johnny. You will speak of her with respect."

He was fourteen years old. He'd lost a father he worshipped a year before, and had turned his back on a mother he barely tolerated when he'd left his new home without permission two months before, to show up on Kate's doorstep asking for — what exactly? she wondered now. A different mother? A home? Sanctuary?

"I'm no mommy," she remembered telling Jack once, and she still wasn't. But she also remembered Jack saying to her, "Look out for Johnny for me" as he lay dying in her arms.

"I hate Outside, Kate," Johnny said in a low voice. He raised defiant eyes. "And I hate Mom for taking me there when I didn't want to go. She knew I didn't want to; I told her. And she made me go anyway."

She looked at him and she saw herself as a child, as aware, as determined, and younger than he was. When her parents had died, her grandmother had taken her to live in Niniltna. After one week of city life, Kate rose early one morning that December and walked the twenty-five miles from the village to the homestead, armed with the little .22 rifle her father had bought her and carrying half a loaf of Ekaterina's homemade bread. There ensued a battle of wills between grandmother and grandchild the echoes of which still reverberated around the Park, and which resulted in Kate moving in with a crusty old widower with four sons, who had the virtue of owning the homestead next to Kate's father's. Abel Int-Hout wasn't a tender or a loving man, but he was a decent and a capable one, and his, for lack of a better word, "stewardship" of Kate allowed her to spend much more time at home than she would have been able to living in town. It had also continued the lessons in self-sufficiency begun by her father when she had begun to walk.

Town in this case amounted to a couple of dozen buildings, a store, a school, an earth station, and a permanent population of four hundred three, which included the dogs. Home in this case meant the one-room cabin she and Johnny were standing in and a semicircle of outbuildings sitting on the bank of a creek that ran through the heart of the Park. Step out in any direction and you'd run into a grizzly before you ran into another human being. Kate liked it that way.

She looked at Jack's son, and said, "I don't want to go away, Johnny. I have to." She shook her head when he opened his mouth to speak again. "If you want to stay here, we have to hire an attorney and work out some kind of custodial arrangement. That takes money. This job will take a month, at most two. No longer than the election."

Two months in the life of a fourteen-year-old was an eternity. "You don't want me here at all," he said.

"No, Johnny, I —"

"You don't care about me," his tone rough. "You probably didn't care for him, either. You practically got him killed!"

His eyes were swimming. Kate took a deep breath and didn't make the mistake of offering an embrace that would undoubtedly be rejected out of hand and which might even spur flight. She had no wish to go chasing through the forest that started on her doorstep after a young man who was too upset to remember any of the survival skills she'd taught him over a series of summer weekends during the last three years.

It wasn't the first time he'd accused her of killing his father. It wouldn't be the last time she didn't deny it. Jack had been at George Perry's hunting lodge because she had been there, plain and simple. She didn't blame herself, exactly, at least not anymore, for his death, but she didn't, couldn't, wouldn't duck out of what she was responsible for, either. Jack had loved her, had followed her into the wilderness, and had not come out again.

"Look out for Johnny for me, okay?"

She waited until Jack's son had regained some of his composure, carefully not looking at him

70

while he did so. The books on the shelves looked dusty. Usually she had them out so often they never sat in one place long enough to gather dust. "And then there's school," she said. "You'll need money for college."

His head came up and he said, voice steadier, "Dad had an education insurance policy. Not that it matters, because I'm not going to college anyway."

"Really," she said. "You're not going to college?"

"No. I hate school. Everybody there's a bunch of do-nothings and fuck-offs. They're not learning anything. They're just hot-rodding around, drinking, doing dope, chasing girls, and stealing radios out of cars."

"I — what?"

"I'll keep going until I'm sixteen," he said, jaw coming out. "Dad explained, the law says I have to go until then. But after that I don't have to, and I won't."

"And you were planning on doing what, instead?"

"I don't know yet," he said. "Fish, maybe. Commercially. Or guide. Or subsistence. Like you."

Kate closed her eyes for a moment and opened them again. "You don't want to work that hard, Johnny."

"Why not? You do." He nodded at the cabin. "And you're doing fine."

"I'm not getting rich at it."

"Yeah, but you're not starving, either. Neither will I."

She stared at him.

"So we don't need any money," he said. "You don't have to go on this job, and I don't have to leave the homestead."

"Yeah," she said, "we do, I do, and you have to."

"I won't."

"You will," she said through her teeth, "if I have to pick you up and carry you."

"I'll runaway," he said. "I don't want to live in Niniltna."

"You have to go to school; you just told me you knew that yourself."

"I'll commute," he said. "I can ride a bike in until it snows and then I can ride a snowmobile. You did."

"You're not staying here by yourself," she said distinctly.

"Why not?" he demanded, words straight and sure as an arrow. "You did."

They glared at each other.

Standoff.

When no one answered the front door, Kate went around to the back, Johnny trailing reluctantly behind. She found Ethan seated on a kitchen chair balanced on its hind legs with its back against the corrugated plastic of the greenhouse wall, shooting slugs off the late crop of red cabbage with a BB gun. On the ground at

72

his right was a twelve-pack of Corona, a lime, and a paring knife. On the ground at his left was a Rottweiler with a slobbery grin and a lordly sense of his own dignity. He rose to his feet and paced forward to touch noses with Mutt. Nobody wagged any tails but nobody growled, either. "Hey, Gort," Kate said, and got a head shoved beneath her hand in reply.

Around the corner came Gort's twin sister. "Hey, Klaatu," Kate said. Klaatu touched noses with Mutt, used the rest of her energy for a perfunctory tail wag, and flopped down in Gort's vacated shade with a voluptuous moan.

Pop! went the BB gun, and another shiny, slimy black slug fell from a leaf, which was mostly holes by then.

"Hey, Ethan," Kate said.

"Kate," he said without looking around. Pop! went the BB gun, thud went another slug, and in celebration Ethan drained the bottle in his left hand.

"This is Johnny Morgan," Kate said. "Johnny, this is Ethan Int-Hout. Abel was his dad."

Johnny looked Ethan over with no visible approval and didn't bother to say "Hi." Ethan looked back and didn't bother to say "Hi" back.

Kate walked over to the twelve-pack and looked inside. There were ten bottles left.

Ethan did look at her then. Seated, his eyes were level with hers, a direct, piercing blue. His hawk-featured face was set, and his rare, warm smile was not around that morning. He hadn't bothered to shave, not for days, and on the olfactory evidence Kate was willing to bet that he hadn't bathed in longer. "Where's Margaret?" she said. She looked around, noticing for the first time how quiet it was in the Int-Hout homestead. Since Ethan had moved back the year before with his family, a jolly, zaftig, red-headed wife and a set of rambunctious and equally redheaded ten-year-old twins, one boy, one girl, she would bet it was never quiet.

"Margaret's not here," he said, squinting down the barrel of the BB gun, seeming to debate whether or not to take another shot. He did. "Damn," he said, "missed him," and lowered the gun again.

"Where are the kids?"

"She took 'em." He leaned the gun up against the greenhouse wall and stood up, towering a foot and a half over Kate. Johnny's eyes widened. "Come on, I'll make some coffee."

The kitchen was a mess, the sink filled with dirty dishes, the top of the cooking stove encrusted with blackened grease. Ethan didn't apologize, and he didn't try to stop Kate when she started in on the dishes while they waited for the kettle to boil.

The coffee was instant. Kate hid a wince and loaded in the creamer. Johnny's cocoa was instant, too, but the marshmallows, though stale, melted in a satisfactory manner. After Ethan cleared the chairs around the kitchen table of unopened mail, dog-eared catalogues, a *Shooter's*

Bible, and a stack of *Aviation Week* magazines, they sat down, still in silence.

Usually, Kate was comfortable with silence. It was why she lived alone on a homestead in the middle of a twenty-million-acre federal park, twenty-five miles away from the nearest village over a road that was impassable to anything but snow machines in the winter and to anything but the sturdiest trucks in the summer.

Ethan's silence was palpable. He was angry, but he wasn't sulking over it. She decided there was nothing for it but to wade in. "I need a favor, Ethan," she said. She wasn't happy asking and, although she tried hard not to let it show, Ethan, when he bothered to look up, could see it in her face. For the first time that day he smiled.

He'd always been able to read her, from the day they shared what was her first kiss at the top of Widow's Peak after an hour's hike one hot day the summer she was sixteen. He was back from his freshman year of college and they were both working for his father, tending the dogs and the farm while Abel was out set-netting with Old Sam Dementieff and Mary Balashoff on Alaganik Bay. They'd spent the morning clearing alders off the airstrip and the afternoon hilling potatoes, and when Ethan suggested a picnic as a reward, Kate had been all for it.

Ethan was the second of Abel's four sons and the closest to her in age. A three-year difference at five and eight or ten and thirteen might as well be thirty, but at sixteen and nineteen the distance had suddenly narrowed. Ethan came home and for the first time Kate noticed how attractive his smile was, how smart and funny his conversation, how capably he shouldered the business of the homestead. Ethan came home and for the first time noticed that Kate had breasts and a figure to go with them, and a smile that, when she bothered to use it, melted him right down to the marrow in his bones. His marrow had been melted before, of course; he was self-aware enough to realize that his looks and his talent at center on the basketball team would get him most of the girls he wanted without too much effort. The girls at UAF did nothing to disabuse him of this notion, especially the girls in the Wickersham Dorm, for whom the jocks of Lathrop Dorm (basement, basketball; first floor, hockey; second floor, swim team) were a specialty.

So when Ethan looked at Kate when he returned home from school that June, it was with the eye of a newborn connoisseur. She was aware of him. He could tell that from the sidelong glances, the occasional soft blush, the not-so-accidental bumpings of arms and hips, but he made no move until his father was safely out of the way. Even then, he waited until the work of the day was done, and felt virtuous in doing so.

Kate at sixteen had never been kissed. Truth to tell, no boy had ever had the courage to so much as try to hold her hand. It might have been the force of her grandmother's personality, or the power Ekaterina had over the tribe, but it might also have had something to do with Kate's air of self-containment, of assurance, of capability. She didn't give off vibes like she needed anybody in her life, let alone a guy. Her classmates saw her as smart, and some of them translated that as arrogant, and some of them translated that as eccentric. She was quiet and some of them translated that as stuck up, others as shy. She had no close friends. She had no boyfriends.

Which was why Ethan's obvious attention hit her like a ton of bricks. Tall, good-looking, funny, smart (even then Kate couldn't abide stupidity), competent at whatever he turned his hand, and best of all, someone with whom she was familiar, someone with whom she already had history, someone who didn't require the elaborate ritual of inane chatter and silly giggles and he-told-my-brother-and-my-brother-told-me conversations and slap-and-tickle games that preoccupied her contemporaries. This was Ethan, and it was obvious that he was interested. It was enough to make every female nerve in her body sit up and take notice. The three weeks between Ethan coming home and Abel leaving were the longest and most excruciating three weeks of her life.

The homestead was at fifteen hundred feet, on the edge of the wide, level valley that made up the center of the Park. Widow's Peak was another thousand feet up, a mere foothill to the

Quilaks looming behind. It was a clear day, and they fancied they could see all the way to Prince William Sound. "Think they're catching anything?" Ethan said as he unpacked their picnic.

Kate shook out an old olive green Army blanket. "I hope so. I haven't had any salmon out of the Sound yet this summer."

Ethan sat back on his heels and narrowed his eyes against the sun. "If I'd known that, I would have brought you one out of the creek myself."

Kate hoped her skin was too dark and the light was too bright for him to see her blush. "No, I meant salt water fish. They're always fatter than the ones you catch in fresh water." She changed the subject. "Do you want a fire?"

"Do we need one?"

She looked up to meet his eyes and flushed again. "I guess not," she said, and reached for the Spam sandwiches.

They ate mostly in silence, because Ethan, after all, also had been raised in what Robert Service had called "the hush of the Great Alone," but when their meal was over and they were packing the debris into their daypacks, he found occasion to brush her hand with his. It felt exactly as if an electric spark had leaped between them, and she jumped. He grinned, and leaned in.

She didn't move during that first kiss, curious at the touch of his lips on hers. He drew back and looked at her. "Come on, Kate," he said, his voice husky, "kiss me back."

She wouldn't admit to not knowing how, but she let him teach her, and oh my, did it feel good. So did his tongue delicately tracing the whorls of her ear, his teeth at the base of her throat, his hand cupping her breast, his knee rubbing between her legs. She felt like she'd been run over by a truck, a big one; she had no breath to protest, and no will to, either.

She was naked, and he was shirtless and starting on the zip of his jeans when the Super Cub buzzed the top of Widow's Peak on a short final into the homestead. It was Abel, flying back from Alaganik Bay after the Fish and Game had closed the bay to fishing for the week, and he got an eyeful.

Abel asked Ethan one question when they got back down to the homestead. "You use a rubber?"

Ethan set his jaw. "We didn't get that far," he muttered finally, when it became evident that his father wasn't going to let it go.

That evening, Abel flew Kate to a one-man placer gold-mining operation near Nizina. Seth Partridge was the miner, and Micah Int-Hout, Abel's third oldest boy, barely thirteen and no competition for Ethan, was already apprenticed to him for the summer. Seth agreed to take Kate on, too. She spent the rest of July and most of August pining for Ethan and the astonishing feelings he had coaxed from her body, and learning how to alter the course of a creek with a D-5 Caterpillar tractor. When she got back to the homestead, Ethan was already back in Fairbanks. The next summer, Abel found him a job in Anchorage.

Two years later, upon graduation from high school and at the insistence of her grandmother, Kate went to Fairbanks and joined Ethan in the ranks of the student body. Ethan knocked on her dorm room door on the day after she arrived. "Hi," he said, and smiled, and she toppled over the same edge she had been teetering on two summers before. She wanted him, she wanted him so much her teeth ached. It seemed that he wanted her, too, and only the fact that they both had roommates kept them out of each others' beds for as long as it did. They necked a lot, squirming together on a chair in a dark corner of the Student Union Building, taking time out up against a tree in the middle of running the Equinox Marathon, in the back row of the campus theater during a showing of *Psycho*. "I think it's going to fall off before I get the chance to use it again," he groaned one evening in the Lathrop lounge, when they were interrupted by a horde trouping in to watch *Dallas*.

He must have taken steps to see that it wouldn't happen, because a week later she caught him with another girl, and that was the end of that. Disloyalty was the one sin Kate Shugak would not, could not forgive.

At Thanksgiving break, Abel, not usually so slow, woke up to the fact that the UAF campus wasn't all that large and that his son the junior and his foster-daughter the freshman were both living on it. In December Ethan transferred to the University of Washington, ostensibly because the wildlife-management curriculum was larger and with better teachers, and would round out his degree. There he met Margaret, and married her the month after he graduated.

Kate, left alone at UAF, went into hibernation, emerging only at the invitation of an inspired English teacher, who taught her how to read recreationally. From that point on, she had never been lonely. She had seen Ethan perhaps a dozen times for brief periods since. She was always civil. He was always courteous. They might have been strangers, instead of almost lovers. Since he had moved back to the Park, family in tow, to start a fly-in bed-and-breakfast on Abel's homestead, she had seen him perhaps half a dozen times, at the Int-Hout homestead when Mandy had wanted to stop in and say "Hi," at the post office in Niniltna, and at the Roadhouse. She was still civil. He was still courteous.

It was obvious by the gleam in his eye that Ethan was remembering a lot of the same things she was. Johnny looked suspiciously from one adult to the other. When Kate looked at him, he sneered, and she could imagine his thoughts. "My dad not dead a year, and you're ready to jump in bed with somebody else." She thought of July in Bering and Jim Chopin, and then she did not. "I need a favor, Ethan," she said again.

"You said that," he replied.

"Yeah," she said, "sorry." She nodded at Johnny. "Johnny's —" She hesitated. "Johnny's staying with me for a while, but I'm going to be in and out for most of the next month or two. I don't want him to stay at the homestead alone, so I was wondering if he could park here for the duration."

Ethan looked at Johnny, who met his gaze with a sullen expression. "He looks like he wants to move over here, all right."

Kate kicked Johnny beneath the table.

Johnny kicked her back, hard enough to make her jump and swear.

Ethan laughed, which transformed his face. Johnny relaxed a little.

Still laughing, Ethan told Johnny, "You're my kinda guy, kid. Sure, you can bunk in here if you want to." The laughter faded, leaving him looking glum. "It's not like I don't have the room."

Voice carefully devoid of anything that might be mistaken for genuine interest, Kate said, "So, when is Margaret coming back?"

Ethan got up and collected their cups. "She isn't, according to her," he said over his shoulder. "She's filed for divorce."

All Kate could think of to say was, "Why?" and then she added hastily, "I'm sorry, Ethan. None of my business."

He snorted. "Like it wasn't all over the Park by sundown the day she left. Where have you been?"

"Out of town," she said. "So what happened?"

He turned around and folded his arms, leaning back against the sink. "She wants to move back to Seattle. That's where her parents are, and her sister. Says she doesn't want the kids growing up all alone in the middle of a wilderness. Says they're going to have a civilized upbringing. I think myself she wants cable back." He sighed. "Breakup was too much for her, I guess. Or maybe it was breakup and the Park in combination. She wasn't raised to it like we were. I probably should have seen it coming. She never did like Cordova much, either, and she sure wasn't happy when we moved back to the homestead. Didn't like the idea of cooking and cleaning up after strangers, so the fly-in B-and-B idea went west. After that it was one big downhill slide. She and the kids left in May, right after school let out."

He looked at Johnny. "You gotta have cable, kid?" Johnny shook his head. "Good. Cause they ain't any such animal here. Or phones. Got lights, though, and hot and cold running water." He hooked a thumb at Kate. "Better'n her dinky little cabin."

A brief silence. "I'm sorry, Ethan," Kate said, sounding as inadequate as she felt.

Johnny gave Ethan a curious look. "Don't worry," he said suddenly, "he's not."

"Johnny."

Ethan stared into the blue eyes so unlike his own. "It's okay, Kate," he said finally. "He's right.

I miss the kids." He smiled again, and again transformed himself from someone who ground men's bones to make his bread into yet another rueful Alaskan backwoodsman who had picked the wrong woman. "But that's about all I miss."

While Johnny was checking out Ethan's old room, still filled with Ethan's old model planes, Ethan walked Kate back to her truck. "I've already got him enrolled in school in Niniltna. He knows how to run a four-wheeler, and he knows how long it'll take him to get there. He's got the schedule, and his books."

"Yeah, but will he go?"

"He says yes."

"That's not necessarily the whole-hearted endorsement I was looking for, Kate."

"He says yes," she repeated. "He's young, but he keeps his word when he gives it. He'll go." At least for the next two years, she thought, and shrugged it off. Time enough to think about that when it happened.

Ethan touched her arm and in an instant it was like she was back on the top of Widow's Peak on a hot, sunny afternoon, with the sky clear all the way to Middleton Island. She moved to one side, out of reach. "What?"

"Why are you leaving him? He hasn't been here that long. Why are you just taking off on him?" He paused. "He's Jack's boy, isn't he?"

"Yes." She looked over his shoulder and concentrated on a stellar blue jay showing off his shiny blue feathers against the dark green branch of a white spruce. She nodded at the house. "He's with his mom now, or he's supposed to be. He ran away."

"Ah, shit."

"Not for the first time. His mother told him if he ran off again, he could stay lost. He hitchhiked here from Arizona, Ethan."

"He's what, fourteen?" When she nodded, he said, "Ballsy little bastard, isn't he?"

Kate ignored the admiration in Ethan's comment. It was strictly a guy thing. "What Johnny doesn't realize is, Jane hates my guts. She showed up last night at Bobby's. Now that she knows he's with me, she won't stop looking."

"Happy Mother's Day."

"Yeah."

"She going to show up out here?"

"Not here, not yet. My place, maybe."

"So you want him here when she does."

She nodded. "The reason I'm leaving myself is, I've got a job. Sooner or later, I'm going to have to hire a lawyer. That takes money."

Ethan scratched his chin. "He's pissed at you, isn't he."

It wasn't a question, but she answered it anyway. "Yeah." It was a relief to share it with someone else, even Ethan. "Yes, he is."

"Mad because his dad went with you and got killed." Again, it wasn't a question.

"Yes."

"All your fault."

She nodded.

"Like my dad," he said, surprising her. "That was all your fault, too."

She gaped at him. Never once had any of the Int-Hout boys pointed the finger at her for Abel's death. Not once had any of them so much as whispered the possibility that she might be to blame for his suicide, that if she had let sleeping park rangers and Anchorage investigators lie, Abel might be alive today. Abel, and now Jack. Her fault, she thought bleakly. Her most grievous fault.

"No, it wasn't," Ethan said, surprising her. "Dad was Dad, an unreconstructed Alaska old fart who never got past 1925 in his thinking. Miller, maybe, was an accident. Dahl was deliberate. He wasn't going to live with that any longer than he had to whether you caught him out or not."

She felt a slackening of tension in her gut she hadn't known was there. His next words made her tighten up again.

"Last year, you got in the middle of a bunch of crazies. You're lucky to be alive yourself." He turned to go, and over his shoulder he said, "And I was damn sorry to hear about Jack Morgan, Kate. Everybody says he was a hell of a good man. I liked him, what I saw of him, when we met at Bernie's that time."

She watched him walk down the trail and she thought, Sure you did.

About as much as she had liked Margaret.

5

Kate hadn't been in Ahtna since the April before last, when the engine fell off a 747 and crashed through the roof of her cabin, along with fifty thousand dollars in compensation that had to be deposited to her account at the Last Frontier Bank. The teller had goggled at the stack of cash, and the manager had to be called over to okay the transaction. He did, after telling Kate three times that all deposits of more than five thousand dollars had to be reported to the IRS. Kate was sure that the moment she left the building they'd been running the numbers on the bills.

After repairs to the homestead and the truck, a new snow machine, tires all around for the four-wheeler, a truck load of new tools, a year's supply of canned goods, and a steady line of mostly deserving Park rats with their hands out, there was less than two thousand left, but when she'd gone to Anchorage that April she'd had money to burn. She'd taken Jack to dinner every night. She'd insisted on buying him a cut-and-style at Jeri's, where he'd once forced her into the chair. When he said, barely a jest, "Just so long as you don't make me wear lingerie," she'd taken him to Nordstrom and had him parade back and forth in a series of sports jackets and yuppy chinos. She would have taken him over to the shoe section if he hadn't rebelled. "Paybacks are hell," she'd said.

"I got paid back that night," he'd growled.

The 172 hit an air pocket, and she was jolted out of her reverie. The pilot, a tall, thin man in oil-stained coveralls with a lantern jaw in perpetual need of a shave touched the yoke absentmindedly, not looking up from the book he was reading. Kate had already checked out the title. *Round the Bend* by Nevil Shute. One of George Perry's favorite authors, along with Earnest K. Gann. Both men wrote about flying like they'd held a plane up in the air a time or two, something George, full-time Bush pilot, part-time A&P mechanic, and sole proprietor of an air taxi, appreciated in full.

The plane steadied into level flight once more. They were fifteen minutes out of Niniltna, another fifteen minutes to go. It was a clear day, the sun high in the sky, and the Quilak Mountains loomed at their back like a bridge between earth and heaven, with the right of way reserved only for a worthy few. Beneath them the Kanuyaq River doubled and tripled back on itself as the foothills flattened reluctantly into a broad plateau. Here and there a roof showed beneath the branches of trees that had been encouraged to grow closely to the eaves, the better to protect the owner's privacy. A skiff was pulled up on a sandbar, the aluminum hull dull in the waning light. A black bear and three cubs took fright at the sound of their engine, and Kate's last sight of them had the sow frantically pushing one cub up the lone spruce tree in the middle of a meadow.

She had bought Jack two of the jackets she had forced him to model, because the one he usually wore for court was a disgrace, one of the pockets hanging by one corner and soft-boiled egg stains down the front, and because she rarely had the opportunity to buy him gifts. She had followed him into the dressing room to make sure he didn't leave them behind. There had been a close encounter in that dressing room that should have got them arrested, and would have if that clerk waiting on them hadn't . . .

Ahtna was a small town of two thousand, built where the northern reaches of the Kanuyaq River met the Kanuyaq River Highway, which connected the Glenn Highway with Valdez. It was one of the first communities of any size in Alaska, after Fairbanks and Nome, started by one of the smarter stampeders who had seen early on that while the miners themselves made little or no money, the businesses who sold miners their supplies made out like bandits. "Mining the miners," they called it. Some of the miner miners were bandits, come to that, Kate thought, reminded of certain members of her own family tree, one of whom had been hung for a horse thief back in 1899. Not that Emaa had ever admitted to it, but Kate had done some research for a paper on local history for a school project, and the story of the hanging had been on the front page what was then the weekly *Ahtna Tribune*. It had been one of the more well-attended public events in Ahtna's early days, according to the reporter, who quoted the newly sworn territorial sheriff in every paragraph.

Now, with her experience as a law enforcement professional, she thought of the article with a more informed perspective. New lawman on the job out to make a name for himself, establish his authority, send out a warning to the other no goodniks in his jurisdiction not to shit in his nest. Poor Zebulon Shugak didn't stand a chance. But he had certainly given rise to a great deal of merriment among the student population of Kate's generation of Niniltna High, which had added not inconsiderably to her own status as well.

And then there had been the bonus of embarrassing her grandmother. Johnny Morgan, she thought, was an amateur compared to Kate Shugak in her prime.

Evidently the sheriff's plan had worked; Ahtna had grown to become a thriving little hub town, and had been the first to embrace flight by building an airstrip out of gravel mined from an oxbow a mile up the river and hauling in tanks to be filled with fuel which was sold at rates just this side of extortion. Ahtna was the Park's banking hub, its marketing hub, its educational hub, with one of the University of Alaska's few remaining regional branches, and its bureaucratic hub, with federal offices for the departments of the Forest Service, Housing & Urban Development, the Air National Guard, and everything in between, including, naturally, the National Parks Service. Raven, the Native regional corporation, was doing a brisk business in erecting HUD-backed subdivisions and renting the results to federal employees, many of whom were by now Raven shareholders. One pocket picks the other, Kate thought as they banked over one such subdivision and came in for a landing with George Perry all over it, light as a feather, straight as an arrow; you didn't know you were on the ground until you'd stepped out of the plane. Bush born and bred, Kate appreciated a good pilot above all else.

"Somebody meeting you?" George shouted over the roar of the engine. Mutt gave George a swipe with her tongue before jumping out to stand next to Kate, and laughed up at him with her guilty tongue hanging out when he swore and wiped his face on his sleeve.

"I'm fine," Kate shouted back.

"Okay," he shouted in reply, although he didn't look convinced that it was. Everyone was treating her like she was breakable these days.

Kate shut the door with more force than necessary. George locked down the handle, and the Cessna taxied down to the end of the runway and took off again.

She hitched a ride with someone she didn't know, a man at least ten years her junior, his profession made known by the buoys and silver seine in the bed of the truck. He offered to buy her a drink and tell her his troubles. Kate was so pleased at this complete ignorance of her identity and recent history that she let him down a lot easier than she might have, and they parted friends in front of the hotel. Mutt even wagged her tail. She never kissed on the first date.

Kate paused for a moment, watching the gray, silty current of the river flow powerfully between high, crumbling banks. A spruce tree had given up the fight to maintain the vertical and was laying on its side, roots exposed, its top just above water. Two skiffs passed in midstream going in opposite directions, the upstream one empty, the downstream one piled high with boxes and cans and crates and cartons, the gunnel almost awash. A flock of Canada geese made a low pass in a ragged vee, honking the call that sounded so joyous in spring and so melancholy in fall.

Mutt stood next to her, the picture of patience. Cars and trucks arrived, doors slammed, gravel crunched underfoot. Some people nodded, others said hello with great care, as if they were afraid she might bite. Whispered comments floated back to her. "— lucky to be alive —" "Did you know Jack Morgan? A great guy —" "— World War III, Denali style —" "— she seems all right, you have to wonder if it was as bad as they say —"

Near them a car door opened. "Miss Shugak?"

Mutt's ears pricked up, and she took a pace forward. The man backed into the doorframe with a thump and said, the words tumbling out, "Mr. Heiman would like to speak to you for a few moments, if you don't mind." He looked from Mutt to the handle of the rear door, torn between his duty and his wish to live. Stretching his arm as far as he could, he managed to snag the handle and maneuver the door open, all the while keeping one foot in the well of the driver's seat.

Kate was always appreciative of a job done against the odds, and she took pity on him. "It's all right. She doesn't bite unless I tell her to." And then because she couldn't resist it, "Or unless she's hungry."

The manner of his reentry into the car was less than graceful.

Peter Heiman was laughing when she bent down to look in at him. When he could he said, "Hey, Kate."

"Hey, Pete," she said.

"Get your ass on in here and set a spell. You, too, Mutt."

With a graceful leap Mutt was sitting down in his open briefcase, papers flying everywhere.

Kate climbed in and closed the door.

"Damn, I love this dog," Peter Heiman said, scratching behind Mutt's ears. Kate couldn't tell for sure, but she thought the backs of the driver's ears looked a little red. "How you been, Kate?"

"Okay, I guess," she said, and at his look added, "Better now."

"Good. I was sorry to hear about Jack Morgan. I know you two were close for a long time. How come you never married, anyway?"

She looked away. "I guess we just weren't the marrying kind."

"I hear his kid is staying with you."

"Yes." He raised an eyebrow, and she said, "He's fourteen. That's all you need to know."

He laughed again. She'd always liked that about him, his laughter. He laughed a lot, over cribbage games at Abel's homestead, over the bar at Bernie's, at high-school versus town-team basketball games in Niniltna. He was as crafty an opportunist as ever did business in the Park, but he had a strong sense of the ridiculous and an even stronger sense of reality, and she respected him as much as she respected anyone in public office.

"So what's up, Pete?" she said. "You looked like you were waiting for me."

His hand still on Mutt's head. "I was." Their eyes met. "Brad? Take a walk, would you? Thanks." The driver got out and the door closed.

"I can't believe you have a driver," she said.

"Pretty uptown for the Park. Aren't you afraid someone will see?"

"I hear you went to work for her. For Gordaoff."

"Gordaoff." Not "Anne" or "Anne Gordaoff," just "Gordaoff." Pete had known Anne since she was in diapers, but there was no pretense at courtesy here. Anne was Peter's opponent in a close race for a seat that by now Kate guessed he regarded as personal property. Using Anne's last name was Pete's way of repressing or even eliminating any personal relationship they might have had over the years. "He's behind," Kate remembered Billy Mike saying of Peter that morning, not once but twice, as if that was the answer to everything.

Maybe it was. Kate hoped like hell it was not. This was the problem in working crime in a place like Alaska, where there was only one person per square mile, with most of them related one way or another, and most of the rest related to her. "I'm getting paid by the Niniltna Native Association, strictly speaking," she said equably, "but yeah, I'm working for Anne's campaign."

"Doing what?"

She thought it over, and decided he'd find out soon enough on his own. "She's been getting some hate mail. Threatening letters, like that. Her campaign manager got worried."

"Darlene Shelikof."

"Darlene, yeah."

There was a brief silence. "You want something to drink?" Peter opened a cooler and knew her well enough not to offer liquor. "Diet 7-UP, am I right?"

"I'm off that," she said. "I'd take a bottle of water if you had some."

He did, and poured a tiny bottle of Jim Beam over a thick mug full of ice. He sat back, sipping, watching her. She drank her water and watched back. His mug had his campaign slogan on it, HEIMAN IS YOUR MAN IN JUNEAU, gold letters on a blue background, just like Alaska's flag. The gold flashed in the late afternoon sun.

Minutes ticked by the way they do, one second at a time. Finally Pete laughed again and slapped his knee. "I should never try to outstare you or outstubborn you, Kate. I know better."

Or try to intimidate me, she thought.

Still laughing, he said, "You want to come work for me?"

"I've got a job."

"I'll double whatever Billy Mike's offering. You'll need the money, now you've got a kid to support."

She drank water, more to give herself time to think than because she was thirsty. "You getting threatening mail, too, Pete?"

"I don't want you on her side against me," he said.

This time she laughed, the sound coming up rough and rusty past the scar on her throat. "Why, Pete, I believe you just gave me a compliment."

"I don't want you on her side against me," he repeated.

"I'm not," she said. "I'm working security. I'm not involved in the campaign, or in the campaign decision-making process in anyway. I'm watching for bad guys. That's it."

"Oh, hell," he said, sighing. "I've never known you to back out of a commitment once you've made it, anyway. But I thought I'd give it the old college try." He gave her a hearty kiss on the cheek and a rough hug and followed her and Mutt out of the Ford. The driver kept the SUV between them and him.

They strolled across the parking lot, Pete's arm around Kate's shoulders, Mutt padding at Kate's other side, and the first person they saw was Darlene Shelikof.

Kate gave her a cool nod and swept by without speaking. "Darlene," Pete said, stopping to put his hand out. "Good to see you again."

"Hello, Peter," Darlene said, eyes darting between him and Kate.

"How's your folks? Your dad still fishing over to the flats?"

Kate moved toward the door and, thankfully, out of earshot.

The Lodge was one of those Ahtna institutions that increased the town's can-do commercial legend, the brainchild of a local welder who had gone to work on the Pipeline and had seen the opportunity inherent in its completion and the wholesale selloff of the remaining supplies and equipment. Artie Whittaker bid for six of the fifty-six man Atco trailers in which Alyeska had housed its temporary work force in twelve camps from Prudhoe Bay to Valdez, finessed transportation costs by taking delivery of them in Ahtna, turned one into a kitchen, one into a restaurant and bar, added some bathrooms to give some of the rooms in the other four trailers private baths, added Arctic walkways to join them together, and opened for business. He was full from the first day, helped by a good cook, a first-class bartender, and that his only competition was a few bed-and-breakfasts in private homes and a run-down motel that catered to philanderers from Valdez up for an illicit weekend's *à deux,* or *à trois* as the case might be. "There are things you just don't want to know about your neighbors," Artie had told Kate once, giving his head a gloomy shake. Considering that her line of work all too frequently put her in the category of Peeping Tom, she agreed with him wholeheartedly. It made a bond between them, and she was looking forward to seeing him again.

But Artie wasn't at the registration counter this afternoon. A dark, slender man with long hair swept back in an artful style and a single diamond stud in his left earlobe smiled at her. "How may I help you?"

"Where's Artie?" she said.

"Artie's in Kona."

"You're kidding."

"Nope. He's retired," he said cheerfully. "I bought him out last October."

"Did you," Kate said. "What's your name?"

He drew himself up and declaimed, "My name is Luiz Antonio Orozco y Elizondo, prepare to die." He grinned. "But you can call me Tony."

"Thank god," Kate said.

Tony laughed. "And you are?"

"Kate Shugak. I should have a reservation." At this point Mutt made her presence known by rearing up to place both enormous paws on the edge of the counter. "Any objection to dogs in the rooms?"

On her hind legs Mutt looked Tony straight in the eye. "If I had, I'd rethink them," he said.

Mutt's tail gave a preliminary approving wag. Kate's four-footed character-defect detector. Except in the case of Jim Chopin, she was infallible. Kate decided Artie had sold well.

The last time Kate had overnighted at the Ahtna Lodge reservations had been entered in an oversized red daily diary, in Artie's famously illegible handwriting, and the keys had hung from a board mounted within reach of the counter. A guest was expected to pick a key, write down their name and room number in the diary, and pay whenever they saw Artie next.

Now there was a computer, which spit out a slip of paper. "Ah, you're part of the Gordaoff campaign," Tony said. "You're all in the same wing." That was the first time Kate had heard the Atco trailers that made up the Ahtna Lodge referred to as "wings." The keys were in little open-ended boxes against the opposite wall. Tony handed one over.

"Thanks. Any messages?"

"No."

Kate looked down at the slip of paper. "Do you know how long I'm supposed to stay here?"

One mobile eyebrow went up, but Tony said, "There should be a departure date on your receipt."

Before Kate could find it, she heard a voice call out her name. It didn't sound friendly. "Kate!"

Kate winced inwardly, and turned. "Darlene. Hi. I just got in."

"I saw," Darlene said. "I'd like to talk to you for a moment." She saw Tony watching and added with a wide, insincere smile, "Please."

"I wanted to take a shower," Kate said, not really hedging. Bathing on the homestead involved a round, galvanized steel tub. A series of long, hot showers in hotel rooms was an added bonus to signing on with the Gordaoff campaign.

"This will only take a minute," Darlene said. She put out a hand to take Kate's arm, encountered Kate's look, and thought better of it.

Kate shouldered her duffel and followed Darlene to a corner.

"Why did you walk in with Peter Heiman?" Darlene said in a low voice.

"He drove up at the same time I did," Kate said.

"What did he want?"

"He's an old family friend." For the hell of it Kate added, "He wanted to offer me a job."

Darlene stepped forward, glaring. "What do you mean, he offered you a job!"

Kate put a hand on Darlene's chest and pushed her back a step. "The only way we're going to make it through the next two months is if you don't crowd me, Darlene."

Darlene took a deep breath and let it out. "What do you mean," she said, spacing out the words, "Peter Heiman offered you a job?"

"I think it comes under the heading of, better to have the camel on the inside of the tent pissing out than on the outside pissing in," Kate said. "Don't worry. I declined his very generous offer." She watched Darlene's face with interest, wondering if the other woman was going to suffer a massive heart attack right before her eyes. She hoped not. Her better nature might force her to give Darlene CPR.

Darlene, with a powerful effort, brought herself back under control. "We want Anne to be safe," she said, spacing out the words with care. "Jim Chopin says that people who write letters generally stick to writing letters. Okay, fine. But Anne's the front-runner in this race, and that draws attention, especially when you're the front-runner against a two-time incumbent who is wired into the Republican majority and has money coming into his campaign from Outside to keep him in office. Especially when you're a Native woman running against a white man. Especially when you're younger and he's older."

Kate waited. Mutt, standing next to her, yawned so wide her jaw cracked.

"You should know I've hired a researcher," Darlene said. "She's looking into Heiman's background."

"Research for attack ads?" Kate said.

Darlene's lips tightened. "Depends on what he throws at us first."

Kate thought Darlene's comment through to its logical conclusion, and didn't like where she arrived. "You think Pete Heiman might be behind these letters?"

"Why not?" Darlene said, adding, the world in two words, "He's behind."

Kate's eyes narrowed. "The only bent thing I know about Pete Heiman is his extreme bad taste in women. I don't recall him ever stooping to hate mail, or anything remotely that tacky." Something any law enforcement professional looked for in a suspect, a history of bad behavior. If you stole a trike when you were four, that was history, and in Alaska, no matter how reassuring the judge was from the bench about your record being expunged because you were a juvenile, that record never went away. So far as Kate knew, Pete Heiman had no record, other than that of being a good son, a successful businessman, a lousy husband, and your ordinary, everyday common or garden variety sold-to-the-highest-bidder Republican legislator. At least Pete didn't get visions from God to guide him through the legislative session. At least Pete didn't introduce a law to legalize billboards in the state. At least Pete knew enough about life in the Bush to get behind rural subsistence, and enough about Alaska Natives to be willing at least to discuss the issue of sovereignty.

"He's behind," Darlene repeated.

I'll earn my keep, Darlene, Kate thought, but some of it's going toward not letting you throw mud all over one of Abel's best drinking buddies. "So I read the mail, I watch the crowds, I follow up on anyone that looks iffy," she said out loud.

"You protect the candidate," Darlene said.

"I can do that," Kate said. "But let me repeat what I said before. Don't crowd me, Darlene."

They stared at each other until a voice broke in.

"Darlene?"

They looked around and saw Anne Gordaoff's husband, Doug, whom Kate had met briefly in Niniltna as Billy Mike was forcing her out of her own retirement. He was of middle height, with a youthful face belied by a thick thatch of gray hair and a quick, charming smile. Too quick and too charming, Kate had thought then, and saw nothing now to change her mind.

"She wants you," he told Darlene. "And the researcher, I can never remember her name, she called and wants you to call her back." He flashed the smile at Kate. "Kate."

"Doug," Kate said, and hoisted her duffel again. "I was just checking in."

"There's quite a crowd of people at the gym," Darlene said brusquely. "Get there as soon as possible." She turned and walked away with Doug.

"Certainly," Kate said to her retreating back, and bethought herself once more of the very large check folded inside her jacket pocket, ready to be deposited in the Ahtna branch of the Last Frontier Bank at 10:01 A.M. the following morning.

6

The Ahtna High School gymnasium, as befit a town that was the hub of its region, was large, with a floor divided into six basketball courts, bleachers that extended from both sides, and a stage that took up most of the third wall. The metal trusses had been painted alternately in the blue and white of the Ahtna Avalanche, the home team, although their color was nearly obscured by the forest of banners hanging from them like so many rectangular bats. Regional championships in basketball, wrestling, and volleyball; state championships in basketball and volleyball, and three retired jerseys were among the trophies, and the smell of popcorn indicated that the freshman pep club had seized upon the evening's event to make a couple of bucks.

The bleachers, Kate saw in some surprise, were crowded, as were the metal folding chairs lined up on the court below. People spilled into the aisles and stood three deep against the rear wall. Someone had propped open one of the fire exits so those inclined could nip out for a smoke and not have to come all the way around through the front door to reenter the building. No alarm was sounding, so they must have disabled it.

On stage, challenger Anne Gordaoff and incumbent Peter Heiman were being miked, and moderator Mary Frances Chernikof stood frowning at a fistful of notes, all three flanked by the stars and stripes on one side and eight stars of gold on a field of blue on the other. In the audience, one woman had brought her knitting, another a mukluk she was trimming with caribou. A group of old men sipped something out of a paper bag and muttered among themselves. A group of young men were bent over a Game Boy. A few young couples were taking advantage of the dimmed lights to neck, and small children ran off an excess of energy in running up and down the steps bisecting the bleachers, shrieking with laughter at the booming noise they gave off. A mixture of Athabascan, Aluutiq, and English made a low background hum, and a crew sporting jackets with the gaudy logo from an Anchorage television station appeared to be having trouble with their cameras.

Billy Mike stood next to Kate looking intent and serious, as befitted the tribal leader of the Niniltna Native Association. Outwardly, he was careful to maintain an impartial air, and Kate saw the incumbent bend a long and thoughtful look on Niniltna's chief. If Anne Gordaoff had

Billy's endorsement as candidate for state senate, Anne Gordaoff was as good as sworn in. Kate could see other Park rats following Pete's gaze and coming to the same conclusion.

"Kate?" a voice said.

Kate looked around and saw a short, plump redhead beaming at her. "Tracy? Is that you?"

"Kate! I heard you were coming, and I couldn't believe it!" The redhead threw her arms around Kate and hugged her.

"Tracy Huffman," Kate said, freeing herself with difficulty. "What the hell are you doing in Ahtna? Last I heard you were reporting for the *Daily News-Miner*."

"I was, from the day after we graduated. I was with them until this April. Then Darlene came knocking at my door with an offer I couldn't refuse." She saw Kate's expression and added, "You couldn't, either, I hear."

Kate, about to deny it, decided to laugh instead. "Yeah, well. I guess I've sold out."

"Doesn't take long, does it?"

"No, it sure doesn't." She looked with affection at Tracy's good-natured face, at the thick hair pulled back from her brow with a tortoiseshell band, at the big blue eyes sparkling with the sense of fun that had gotten them all into trouble more than once way back when. She was dressed in a long-tailed green silk shirt, black stretch pants, and ballet slippers. There was a black portfolio over one arm and a clipboard in the other. "What are you doing for the campaign?"

"I'm the flack." Kate looked puzzled, and Tracy translated. "Media consultant."

Kate provided her own translation. "You talk to reporters."

Tracy's blinding smile beamed out again. "You've always been better than average bright, Shugak. I've always liked that about you."

Mutt interjected with a polite sneeze, and Tracy looked down. "You must be Mutt." She offered a fist, palm down. Mutt sniffed it, sneezed again, and looked at Kate as if to say, I've had enough of dodging people trying to step on my toes, thanks.

Kate looked around, assessing the room, and picked a spot against the wall opposite the stage. Moving toward it, she said, "I got your letter, and the poem. It meant something, Tracy. Thanks."

"It helped me some when my dad died. I thought maybe it might you, too. Look, Kate, I won't go here more than once, but I want you to know I'm sorry as hell about Jack."

Kate could tolerate Tracy's sympathy, just. "Thanks."

"I have to say, I'm glad you made it, though."

"Yeah."

Tracy gave her a sharp look. "One day, you'll be glad, too."

I don't know, Kate thought. I don't know if I want to be.

"So," Tracy said, giving a group of men standing not very far away an obvious and provocative once-over, "I hear you're our new security."

Kate found an overlooked chair, unfolded it, and stood on it. "That's me."

Tracy's attention was divided equally between the group of men, who were by now looking back, and her conversation with Kate. "Jim Chopin talk you into it?"

Kate looked down from her scan of the crowd. "No. How does he come into it?"

"He's the one who told Darlene to hire you." Looking toward Darlene standing on the stage conferring with Anne, Tracy added, "I'd have liked to have been in the room when he did to see just how well that went over."

"I thought it was all Billy's idea."

Tracy shrugged. "I only know what they tell me." She gave a theatrical sigh. "Who's the famously hunky Jim Chopin sleeping with nowadays, anyway?"

Kate stared hard at a high school boy who was lighting up what she was fairly certain was a joint. He saw her looking and choked on the first inhalation. The smoke went down the wrong way. Coughing, tears streaming down his face, he stumbled out of the building. "I wouldn't know."

"Because I am most definitely available."

"Congratulations," Kate said.

"What's wrong?" Tracy eyed her with an appraising expression. "You sound a little —"

"What?"

"I don't know, a little testy, I guess."

"Just hungry, I missed my dinner. I met the

109

new owner of the Ahtna Lodge when I checked in."

"Who, Tony? Isn't he precious? No hope there for the heterosexual woman, I fear."

Kate grinned. "All I care about at the moment is how good his cook is."

Tracy sighed. "Still thinking with your stomach, Shugak. I feel like I'm right back on the fourth floor in Lathrop Dorm." She watched Darlene aim a long, expressionless look at Kate. She watched Kate meet it with a long, expressionless look of her own. "Oh yeah, right back there. You still pissed at her? It's been a long time."

"I never did like her much," Kate said, "even before."

"I noticed," Tracy said. "We all did. You didn't have two words to say to anyone that first year, but you had even less to say to Darlene Shelikof. Did you guys know each other before UAF?"

Kate watched a thin young man wedge himself into the first row of the bleachers on her left, his head shaved bald beneath a Cordova District Fishermen United cap. No visible tattoos. He was alone — no, a woman appeared and plunked down in his lap and he laughed and kissed her. Kate dismissed him as a suspect at once. Skinheads never laughed, and they almost never got laid. "No," she said to Tracy. "I didn't know her before."

A stocky young man with his mother's dark

hair and eyes and his father's quick grin had been introduced to Kate as the candidate's son, Tom. He came up to them, his eyes admiring the red-head. "Hi, Tracy." He spared Kate a brief glance and no greeting. "Mom wants you."

Tracy hitched up her portfolio and said, "Duty calls. Later, Kate."

"Later," Kate echoed.

The group of men watched Tracy walk past with identical needy expressions on their faces. One of them was the fisherman who'd given Kate a ride in from the airport. Never say die.

There were two television cameras trained on the stage, one at the head of each of the aisles formed by three blocks of metal folding chairs, by now most of which were full. So were the bleachers.

The Gordaoff family was in the center of the front row, and a stream of what Kate from her experience with Emaa holding court at public functions instantly recognized as wannabe toadies formed a more or less continuous line in front of them. Erin, the candidate's daughter, had a nondescript face and a build that combined her father's lean with her mother's padding to make a figure that gave every man in the room whiplash when she walked by. She sat next to a tall blond man, introduced as Jeff Hosford and Erin's fiancé. Erin's senior by at least ten years, he had the blunt features and the pumped-up look of a weight lifter. His right hand rested on the back of Erin's neck. Erin stayed motionless beneath that hand, as if she were on a leash. Kate had been surprised when he was introduced as an attorney with a firm in Anchorage and the campaign's chief fundraiser. He looked more like muscle for the mob. His smile had been automatic and without feeling, his handshake damp, and he had tried a little too hard.

Peter Heiman came in and was immediately surrounded by supporters of his own, fewer in number, and whiter. Kate wondered how indicative this was of the district as a whole. Maybe Darlene was right, although she hated to entertain that notion for more than a second at a time.

The two candidates took up positions behind their podiums, the two people vying to represent one of the most geographically, culturally, ideologically, and economically diverse regions in a state where, in a gathering of four people there are five marriages, six divorces, and seven political parties. Kate thought of the Park, and she thought they were both crazy, one to want to keep the job, and the other to want to take it away from him.

The Park, twenty million acres of mountain and glacier and river and plain, deep in the heart of Alaska. North and east were the Quilak Mountains, south was Prince William Sound and the Gulf of Alaska, west was the TransAlaska Pipeline and the Alaska Railroad. Its biggest river was the Kanuyaq, two hundred and fifty miles of twist and turn, broad and shallow and filled with sandbars to the south, narrow and deep and boulder-filled to the north, with a thousand creeks and streams draining into it. It's biggest mountain was Angqaq Peak, known to mountain climbers the world over as the Big Bump, eighteen thousand feet and change of rock and ice, attendant peaks of twelve and fourteen and sixteen thousand feet forming an entourage.

For every mountain there was a glacier, thick tongues of millennial ice receding reluctantly to reveal a wide, high plateau that sloped into rolling foothills and a long, curving valley that drained into the Kanuyaq. The Kanuyaq was the Park's well and its breadbasket. It was also the Park's major highway, navigable by boat in summer and by dogsled and snow machine in winter.

One road led into the Park, maintained, barely, by a single grader stationed at Ahtna, the town that marked the junction between the Kanuyaq River Highway and the spur of gravel leading to Niniltna. The grader took a week to scrape the road one way into Niniltna, spent the weekend at Bernie's Roadhouse, and then took a week to scrape back to Ahtna. The road stood up under this assault, as it had been first laid down as a railroad grade a hundred years before, engineered to get the copper out of the Kanuyaq Copper Mine and down to the port of Cordova. When copper prices fell in the thirties, the mine closed and they pulled up the tracks of the Kanuyaq River & Northern Railroad. Park residents followed behind, digging out the ties for use as needed in shack foundations, raised-bed gardens, creek bridges. Bernie had scavenged the last of them, back when he built the Roadhouse in the early '70s, to hold up the bar. The railroad roadbed was still flat, more or less, and still driveable, more or less, or it was in summer. In winter it wasn't plowed, and the Park lay inviolate behind twelve-foot drifts of impassable snow. The most important traffic over it was the fuel truck, and the most important trip it made was the last delivery before Labor Day.

Boats, snow machines, and dogsleds were all very well, but the preferred method of transportation was always and ever air. Everyone with a homestead had their own airstrip, and for those with lesser acreage there was the forty-eight-hundred-foot strip that ran right through downtown Niniltna, which served as the base of operations for George Perry's semi-irregular air taxi service. When George wasn't beating the water at Rocky River, or trysting with the latest girlfriend at his hunting lodge south of Denali.

Kate shut down on all thought of George's lodge and focused on the stage. It was cool in the cavernous room but with this many people it wouldn't stay that way for long. The smells of dried salmon and fresh moose and curing hide and wood smoke saturated the air. She knew many of the people there by sight; others were new to her. Nobody looked like they were carrying, other than those who had knives strapped to their belts, although with Alaska's new concealed-carry permit, available to anyone who trundled themselves down to the local police station to take the class, someone in this crowd could have a rocket launcher stuffed into their boot and she'd never know it.

There was constant motion. In a crowd this big, there were always people on their feet, moving to a new seat, to the water fountain, to the bathroom, outside for a smoke or a drink or a toke. But on the whole, attention was focused on the stage, and on the debate. It surprised her. She had thought that rural Alaska had given up on politics years ago. Of course, Anne Gordaoff was one of their own. She was probably related to more people in the Park than Kate was.

Anne Gordaoff was forty-six years old, a chunky woman with short brown hair in an untidy Dutch boy haircut, big brown eyes with laugh wrinkles fanning away from the corners, a pursed rosebud of a mouth that opened to reveal large, white, even teeth, and a double chin that went away when she raised her head to smile. She smiled a lot.

She was dressed in a conservative brown pantsuit that looked straight out of the Eddie Bauer catalogue, and Kate was willing to bet that the lightweight T-shirt beneath the blazer was one of a dozen in the same color. All the better to disguise the wear and tear of travel. Practical. Comfortable. Conservative, except for the dancing-shaman brooch that dominated a lapel. If Kate had had a left nut, she would bet it all on the possibility that a Park artist had made the brooch and that the artist was in the audience tonight.

The debate moderator was a plump woman with a neat cap of short blonde hair. She was also smart, articulate, and well informed on Alaskan issues. She pushed both candidates right into the deep end with a question on subsistence. Anne came down hard in favor of rural preference, Peter playing the same tune in a lower key and, as a consequence, sounding less radical and less angry.

"The people who have been hunting and fishing these lands for the last ten thousand years ought to be the ones who have preference, especially in times of shortage," Anne said in reply. "It is unconscionable for the state government to say to the upriver Athabascans and the downriver Yupik, 'You cannot fish the Yukon River this year because we must meet quotas for the commercial fishermen.' "

Jeff Hosford walked by Kate's chair, talking into the cell phone that seemed to be permanently attached to his right ear. He looked up and saw Kate watching him. His smile was slow and insolent, and he stripped her with his eyes. It was obvious from his expression that she was now expected to leap into his arms and wrestle him to the floor. When she let her gaze drift past him as if he weren't even there, he couldn't stand it and walked over. "Ms. . . . Shugak, isn't it?"

"Mr. Hosford."

"You're our campaign security?" The amused disbelief in his voice was provocative.

"I am."

"A cute little thing like you?"

"Yup."

"I've heard about you, you know. Everybody has. I don't figure half of it's true."

"Could you step to one side, please? I need a clear view of the stage."

He lurked around her peripheral vision for a few more moments, and then moved on. Jerk.

"Well, now, Anne, in times of shortages, I'd have to agree with you," Peter said, and gave the issue an adroit twist. "But what about the Natives living in Anchorage? There's about thirty thousand of them, at the last census, and more moving in every day. They call Anchorage Alaska's largest Native village. Are you saying that because they have chosen to live in an urban environment that they have lost all rights to fish and hunt where their parents and grandparents did?"

Peter was trying to get Anne to say that she preferred Native preference, period, for hunting and fishing priorities, which was almost certainly true but which would lose her a lot of non-Native votes in the district and probably the election, but Anne was too smart for that.

"I am saying, Peter, that the people who live off the land should be allowed to do just that in times of shortage, and that the people who have a cultural history of subsistence hunting and fishing should also be allowed to continue to do so."

Thus neatly including all non-Native Bush rats in her stand on rural subsistence, too. Anne smiled primly straight into the camera recording the event for later broadcast over the statewide television channel, ARCS, and that was when Kate realized that Anne Gordaoff had plans to run for governor. Kate looked at Pete and wondered if he knew. Probably. He might even vote for her.

Doug Gordaoff passed her, his eyes fixed on the swinging behind of a young woman in very tight jeans, who tossed flirtatious glances over her shoulder as if she were leaving a trail of bread crumbs.

The next question was about sovereignty. Again, Anne came down on the side of self-government for Native villages. "Why not?" she said, softening her voice in an immediate response to Peter's lower key that Kate could only admire. "What have we got to lose? The whole theme for the Nineties was 'taking responsibility for our actions,' we were all supposed to shoulder our own weight, stop leaning on the federal government to take care of us. Well then, let us try, let the villages assume some of the duties and responsibilities of self-governance."

"For example?" the moderator said.

"Law enforcement," Anne said immediately. "There is no such thing as law enforcement in too many Native villages, who never see a state trooper from one year to the next unless there is murder done."

Kate thought of Jim, and of how he spent as much time in the air going from crime to crime as he did on the ground investigating them, and thought Anne had a good point.

But this was too much for Pete. "There are only two hundred and seventy-three troopers in the state of Alaska. They can't be everywhere at once."

"Yes, and why is that, Peter? Could it be that the state has failed to adequately fund the Department of Public Safety, so that there aren't enough troopers to respond to any but the most serious crimes in the smaller communities?"

Darlene was sitting in the front row of the folding chairs directly in Anne's line of sight. She raised her hand in a signal that Kate couldn't quite make out, but it made Anne, who had been gradually leaning forward, straighten in her chair and take a deep breath.

Peter, who had come without handlers, yanked on his own invisible leash and dropped his voice, once again the voice of sweet reason. There was no arguing Anne's point, so he didn't try. "Anne, this issue was supposed to have been resolved with the passage in 1971 of the Alaska Native Claims Settlement Act. For forty-four million acres and a billion dollars, the Native tribes of Alaska would cede aboriginal lands for the TransAlaska Pipeline right-of-way and form corporations to see to the needs of their peoples."

"Yes, and all ANCSA required in return was that Alaska Natives become white," Anne flashed back. "We live in the Bush, not in boardrooms."

"What's next, Anne?" Pete said coolly. "What comes after Natives gain sovereignty? You going to follow the ways of Outside Indian country? You going to open a casino in Niniltna?"

A statement guaranteed to win all the votes there were from the religious right wing of Pete's party.

It was at this point that Kate realized that Peter Heiman might have gubernatorial ambitions of his own. She didn't think Anne would vote for him, though.

Peter had won this round on points, but Anne had him on passion. Darlene tiptoed over to Tracy, standing next to the television camera and flirting with the cameraman, and whispered something to her. Tracy nodded and hurried out of the building. The cameraman yearned after her with a mournful expression on his face. Darlene pulled out her cell phone and speed-dialed a number.

The next question concerned each candidate's reaction to the recent initiative passed by an overwhelming majority of Alaskan voters to make English the official language of the state of Alaska.

"A slap in the face to every Native in the state," was Anne's comment.

"Unnecessary," Peter allowed, and grinned. He had an attractive grin and he used it well. "I hear Tuntutuliak has passed an ordinance establishing Yupik as the official village language. I hope every time a federal bureaucrat has to fly in there to do business that he has to hire a Yupik interpreter, and I hope those Tuntutuliakers know enough to charge the red-shift limit for the service."

Even Anne laughed. Kate looked for Darlene to see how she took this, and couldn't find her in the crowd.

Erin Gordaoff, looking lost without Jeff Hosford at her elbow, scurried past. Kate watched her go into the ladies' room.

The moderator gave each candidate two minutes to sum up. Anne touched on her background in the health care profession, of her service to the community on various governmental committees, of her stint as a member of the University of Alaska's Board of Regents. She invoked family icons, the how-many-times great-grandmother as a direct descendent of Baranov, of the grandfather who was a delegate to the Constitutional Convention in 1955, of the aunt who worked on ANCSA. She thanked her campaign manager and cousin, Darlene Shelikof, and the rest of her supporters for getting her this far.

She was articulate, humble, and smart enough

not to attack Peter. Mudslinging didn't work in Bush elections, where Native villagers in particular were unfailingly polite to candidates of either party whether they voted for them or not, and expected their children to be, too.

She was also a younger woman to Peter's older man, and Pete didn't hesitate to point that out, referring to his many long years in Alaska, summoning up family apparitions of his own going back three generations of Alaskan history, his record as a successful businessman and employer of over a thousand Alaskans, his two terms in Juneau.

The audience applauded, the stage lights overhead dimmed, and everybody shook everybody else's hand. Comments from the crowd held the honors of the evening to be about even. More than one person was laughing over Pete's Yupik interpreter, and Kate heard someone say, "Think Dan O'Brian'd like having to do business for the Parks Service in Athabascan?"

"So?" Billy Mike said.

"I admit," Kate said, "I'm impressed."

His round moon face was split by a wide, and what could have been relieved, grin. "Good. Great."

"I don't have to like her to keep her safe," Kate said. "I don't even have to vote for her." He laughed, scoffing at the possibility. "Tell me, Billy, this advance I've got in my pocket. It's drawn on the Niniltna Native Association bank account. I'm wondering how the other three hundred and forty-six shareholders would feel about this use of the tribal chief's discretionary portion of the general fund."

"The board okayed it at Monday night's meeting." He looked back at the crowd and said, "So? Do you see anyone suspicious?"

"Well," Kate said, watching the crowd gather around the tables dispensing cookies and Kool-Aid, "other than the joint I saw Michael Moonin sucking on, Rudy Brooks selling six hits of what I figure was cocaine, too many people drinking too much Windsor Canadian out of paper bags, and the narrowly averted infliction of what would have been statutory rape by Nathan Kvasnikoff upon the person of Carole Pyle — although I must say Carole looked more than willing until her dad, Ray, showed up —" She looked at Billy, whose laughter had faded into round-eyed dismay. "No."

Billy looked from one side of the crowd to the other. "What? You saw all that? Here in the gym? What — why —"

"Billy," Kate said, and he turned back to her. He looked so hurt that she was moved by an unaccustomed stirring of sympathy. "There are over eight hundred people here tonight, maybe more. You get this many people together in one place, you're bound to have some of that stuff going on."

"Why didn't you stop it?"

"None of it was anywhere near Anne," Kate said. "That's what you hired me for, remember?

123

To protect Anne Gordaoff."

"I know, but —"

"Billy."

He lapsed into unhappy silence.

Tracy appeared, the ghost of a grin on her face. "So. Bathed in the presence of the candidate, have you now become a true believer, ready to walk in the paths of righteousness?"

"Ask me tomorrow morning."

"Why tomorrow morning?"

"Tomorrow morning, the check clears the bank," Kate said.

Billy winced, and Tracy laughed. There was a scrabble of canine feet, and Kate looked down to see Mutt on tiptoe, ears straight up, nose pointing at the door. "Mutt?" She hopped down from the chair. Mutt streaked away through the crowd. Kate looked around for Anne and found her still on the stage. "Go to Anne, Billy."

"What?"

"Go to Anne, now. Stay with her, I don't care where she goes or what she does, until I get back. Got it?" He said nothing and she raised her voice. "Got it?"

He looked shaken, but he said, "Got it," and stuck his chubby little chin out like he meant it. He began pushing his way through the crowd to Anne, and Kate took off after Mutt.

She found her finally, in the parking lot, whining at the blue van Doug and Darlene had driven from the lodge to the gymnasium.

Inside was the tall blond man who was the

124

candidate's daughter's fiancé.

And if the gunshot wound in his chest was any indication, he was riding shotgun for the last time.

Nome

July 1900

The little girl had long dark curls done up with pale pink ribbons that matched the trim on her dress. She stood in the doorway of the Aurora Saloon and gazed inside.

A tall man wearing a big gray hat and a black suit came to the door. "I have to say you're the youngest customer I've ever had in this saloon, little girl. What can I get for you? Maybe some lemonade?"

He had a nice smile and she liked his voice, which was deep and soft. She pointed. "That lady doesn't have any clothes on."

He looked over his shoulder at the painting of the reclining nude hanging in back of the bar. "She sure doesn't. Why don't you have a seat on the porch, and I'll bring you a glass of lemonade. Real lemons, fresh off the boat, and you can tell me where to find your mother. Here —"

There was a rustle of silk, and a woman with dark red hair and tired eyes rushed forward to scoop the little girl into her arms. She glared at the man. "Leave her alone!"

The big man looked surprised. "Is she yours, Angel? I thought —"

"No, she's not," the woman said, and the little girl squirmed when the woman's arms tightened around her. "But she has no business in here, and you have no business with her, so just leave her alone."

The man's face darkened, and the little girl was suddenly afraid. "I wasn't doing anything except getting her a drink. I didn't —"

"A drink!"

"Not a drink drink, goddamn it, just some lemonade to keep her settled while we looked for —"

"Victoria!"

Everyone's head turned to watch the woman wade through the mud from the other side of the street. "Victoria Mae Wilson, I told you not to stray!" She saw who was holding her daughter and flushed. "How dare you! Give me my daughter!" She snatched the little girl from the red-haired woman's arms and glared impartially from the woman to the man. He looked resigned. The woman's expression was harder to define. She looked weary and apologetic and, for a moment perhaps, even on the verge of tears.

The little girl watched them both over her mother's shoulder as she was borne off down the street, her mother trailing righteous indignation like the wake of a large ship.

There was a silence between the two people on the steps of the saloon. People, mostly men, pushed past, some pausing to touch their hat brims to the man, some to give the woman a familiar chuck under the chin. They stood as the mother and child had left them, watching the throng of men panning elbow to elbow for gold in the icy waters of the Bering Sea on the beach that formed the other side of the main street. The Arctic summer sun didn't so much set at this time of year as it circled the horizon, weakening in intensity toward the late evening hours but never entirely waning. "Angel —"

"Don't," she said.

His lips tightened. "I don't know how much more I can stand it, watching him treat you like he does."

"It's none of your business," she said without anger. Anxiety always brought out her accent, and this was no exception. He had to work to follow her words. "And he'd kill you, if you tried anything. He'd kill you, Matt."

"Would he, now?" he said thoughtfully, his hand raising to settle on the butt of the pistol strapped to his side. "Would he, indeed?"

She put a restraining hand on his arm. "Don't, Matt." She tried to smile and almost succeeded. "Just don't."

His hand came up to grasp hers. "What hold does he have on you, Angel? You don't have to do this, you could go back to just dancing. God knows my customers love your Flame Dance." He grinned and added, "I don't mind saying it keeps my heart ticking over nicely, too."

Her smile was more the real article this time.

"I don't know for how much longer, though," he said. "Nome's about played out. I hear tell how Alaska Steam is cutting the price of a ticket Outside

to fifteen dollars. That's down from seventy. I figure a lot of people are going to take advantage of that to get the hell out once and for all. I might myself." He looked at her. "How about you?"

She looked away, back at the beach front and the path of gold the sun was making over the ocean behind them. "I don't know. He hasn't said."

"Is it that kid of yours?" he said suddenly. "Has he threatened your baby?"

Her smile vanished and she turned to go back inside. He restrained her. "Is that it, Angel?"

"I told you never to call me that," she whispered. "I'm sorry I ever told you."

"Told me what? Your real name? Why not? It suits you." He raised a hand to smooth back a lock of hair, still red, still lustrous, that had fallen forward on her brow. "It's beautiful. Like you. I want to call you by it."

"You can't," she whispered. "I don't want you to."

"Is it the baby?" he said again. "Because if it is —"

"Because if it is you'll do what?" The Greek's suit was tailored of fine tweed, and his boots were well-made and shined to a mirror finish, but nothing would ever hide the rapacious expression in his cold dark eyes. His teeth flashed when he smiled at the two of them. "You're losing me money, Darling, standing around on the porch talking."

Matt made a sudden movement, and a long-barreled Colt appeared in the Greek's hand.

Once again silence descended. Men froze in the doorway, watching, ready to dive out of the line of fire.

Matt's face darkened. "You want to be careful

129

with that pop gun of yours, Alex," he said evenly. "Somebody could get hurt."

Alex Papadopolous smiled. "Somebody sure could," he agreed, and caused the Colt to disappear again. He stood back, looking at the Dawson Darling, still smiling.

The redhead raised her chin and swept past him into the saloon.

Matt was right, Nome was on its last legs as a stampeder town. The Poor Man's Gold Rush was almost over. The only thing that made for more business in a whorehouse than a boom was a bust. Men stood in line for their turn, and she was exhausted when morning came. Alex would have kept her working right around the clock — "Hell, the sun's still up, ain't it?" — and it was after five before she dispatched the last customer. Tired as she was, she made the time for a quick bath before tumbling into bed and falling instantly asleep.

It seemed only moments later when a faint scratching at the door woke her. She repressed a groan. "Whoever it is, go away," she called. "Come back tonight."

"It's Matt," came the reply. "Open up."

There was another sound, a faint mewling, that had her on her feet and at the door in an instant. She wrenched it open and Matt held out the child in his arms. "Percy!"

Percy was thin and pale and almost asleep. "Mama?" he said, and nuzzled his face into her shoulder.

"How did you get him? How did you know where he was?"

"Alex had to pay the woman he had looking after him. One day I followed him." He smiled. "He's a cheap bastard, Alex is; she wasn't happy with what he was paying her. From the looks of that kid she didn't spend much of it feeding him, either." He shrugged and cast a look behind him before he stepped inside and closed the door. In a low voice he said, "Get dressed. I've got you a ticket on the boat to Fairbanks."

She stared at him, open-mouthed.

"He'll think you went to Seattle," he said. "Anybody could scrape fifteen bucks together. He won't figure you went to Fairbanks, so that's where you should go." When she didn't move, he put firm hands on her shoulders and turned her toward the wardrobe. "Hurry up now, before he gets back."

She took a step, stopped. "Matt," she said. "Why?"

He didn't pretend to misunderstand her. "Because you're not like the rest of them. You got yourself forced into something you don't want to do." He paused. "I could have outbid Halvorsen, you know."

She stared at him. "Is that what this is about? You feel guilty because you didn't win the bidding that night?"

"I know you want out," he said, ignoring her words, "and I aim to get you out." He handed her a small leather bag, and she knew what it was from the weight.

"Matt, I —" She swallowed, and tried again.

He shook his head, his smile a little twisted. "I'm

131

not coming with you now. I've got a saloon to run. Maybe later, when the stampede's over, I'll catch up to you. But now, you've got to go. Speaking of which, pack your bag, woman, you've got a boat to catch."

"The hell you say," Alex Papadopolous said from the doorway, and fired from the hip. The gunshot echoed around the room and startled Percy, who began to cry.

Matt spun around, pulling his pistol and trying to aim. Papadopolous fired again, and Matt fell backward, his head at her feet. She stared down at him, and he raised his hand to her, the one holding the pistol. She took it, as if in a dream, and raised it with a trembling hand.

Alex laughed at her, the same laugh he had laughed at her when he stood in the door of the cabin Sam had built for her, the same laugh he had laughed when he took her to the bed she had warmed for Arthur.

She fired.

7

The Ahtna police chief was a big, beefy, red-faced man with a five-o'clock shadow, a beer-belly gut, and a handlebar mustache. He could have come straight out of central casting to answer a call for "Cop, Small Town, Generic." His eyes were cop's eyes, watchful, shrewd, wholly untrusting. He was every speeding driver's sinking heart coming up in the rearview mirror, every perp's terror when he came into the interrogation room, every watch commander's pet, every conservative's wet dream come true, every liberal's worst nightmare. A cop's cop.

"Hey, Kenny," Kate said.

"Hey, Kate," Kenny said. His grip was warm and solid, and he didn't say anything about Jack, for which that alone she could have kissed him. He was dressed in full uniform, black shirt tucked into black pants cuffed over shined black half-boots that Kate would bet all of her campaign paycheck had steel toes. His badge was gold and shone brightly from the pocket over his

133

left breast: his tie matched the color of his pants and was neatly knotted with the tail tucked between the buttons of his shirt, marine-fashion. Everything had been recently cleaned and fit very well. Kenny knew the value of appearance, and he looked every inch the part.

"So, I'm not liking the hell out of this," Kenny said, indicating the report on his desk. He settled in his chair. It was large and comfortable, with arms and a headrest, and sat in front of a large and comfortable desk in a large, comfortable, and well-appointed room. Diplomas, neatly framed, were hung with military precision on the wall, the filing cabinets were dust-free, the carpet freshly cleaned, and the walls newly painted. Kenny had somebody out front to answer phones and mind the prisoners, if any, in the four-cell jail down the hall. The sour smell of vomit, common to so many cop shops, in the Ahtna Police Department made itself conspicuous by its absence.

Kenny Hazen was the chief of police for Ahtna, which had remained defiantly unincorporated from its founding in 1892, through all of the following century, and entered the next the same way. Local taxes were confined to an eight percent sales tax on everything except food and drugs, which was one reason it attracted businesses from all over the state and why big-box chains like Wal-Mart had been heard to have been investigating into the possibility of locating there.

From that eight percent sales tax, which everybody paid, local and tourist and the weekend fisherman from Anchorage alike, came the funds to run the city. Which was why Ahtna had a one-man police force, but then that was the way Ahtna residents liked it. Ahtnans preferred to handle their own domestic problems, so that by the time Kenny, retired from the Anchorage Police Department after he got in his twenty to take up the job of Ahtna's chief of police, arrived on the scene, all the guns had been hidden, all the blood had been mopped up, and everybody had the same story to tell. The chief had no Indians, but then neither did he have much to do, and he did it at a handsome salary that kept him middling honest. Ahtna could assure prospective businesses thinking of opening a branch office on the Kanuyaq that the local police force was efficient and reliable and fully supported by the local community.

"I'm not liking it much, either, Kenny," Kate said. "It happened on my watch."

A voice said from the doorway, "No shit, Shugak."

She looked up to see Jim Chopin towering over her. Mutt gave a joyous bark and bounced to her feet, nudging at his hand with her head.

"What are you doing here?" Kate said.

Jim grinned his grin at Kate, the one that should have been posted next to a photo of a great white shark over the caption, "Separated at birth? You be the judge."

135

"Anybody'd think you weren't happy to see me. I'm hurt."

She snorted. "Yeah, right, that'll happen."

"You don't always know everything there is to know about everyone, Shugak," he said. The fine edge underlying his words was a surprise. He saw the odd look on Kenny's face as he sat listening to them, and got himself back under control. "I'm here because Darlene came to me first about the letters, and now because somebody who's working on her campaign has been murdered. Kenny called me last night. I flew in this morning. Not that I'm answerable to you for my actions."

"Nobody said you were," she said, taken back.

He looked at Kenny. "What have you got?"

"A GSW to the chest, straight into the heart. Powder burns on his jacket. Small caliber, probably a twenty-two."

"I don't suppose the killer was kind enough to leave the weapon at the scene, say, oh, laying under the dash, with a perfect set of fingerprints on the grip?"

"Nope."

"Hell." Jim thought. "Killer was close."

"Real close. Semen on the vic's underwear and on the seat of the car, and whoever zipped him up after caught a piece of his pecker in the zipper."

"Ouch." Jim winced.

Kenny shrugged. "He didn't feel it. He was dead by then. Anyway, that's why I figure a pistol. Wouldn't be room to maneuver a rifle, even with Hosford otherwise engaged."

"Hard to carry a rifle concealed, too," Jim said.

"There is that."

"So you're figuring a woman met him at the truck, rode him on the seat, and just when he was distracted, lights out." Kenny nodded. "Got a suspect?"

Kenny nodded again. "About three hundred. That's how many women there were in the gym last night."

"Any witnesses?"

"About eight hundred. That's how many were in the gym total. None of them saw anything."

"Great."

"Yeah, that's what I'm thinking." Kenny nodded toward Kate. "She got the scene isolated, and we got the body on a plane for the crime lab in Anchorage this morning."

"Maybe some fluids?"

"I'd say almost certainly, but we'll need a suspect to match to them before we get anywhere."

"What about the other members of the campaign? That's who you're going to look at first, right?"

Kenny looked at Kate. Kate said, "I was standing on a chair in the back of the crowd for the whole debate. At any one time I saw the entire entourage sitting in the front row right in front of the stage. I saw Tom, the son, everywhere, usually in company with one pretty girl or another. I saw Doug walk by at least once. I saw

Darlene get up and confer with Tracy. I saw Tracy leave the room. Later I looked for Darlene and couldn't find her. Erin, the daughter, went to the bathroom at least once. Hosford I never even saw leave, by himself or with anyone. There were just too many people there." She looked at Kenny. "Can I make a call to Anchorage? I want to check something out."

"Sure. Use the one at the empty desk in the outer office. The door closed behind her and Kenny looked at Jim.

"Don't say it, Hazen," Jim said. "Just don't fucking say it."

"Brendan? It's Kate Shugak."

There followed another of those silences that she was starting to get used to whenever she greeted someone she hadn't seen in a while. You'd think I'd come back from the dead, she thought, annoyed. "Brendan?" she said again.

There was a feminine murmur in the background, and the receiver was muffled when he replied to it. "Yeah, I'm here, Kate. Long time no talk. Just a minute, honey," he added, presumably not to her.

"Yeah, I know. I'm sorry to call so early, and on a Saturday morning, too." Brendan McCord was an assistant district attorney in Anchorage, with whom Kate had worked during her five and a half years on the investigator's staff. "You didn't get married, Brendan, did you?"

"Jesus, no!" Brendan's voice was truly horrified. "Don't say things like that, Shugak. My heart's not as strong as it used to be. Besides, you know I've been waiting for you."

Kate grinned into the receiver as she heard another murmur, less languorous and more annoyed this time. "Sure you have." Enough with the pleasantries. "Do you know Anne Gordaoff?"

"I know of her. She's running for state senator from District 41, isn't she?"

"Yes. I'm working security for her." She told him about the threatening letters.

"Kind of comes with the territory, doesn't it?"

"That's what I said, but then they waved a bunch of money at me."

"Were you cheap?"

"No, but I was easy," she said, and they both laughed.

She sobered. "Things just got worse, Brendan. Someone's been killed, someone working on the campaign."

He was instantly on the alert. "Who?"

She told him.

"Kenny Hazen's a good man," he said thoughtfully. "The body on its way to town?"

"Yeah, and Jim Chopin flew in this morning." She left out the activities of the early evening because she'd had enough men yelling at her for one day.

"Ah, the Man in Blue. Yeah, and?"

"You know this Jeff Hosford?"

A moment passed. "Attorney?" Brendan said.

"In his former life, yes."

"Dischner, Seese, Christensen, and Kim."

Unconsciously Kate straightened in her chair. The dispatcher's voice behind her faded away. "Dischner? As in Eddie P.?" As in whose offices she had burgled in company with Mutt, Jack Morgan, and the FBI less than two years before?

"Yup. He's a gopher. Go for this, go for that. Or he was."

"You sure? He's Gordaoff's fund-raiser. He was flashing a lot of money around for a gopher."

"I wouldn't know about that. In town he runs — ran — in and out of the courtroom with notes. Like that. A newbie they are breaking in. Or they were. I haven't seen him around for a while. Explains it if he was working for Gordaoff."

"He was a little old for a newbie."

"Took him seven tries to pass the bar."

"You're kidding."

"I never kid about the bar exam."

"My mistake," she said. "Can you check him out for me?"

There was the rustle of paper, the scratch of pencil. "Okay, Jeff Hosford, I'll make a few calls. Can you call me back this afternoon?"

"Yes."

"I should have something by then."

"Great. Thanks, Brendan."

He hesitated, and she said, "What?"

"Good to hear your voice, Kate, that's all." He hesitated again, before adding, "I miss the hell out of Jack."

"Me, too," Kate said, and slowly took a breath, in, out, managing the pain. "Me, too," she repeated, and hung up before they were both in tears.

She went back into Kenny's office. "Guess who Jeff Hosford used to work for?"

"Who?"

"Eddie P."

Jim sat up, dislodging Mutt's adoring head, which had been resting on his knee. She gave him a reproachful look. "Edgar P. Dischner?"

"That's the guy."

"If he was working for Eddie P., he was bent," Jim said.

"Tell me something I don't know, Chopin," Kate said. "Brendan McCord's going to ask around about him. I'm supposed to call him back on Monday." She looked at Kenny. "I'll let you know what he says."

"Eddie P.," Jim said. He pulled off the blue ball cap with the trooper seal on the front and ran his hand through his hair, a thick, dark mane he kept trimmed to just within the regulation length and no shorter. "If Eddie P. is mixed up in this, things just got a whole lot more complicated. Eddie P. is asshole buddies with every mover and shaker around. Well. The ones not already in jail."

"Damn it," Kenny said. "I hate this political shit. Give me a straight-forward Spenard divorce every time."

Kate shrugged. "Absent physical evidence,

141

and no witnesses . . ." Her voice trailed away.

"I really do not like this," Kenny said.

"Me, either," Jim said. He looked at Kate. "How's life on the campaign trail?"

"Haven't had to throw myself in front of a bullet yet." An unfortunate choice of words, given the present situation, but she didn't eat them.

"Keep it that way." Jim got to his feet, nodded to Kenny. "Keep in touch. Let me know what McCord has to say."

"Will do." The door closed, and Mutt stood with her nose pressed to the crack. She wasn't whining, exactly, but she was definitely hankering.

"Mutt," Kate said, and Mutt abandoned the crack with reluctance and returned, to plunk down with a deserted air.

"What do you do next?" Kenny said.

Kate shrugged. "I've got a job. They've already paid me. I'll do it. I'll keep my eyes open. You and I both know that the killer was most likely someone he knew. Which means someone connected with the campaign."

"With Dischner involved . . ."

"I admit, it throws us a curve. Still."

"Still," he agreed. "I'll start talking to the list of names you collected at the gym. In the meantime? Watch your back, Kate."

She grabbed Mutt's ruff and shook it. Mutt's great tongue lolled out as she laughed up at Kate. "I've got Mutt to do that for me."

They spent the first two weeks of October traveling around the Park. Kate had never been on a campaign trail, and within the first week she knew enough to know that she'd never go on another, no matter how good the pay was. Anne knocked on the door of every homestead on the road to Glenallen. She visited every house in the village of Niniltna. She visited the Step so Dan O'Brian could harangue her on the issue of subsistence, although he pretty much phoned it in because he was one of the few rangers in the state smart enough to manage his park with the advice of Park elders, Native and non-Native alike. When Billy Mike told him the black bear population in the Quilak foothills had dropped by a quarter of what it had been twenty years ago, Dan closed the Park to black bear hunts for five straight seasons, until the black bear population had turned around, and even then he allowed hunting only by subsistence permit the first two years. For a fed, Dan O'Brien looked suspiciously like one of their own to Park rats. Peter Heiman, who had a lot of financial supporters who lived in Anchorage and hunted in the Park, had been trying to get him fired for the last eight years.

There wasn't a meeting or an event or a festival, no matter how small, that Anne missed during those two weeks. The Park Sledders snow machine club met in Valdez and she was there, keeping her mouth shut when they voted unanimously to forward a request to the state legislature to open the entire Park to snow machining. When Auntie Joy hosted a quilting bee in Glenallen, Anne was there, needle in hand. That night a pair of instructors showed up from the Fred Astaire Dance Studio in Anchorage to teach the cha-cha at the Nickel Creek Lodge, and Kate had the privilege of watching Anne and Doug fumble their way through crossover breaks. She was then treated to the sight of Doug hitting on the female instructor, a buxom blonde named Cheryl who won Kate's heart when she transformed Doug's attentions into a request for further instruction and proceeded to work his ass off, literally, with thirty minutes' focus on Latin motion. Doug hobbled off the floor looking like he'd thrown his back out. Anne, working the room a table at a time, didn't appear to notice.

The Plum Bob Lake Mycological Society met for a seminar, and Anne took a test on how to recognize the good morel mushroom and passed it. The Tok Little Theater staged a presentation of *Bus Stop* and Anne was in the front row. The annual dinner of the Park Pioneers was held in Eureka and Anne was the featured speaker. She never drove by a bar, always stopping to go in and introduce herself.

Each day began at breakfast with whatever passed for the local chamber of commerce in whatever village or town they had gone to bed in the night before. This was usually followed by

144

an appearance at the local school, talking to the high school civics class. Lunch, invariably hamburgers with the fat congealing on them or very bad pizza, was eaten on the run, unless it was eaten in the school's cafeteria.

The afternoons were dedicated either to travel to the next town, village, homestead, or wide spot in the road, or to more knocking on doors. Dinners were command performances by the candidate before organizations with names like the FAS Support Group, the Alaska Miners Association, Mutts and Mushers, and the Nabesna Hospital Guild. Entrées featured chicken in every imaginable form and halibut way past its prime, with vegetables fresh out of the can. Kate had never eaten so much bad food for so long in her life.

Darlene was at the candidate's elbow at every stop, during every appearance, cueing her at every event. Kate saw Darlene whisper the name of a voter five seconds before that voter got to Anne, and watched Anne call the voter by name with an outstretched hand and a beaming smile that contrived to give the impression she reserved that smile only for them. When somebody asked Anne a question she couldn't answer, Darlene was ready with the relevant information or with a smile of her own, and a "We'll get back to you on that, Mr. Corley." When during one of the high school visits Tom made a move on a girl who was obviously underage, Darlene broke it up and led Tom, scowling, back to stand in his mother's shadow.

Posters began to appear, on the windows and walls of bars and restaurants, on posts stuck into the ground in front of people's homes, plastered on telephone poles. There were buttons, too, metal rounds with Anne's picture on a blue field and red letters that said, VOTE GORDAOFF! Kate began to see bumper stickers — PUT GORDAOFF IN HER PLACE — THE STATE SENATE! — on the occasional truck and not a few four-wheelers. She picked up a copy of the *Ahtna Tribune* at the end of their first week on the road and found a full page ad on page three, Anne Gordaoff and her whole family grinning at the camera with a caption that read, "Alaskans for Alaska! Vote Gordaoff for State Senate!" The next week the same page, a different picture, this one of Anne alone, much younger and dressed in nurse's whites. "Anne Gordaoff has Made a Career out of Caring for Alaskans — Vote Gordaoff for State Senate!"

Kate slept in a lot of different beds, and some were comfortable and some were not. She ate a lot of her meals standing up or out of a bag. She became sick of the sight of the back of Anne Gordaoff's head. She became very tired of Darlene getting her up at five every morning to prep her on the day's schedule. Doug Gordaoff hit on her. Tom Gordaoff hit on her. Erin Gordaoff drifted around like a ghost, white, wan, tear-stained, bereft. Anne refused to let the young woman go home and grieve, insisting

146

Erin stay with the campaign. Kate couldn't decide if this was the best solution Anne could devise to comfort her daughter and not stop campaigning, or if it was because Erin's bereavement gave the campaign more sympathy, or if Erin's presence went to show that while Jeff Hosford was gone, he was not forgotten, and by extension, Anne's loyalty to her employees, past, present, and future.

Kate still couldn't decide if she liked Anne Gordaoff or not. She had thought so, that evening at Bobby's when Anne had spoken in such forceful manner against the cult of the Native victim, something Kate had despised all her life. Since then, she had seen too much of Anne the pragmatic politician to leave her admiration undiluted. It was easier to draw her paycheck, watch the crowds for potential assassins, and not think about it. As a result Kate played a lot of late-night, cutthroat pinochle with Tracy Huffman and George Perry, whom Anne had hired to be the campaign's chief pilot. Anne Gordaoff was wise in the ways of local hire, yet another hot-button issue in a state with too many Outside employers.

Anne herself was tireless. She spoke with patience to students, she addressed their parents as equals, and she listened with respect to elders. There were a lot of Republicans in the district and she marched up to their doors, too, and Kate was surprised when none were actually slammed in her face. It seemed that Anne

Gordaoff was determined to speak to every single person who lived in District 41. She wanted the job, and she was willing to work hard to get it. Kate had to respect her for it, but thought that eating freezer-burnt halibut every other night might be too high a price to pay.

Once in a while Kate saw people she knew. Demetri nodded at her from a seated crowd in the Niniltna High School gym. Auntie Balasha brought her hot fry bread at a potlatch in Gakona. At a home show in Glenallen a big, beefy man in Carhartt's that looked as if he'd just finished fileting a dozen silvers picked her up off her feet and squeezed the breath out of her.

"Hey, Burt," Kate said. "Mind putting me down now?"

He laughed, a big, booming laugh, and she thumped down once more on terra firma. "The last time I saw you, you were fresh outa Anchorage with a scar across your neck made you look like you'd gone one on one with a grizzly." He poked a blunt forefinger at the open collar of the blue plaid shirt she wore over a white T-shirt, and she endured it because Burt Kennedy had known her as long as anyone had and had been around longer than most. "Looks better now."

"Yeah."

"So how the hell are you?"

"I'm good."

"I'm glad."

"Thanks," she said, and meant it, for the tact

that kept his concern brief. "How's the mine?"

He flapped a dismissive hand. "Price of gold what it is, I oughta pay people to buy what I dig out." A sly grin kept her from taking him seriously. He jerked his chin in Anne Gordaoff's direction. "You working for her?"

"Sort of," she said, realizing for the first time that her presence on the Gordaoff campaign trail could be taken as an endorsement by Ekaterina Shugak's granddaughter. She caught Darlene watching with a smug expression, and cursed herself for her own naïveté. A political animal she was not, that gene of Emaa's having passed her by.

"Well, hell, introduce us," Burt said. Kate did; Anne seduced him by knowing that day's price per troy ounce of gold, silver, and platinum and per pound of lead, and Darlene looked even more smug. For just an instant Kate debated heading for the first flight out. Her most recent paycheck crackled in her pocket. She gritted her teeth and carried on.

One memorable evening in Tanada members from the congregation of the Chistona Little Chapel picketed the opening of a new branch of Planned Parenthood, to which Anne, to her credit, was lending her presence. Kate looked for Pastor Seabolt and wasn't surprised when she didn't find him. Seabolt's self-imposed role was always as the man behind the curtain, the unseen hand pulling the invisible strings. She wondered about his grandson, which led inevitably to thoughts of Johnny.

She'd seen him twice, on flying trips into Niniltna. He still looked at her like he hated her guts. He still refused to leave. Ethan said they were getting along fine, just fine. "No, his mom hasn't been around. Word is she had to go back to Anchorage so she didn't lose her job." He looked down at her and his face softened. "The best thing you can do for him is to leave him alone," he told Kate.

"I don't want to leave him alone so much he starts to think I don't care."

"First thing you do when he gets here is take a job that'll keep you off the homestead and all over the Park. He's thinking that already."

Kate set her teeth. "I explained, I told him why —"

"He's fourteen. Explanations don't mean shit to a fourteen-year-old. Leave him alone, Kate. He's going to school, pulling down okay grades in spite of not liking it much. He's tall for his age so Bernie's after him to try out for the junior varsity basketball team. That'll help."

"You're getting along okay?"

Ethan grinned. "Oh yeah, we're getting along fine. He hates women almost as much as I do."

She laughed in spite of herself.

"You should do that more often, Kate," he said, looking down into her face.

"What, totally screw up a fourteen-year-old boy, and get myself arrested for kidnapping while I'm at it?"

"Laugh," he said. "You look good when you laugh."

"Johnny," she yelled toward the stairs, "I'm leaving!"

Johnny didn't come down to say good-bye. Ethan shrugged and raised a brow. "Give him time."

She knew Ethan was right, but it didn't make any difference. She felt like she was letting Jack down.

The murderer of Jeff Hosford was still at large. Brendan McCord had been unable to add much to his initial report of the dead attorney. He'd been in the state seven years, for five of those years working for Seese, Dischner, first as a clerk and then, when he finally passed the bar, as an attorney. He owned a condo in Park Place, an uptown Anchorage neighborhood with very high rents. He'd been unmarried and something of a ladies' man. "I'm sorry, Kate," Brendan had said. "Hosford was practically the invisible man. I ran a check on him through Motznik and he owned one car, a Ford Explorer; he voted in every election; he paid his taxes in full and on time. He wasn't a member of any political party that I can discover. I went over to his condo and talked to a few of his neighbors. They said he was out of town a lot."

"Out of town where?"

"They didn't know."

She reported on this happy state of affairs to Kenny Hazen.

His response was predictable. "I really do not like this, Kate. I really do not like it at all."

Five days later, or maybe it was thirteen, Kate had lost track of time, Anne and Company were back in Ahtna for yet another appearance, this one the opening game of the basketball season in which the Ahtna High School was heavily favored to win the Class-B state championship, at which Anne tossed up the jump ball. The game was followed by yet another rubber chicken dinner, although this one was rubber salmon, with the Chamber of Commerce, only this one was with the Kegturyaq Native Association's board of directors. Kate checked out the gym and the dining room for the usual suspects, as usual didn't find any, and ducked out early for the hotel with the uneasy feeling that she was not earning her keep. There had been no more letters, no one had so much as sneezed in Anne's direction, unless you counted the drunk in the Alaskan Bar in Cordova who pinched her ass and propositioned her with her husband standing right next to her, and nobody did.

Darlene hadn't said anything about letting her go, though.

And here she was again, in beautiful downtown Ahtna, once again checking into the Ahtna Lodge. Tony simply beamed when he saw her coming, and this time he was ready for Mutt, a package of beef jerky open and waiting. Mutt accepted a piece, laid it down carefully on the floor, trotted behind the counter to rear up, place both paws on Tony's shoulders and give him the traditional salutary tongue bath. "You are so cheap," Kate said when she came out again. Mutt wagged her tail furiously and went for the jerky.

"How's life out on the campaign trail?"

"Pretty dull," Kate said, signing the receipt he handed her.

"Probably you'd like to keep it that way." By now Tony, an inveterate gossip, knew more about Anne Gordaoff's campaign than Anne did.

"Probably," Kate agreed. "Is the water hot?"

He pretended to be puzzled. "Hot water? What would you need with hot water?"

"Don't toy with me," she told him, and he laughed and gave her a key. "Same wing, same room. Restaurant's pretty full this evening, might be a wait." He cocked an eyebrow. "I could bring a sandwich to your room."

By this time Kate had met and bonded with Tony's cook, Stanislav, who was also his partner, in business and in life. She shook her head. "Forget it. I've been looking forward to one of Stan's steaks for . . . how long have I been gone?"

"Eight days," Tony said, grinning.

"Whatever. I'll stand in line for Stan."

"Be our guest."

She dumped her bag in the room with the two twin beds, television, and communal bathroom down the hall. "You coming?" she said to Mutt, who gave her a look of disdain and curled up on the second bed in the room with her beef jerky.

At the restaurant a waitress said, "Do you mind sharing a table?" and without waiting for an answer grabbed a menu and led the way to a table against the far wall, next to a window that overlooked the river. "Do you mind sharing a table?" she said to the woman already sitting there, and also without waiting for an answer slapped the menu down in front of the seat opposite her before heading at high speed for the bar.

"I guess I don't," the woman said, looking up at Kate.

"I guess I don't, either," Kate said, and they both laughed. Kate held up a book. "We don't have to talk."

"Good," the other woman said, indicating a three-subject notebook with the pen she held in her hand. "Sit down, it doesn't look like my date's going to show."

They smiled at each other again, and Kate sat down. Eventually the waitress came back with water and took Kate's order, and went away again.

Kate didn't open her book immediately, as the moon had risen and was painting pictures on the surface of the river as it flowed past. It was low and slow at this time of year, all the fish up the creek, all the meltoff out in the Gulf, but it was still beautiful. Kate had grown up next to it, on it, sometimes in it, and still it never failed in its allure. One of her favorite books as a child it was still one of her favorite books, she reread it every spring — was *The Wind in the Willows* by Kenneth Grahame. Now there was a writer who understood rivers.

She wondered if Johnny had read it, or *Life on the Mississippi*. The last time they'd had a civil conversation on the subject of books, he'd been head down in the collected works of Robert Heinlein. Her steak came, a porterhouse with garlic mashed potatoes and steamed broccoli topped with toasted almonds. Kate had difficulty in repressing a moan of ecstasy. The other woman had been served before her, and they ate in not incompatible silence. Other people finished meals and adjourned to the bar, which got even noisier as the restaurant emptied out. Music started from somewhere and the four-by-eight dance floor filled up.

Kate pushed back from her empty plate with a satisfied burp, and raised her eyes to see the other woman smiling at her. "You were hungry."

"I was starving," Kate admitted. "I think I'll live now."

The other woman's notebook was open. It looked to be almost used up, as well as stuffed with scraps of paper and envelopes and flyers, all with notes written on them.

The waitress appeared. "Coffee?" she said, gathering up their plates.

"Yes, please," Kate said. "With cream."

"Twice," the other woman said.

"All we've got is creamer," the waitress said, and was gone.

The other woman went back to her notes, Kate to her book, a novel set on another world where the human settlers left their ship in orbit to control the weather and had bioengineered angels to fly up to talk to it. The only problem was that hundreds of years had passed, and the people on the planet had come to believe the ship was a god. It was a terrific book, and Kate was going to look for more by the same author as soon as she possibly could, but it was failing to hold her attention this evening. Maybe it was the noise from the bar. Maybe it was the woman sitting across from her. She was a large, untidy woman with eager, inquisitive eyes, carelessly dressed in blue jeans a size too large and a teal turtleneck sweater a size too small. She wore no makeup and no jewelry that Kate could see.

The woman said abruptly, startling Kate, "I'm a writer."

Kate had never been one for small talk, but a writer was interesting. "What do you write?"

"Books." The other woman flushed, laughed a little. "Well, I'm writing one book."

"A novel?"

"Yes." She nodded at the book in Kate's hand. "Not science fiction."

"You don't like science fiction?"

"I like just about anything," the woman said.

"You should see my library. My trailer is mostly books."

"My cabin's insulated the same way," Kate said.

The woman grinned. "Wonder what the R factor is on books. My name's Paula."

"I'm Kate."

"Where do you live?"

"Niniltna. You?"

She jerked her head. "Right here. Ahtna."

"You writing a book about Ahtna?" The idea amused Kate.

"Yes. Well, no, only sort of." The other woman gave a self-conscious laugh. "That sounds like I really know what I'm doing, doesn't it?"

Kate looked up to see Mutt standing outside the door with her nose leaving prints on the glass pane. Evidently the allure of beef jerky had worn off. She only hoped Mutt hadn't scared the maid who must have let her out of the room too badly to make the bed the next morning; they were staying two nights in Ahtna. She let Mutt in, and Mutt followed her back to the table, sitting next to Kate's chair and looking at the other woman with inquiring yellow eyes.

"God, he's gorgeous," Paula said.

"She," Kate said, knotting a hand in Mutt's ruff and giving it an affectionate tug. "Don't tell her that, she's already got enough ego for ten."

"She looks like a wolf."

"Only half."

The woman's eyes widened. "You trust her around people?"

157

"She's very well trained."

"I guess." The woman looked doubtful but didn't run screaming for the nearest exit, either. She pulled her notebook toward her as the waitress showed up with the coffee pot. "We'll be closing soon," the waitress told them.

"Leave the pot and bring us our checks," Kate suggested. Mutt stirred beneath her hand. Hunting birds along the Kanuyaq was lousy in September, and lousy in Ahtna all the time. "Have you got a steak left back there?"

"What kind?"

"Raw."

The waitress looked at Mutt. "Sure." She smiled for the first time. A dog person. "And maybe some bones."

Mutt got a slab of prime rib and a nice little pile of bones besides, and lay down to munch with a contented expression. The waitress charged Kate only for the cost of the meat, not the full dinners. Kate doubled her tip. What the hell, it wasn't her money.

The lights in the restaurant, never bright to begin with, dimmed. The crowd at the bar began to mellow, and the songs they danced to got slower and sexier. A short plump man in the standard Park uniform of jeans, checked flannel shirt, and boots drifted over. "Would you like to dance?" he asked Kate.

She shook her head. "No, thanks."

He looked at Paula. "Sorry," she said.

He drifted off again mournfully, to be re-

ceived back at the bar by his friends with com-
miserating backslaps and another round of
Heineken. Kate's eye moved down the bar,
checking faces against a mental database of
known felons, the invariable habit of the practicing policeman and one she had never bothered to break once she left Anchorage. There
was the usual assortment of people wanting to
fall in love for the night, a man bundled in a
down parka too hot to wear inside, and — she
backed up a couple of faces. Tom Gordaoff was
bellied up to the bar with his arm around the
shoulders of a girl who looked like she ought to
have been carded at the door and turned away.
They clicked glasses and drank, after which
Tom leaned in for a long, slow wet one, his
body crowding hers against the bar, one knee
forcing her legs apart. Her hands settled on his
hips, pulling him in. Perhaps not that young
after all, Kate thought, and left them to it.

Her dinner partner was writing in her notebook, hasty scribbles that Kate, usually a good
upside-down reader, couldn't decipher. She
wondered if she and Mutt were going down into
literature as the woman with the wolf. The other
woman looked up to see her watching, and colored. "Sorry. I have to write the ideas down as
they come to me or I'll lose them."

"You must go through a lot of notebooks," Kate
said. This one looked like it was on its last legs,
held together by two enormous rubber bands.

"I buy them in bulk on Costco runs into Anchorage. I've got one everywhere, on the kitchen counter, in the bathroom, next to my bed. And two or three pens each. You never know when you're going to run out of ink."

Kate didn't usually waste a lot of time on strangers, so she surprised herself by asking, "Tell me about this book you're writing."

The woman's big brown eyes brightened, making her look like a ten-year-old. She had about her that childlike quality of instant, innocent enthusiasm, although she had to be in her mid-to-late forties. "It's an historical novel about Alaska, featuring three generations of women. One comes up with the stampeders during the Gold Rush, her daughter is an Army nurse who flies medivacs to the Aleutians during World War II, and her daughter is a roustabout on the North Slope during the oil boom." She hesitated. "It's sort of a history of the last hundred years of Alaska, seen through their eyes." She hesitated again. "They kind of are Alaska, if you know what I mean."

Kate nodded.

"Do you mind if I ask you a personal question?"

"You can ask," Kate said.

"Are you Native?"

Kate laughed. "Like you couldn't tell."

The other woman blushed. "I'm sorry, that was rude."

Kate shrugged. "Asked and answered. I'm Native. Aleut, mostly. Why?"

160

"Aleut? Was your family evacuated out of the Aleutians during the war?" Kate nodded. Paula's eyes gleamed. "Wow. So now the family lives in Niniltna."

"All over the Park, some in Prince William Sound, a lot of us in Anchorage."

"Do you think. . . ." The woman paused.

"What?"

"I wanted Natives in my book, but I'm having a hard time getting a handle on what they've been doing in Alaska during the past hundred years. I mean before ANCSA. I mean original source material from actual Natives. All the records are written by whites. Even the records of Castner's Cutthroats. It's irritating as hell."

"No Alaska tribe had a written language. The Native tradition is oral. And given the way many of them were treated, there were a lot of mixed-race kids who didn't admit to their Native blood if it didn't show on their faces, so a lot of the oral tradition was lost." It was Kate's turn to hesitate. What the hell. "My father served under Castner."

"No kidding!"

"No kidding."

"God. Did he go ashore at Attu?" Kate nodded. "God," Paula said again, with reverence. "I've read about that. The Japanese didn't give ground easy."

"Nope."

"Is he still around, your dad?"

"No."

"I'm sorry," the other woman said automatically, although it was obvious that she was sorrier not to be able to interview Stephan Shugak than she was for Kate's loss. She looked up and caught Kate's eye. She flushed again. "Truly, I am sorry."

"It's okay. It was a long time ago."

"It still hurts, though," the other woman said, and when Kate's expression changed, repeated, "I'm sorry. There's nothing worse than unsolicited sympathy."

"No, there isn't, but it's still okay," Kate said, and was surprised to find that it was true. Sympathy for something other than Jack's death was almost a relief.

They sat in silence. The moon was high in the sky now, and through the window some of the brighter stars could be seen, Rigel, Betelgeuse. Kate craned her neck to see if the Pleiades were in sight. They were, keeping always and ever just out of Orion's reach. An exquisite torture devised by the goddess of the hunt, one of whose followers Orion had raped. Kate wouldn't have minded Artemis sitting on the parole board when a few of the people she'd arrested came before them. No GET OUT OF JAIL FREE cards for them. She pointed at the notebook. "What was your big idea?"

Paula hesitated. "I don't know. Sometimes ideas sound kind of dumb when you say them out loud. Especially mine."

"Try me. I promise not to laugh."

Paula gave her a long look, glanced down at Mutt, gnawing on a T-bone with a blissful expression, and decided Kate was trustworthy. "I do a lot of research. Just recently I found a story about a woman who was murdered in Niniltna back in 1915, a woman they called 'the Angel,' one of the good-time girls who came up with the stampeders to mine the gold miners in the Yukon, and who came down to mine the copper miners along the Kanuyaq afterward." She grinned. "You talk about Natives not wanting to admit the past, you should try to get some Anglo whose family has been in Alaska more than three generations to admit to having a good-time girl in theirs."

"I remember hearing a little about that. A lot of the women who worked the Fairbanks Line wound up marrying into respectable society, or what passed for it back then, didn't they?"

"You better believe it," Paula said, punctuating her statement with her pen. "Some of them had the guts and determination to climb the Chilkoot Trail and brave the Lake Bennett rapids right next to the men, and went on to marry some of the founding members of the state, and their grandchildren and great-grandchildren are in public office and are running some of the biggest businesses around the state today."

She leaned forward, her eyes bright with discovery. "You know what? I think my Gold Rush grandmother just became a dance-hall girl who was selling some on the side."

"I'll buy your book," Kate said. "And I'll read it, too."

Paula flushed. "Thank you," she said, ducking her head. "I mean, really. Thanks."

8

Kate walked back to her room thinking that it was a shame that interludes and conversations like that one were few and far between. On the other hand, maybe one that good was what gave the job meaning. That and her paycheck, which was beginning to swell her bank balance to comfortable proportions. She was thinking about calling an attorney, maybe the one Jack had used in his fight for custody. Kate had never met her, but the way Jack had described her made her think of a pit bull. She would need a pit bull to go up against Jane.

Deep in thought, she walked right into Doug as he was coming out of Darlene's room. "Oh. Sorry."

He caught her by the shoulders in an automatic gesture. "That's okay."

Mutt snapped at him, a short sound, not loud, but the meeting of teeth was audible. He released Kate and stepped back.

She got a good look at him then, and saw that

his shirt had been rebuttoned wrong, that while his jeans were zipped his snap was undone, his feet were bare, and his usually perfectly combed head of gray hair was tousled, as if someone had been hanging on to it recently with both hands. He held a towel in one hand.

"Lose your way to the bathroom?" Kate said.

He didn't even look embarrassed. "I guess."

She snorted. Mutt, taking her cue, gave a soft growl. They watched him pad down the hall to the communal bathroom.

As a matter of security, she knew that Doug and Anne's room was the only one among the campaign staff that had its own bathroom.

Well, she was only there to look after the candidate's physical safety. She let herself into her own room and shucked out of her clothes and into an oversized T-shirt that hit her about mid-thigh, with a brightly colored parrot celebrating Jimmy Buffett's Y2K party on the front. As she was about to climb into bed, there was a knock at the door. She opened it and found Doug standing there. "You lost again?" she said.

"I just — let me talk to you for a minute, okay?"

She didn't want to be caught talking to the candidate's husband in her nightshirt after midnight, so against her better judgment she let him in. She didn't invite him to sit down but he did anyway, on the bed she had been ready to climb into, a violation of her personal space that she fully appreciated. Mutt didn't like it, either, but Kate made a gesture with her hand and Mutt lay back, chin on her paws, yellow eyes fixed un-blinkingly on Doug.

"What do you want, Doug? It's been a long day, and I'd like to get some sleep."

"Look," he said, "I don't know what you thought you saw, but —"

"I know exactly what I saw," Kate said. "I'm a grown-up; you don't have to pretty it up for me. In fact, please don't waste my time trying."

"I wouldn't want you to — I'd hate to think you'd —"

"What? Tell Anne? That's not my job."

"It's just that —"

"Doug, give it a rest and let me get to bed. If Anne can't keep you in her bed, it's not my business to tell her so."

"It's not that," he said.

Kate sighed. He was determined to tell her what it was.

"It's just that — Anne's kind of hard to live up to, you know?"

Kate maintained an unhelpful and she hoped unfriendly silence.

"Sometimes a man needs a little warmth, a little affection."

Kate yawned.

"Before the campaign all she had time for was her patients. And before that she only had time for the kids. Now she hasn't got time for anybody but those people in District 41 old enough to vote who haven't already signed onto her campaign."

"I see," Kate said.

"You do?" he said. He sounded plaintive without being self-pitying, wistful for those wonderful days when Anne had had time for him, reluctant but willing to sacrifice their relationship for the greater good of the community, only a man seeking some comfort in the trying days and weeks ahead.

Kate hoped she wouldn't vomit. "You have made it all very clear. Your wife doesn't understand you, and her campaign manager does. Go back to your own room now, please."

He was good, he stayed in character, he kept the sad expression of the chronically misunderstood in place all the way to the door, where he paused to rest a hand on Kate's shoulder. "Thanks for listening."

She shrugged. His hand wouldn't move, and he was standing very close to her. "Doug," she said, "in spite of your incredible sex appeal, I am going to give you two seconds to get out of this room. Then either I'm going to take you apart, or I'm going to cede that pleasure to Mutt. I promise you, either way, it will be painful."

His smile was sorrowful as she took her place in the ranks of the legion of women who didn't understand him, and, finally, he left.

After that, she couldn't get to sleep. She understood, all right, better than either Doug or Darlene would like her to, she'd bet money on that. Doug was a rounder; she'd spotted that the minute she'd met him. Darlene, on the other

168

hand, wanted her candidate elected and would do anything to make that happen, including sleep with the candidate's husband to keep the adultery in the family. Better than having him cat around among the constituency. Although he was probably doing that, too, a rounder rounded, that's what rounders do. She thought of Jim Chopin.

She tossed and turned and cursed Doug and Darlene equally, and wondered if Tracy knew. Kate didn't know much about politics but even she could see this was a campaign nightmare in the making.

She wondered if Anne knew. If she did, she also knew how to keep her feelings hidden. Or maybe she just didn't care. Maybe part of what Doug said was true; maybe Anne didn't have time for anyone but her would-be constituents.

Tony, bless his heart, in the interests of modernizing the Ahtna Lodge, had installed televisions in each room. With any luck there would be an old movie on. Instead she got a new one, with some guy running around peeling other people's faces off his own and blowing up things right, left, and center. It bored her in three minutes, and she turned it off and reached for the latest of many books that had accompanied her on the tour with Anne Gordaoff, the story of a Southern Baptist minister who hauled his wife and four daughters to the Congo in the fifties and proceeded to offend every single local custom that he possibly could and whose wife and daughters, naturally, suffered most for it. It reminded Kate of Pastor Seabolt and his son, Daniel, and his grandson, Matthew. She wondered, as she often did, how Matthew was doing, and felt again, as she always did, guilt that she had not been able to help him. It was an evocative book, all right, rich with personality and description, and Kate only dozed off because she hadn't had any real sleep in two nights.

She was wakened by a knock at the door. She groaned and rolled over to look at the clock on the night stand. Two-thirty in the morning. "Go away," she said loudly, testing the need of whomever was waiting on the other side of the door.

The knock came again.

"Hell," she said, and climbed out of bed to pull on her jeans. Mutt was already at the door, her nose pressed to the crack, and Kate kept the chain on when she opened it. "What?"

It was Darlene. Her hair was wet and hung in strings around her white face. She had another letter in her hand.

Poison Pen had struck again, and Kate had slept right through it.

"Anne found it on the floor of her room."
"Where on the floor?"
"Just inside the door."
Kate nodded, and read the letter again. PAY UP OR ILL TELL.

"He's here, Kate," Darlene said. She was pacing, around the end of the bed to the window and back again.

Tell what? Kate was thinking. Pay what? And to whom? This was the first letter that sounded like blackmail. Did Poison Pen know about Darlene and Doug? It seemed odd, then, that the letter would not go to one of them. Or was Poison Pen under the impression that Anne Gordaoff would do anything to get elected, include pay to keep her husband's affair with her campaign manager a secret?

It was the same writing with the black marker pen, on the same sheet of stationery, inside the same envelope. No postmark this time.

"He's right here in this hotel," Darlene said, pacing. "He must have followed us from the dinner."

"Or he's been with you all along," Kate murmured.

"What?" Darlene said, not understanding, or too worried to try to. "I'm calling the cops, Kate. I don't care what Jim says, this has gone on long enough. It's one thing when they come in the mail. But this guy went right to her room. I'm calling the cops," she repeated.

"Ahtna's only got one," Kate said dryly. She dressed: white T-shirt, black jeans, blue sweatshirt with the gold UAF nanook on the front, white anklets, black-and-white Nike tennis shoes. The face that looked back at her from the mirror over the dresser was tight-lipped,

171

hazel eyes intent. Her hair needed trimming again. She gave it a few swift strokes with the brush, tucked it behind her ears, and forgot about it.

"What are you going to do?" Darlene said.

"I'm going to make a call," Kate said, and went to the pay phone down the hall, where she dialed a number from memory.

" 'lo," a thick voice said after five rings.

"Kenny, wake up. It's Kate Shugak."

Nobody said anything for a moment. "Ah shit," the voice said finally, "who's dead now?"

"Nobody," Kate said, and Kenny responded gloomily, "With you around it's only a matter of time."

"Up yours, Hazen," Kate said pleasantly. "Anne Gordaoff just got another letter."

There was a brief silence. "At this hour?"

"Sorry."

"Me, too. Who found it?"

"Anne. She got up to go to the bathroom. It had been slipped under her door."

"And this couldn't wait until morning?"

"The whole campaign staff is in the Ahtna Lodge tonight, and I want to go around knocking on doors before they're awake enough to think up lies about their recent correspondence. I could use a uniform to back me up. More official, you know?"

"I know. You've got the letter?"

"And copies of the previous letters, and the envelopes they came in. And you might give Jim

172

Chopin a call." If she had to be up before the dawn, why shouldn't everyone else be?

"I'll be right down."

"I owe you one, Kenny."

"Don't kid yourself. You owe me at least ten, Shugak," he said.

She gave him her room number and hung up. "Kenny Hazen's coming down, he's the Ahtna police chief. We're going to talk to the campaign staff one at a time, starting with Anne. And then we're going to talk to everyone else who rented a room in this trailer."

"What?" Darlene stood up. "Why the staff? And we can't get Anne out of bed; it's almost three in the morning; she just got to bed and she's exhausted; she's got to get up early in the morning and go to —"

"I doubt that she's asleep after this," Kate said, nodding at the letter, "and I don't care if she is. I want to talk to everyone to do with the campaign, ask them if they saw anything. We're all in the same trailer, right?"

"Yes, but —"

"Good. Maybe we'll get lucky and somebody will have seen something."

"Kate —"

"This is what you hired me for, Darlene," Kate said, meeting her eyes squarely. "You said you were worried about Anne's safety. I admit, I wasn't very impressed by the threat. Then Jeff Hosford was murdered."

That stopped Darlene. Kate got the distinct

impression that Darlene had forgotten all about Jeff Hosford.

"Maybe Jeff's murder had something to do with the letters, maybe it didn't, but something is going on here. I don't know what it is, but I don't like it. As far as this letter is concerned, well, a lot of people in public life get threatening letters. Not a lot of people in public life get them shoved under their hotel room doors. This means whoever is writing the letters is very close by. If you want to catch him, this is the luckiest break we could have. The longer we wait, the colder the trail gets. I'm talking to all of them tonight, or this morning or whatever, I don't care what time it is."

Darlene stared at her. "You think it's one of us," she said. "I said he must have followed us from dinner and you said, 'Or he's been with us all along.' "

Kate looked at her.

"Bullshit, Kate," Darlene said, her voice rising. "That's just —that's bullshit. Who the hell working for us would do that? It makes no sense! We all want Anne elected; we're working our butts off to get her to Juneau. Who the hell among us is going to write her hate mail?"

Kate looked at her with no expression.

Darlene flushed.

Someone thumped on the other side of the wall at the head of Kate's bed. "Hey, keep it down in there, will you? I'm trying to get some sleep here, crissake!"

"Woof," Mutt said, distributing the effect between the thumper and Darlene. Like Kate, Mutt didn't care for a lot of loud noise about her person.

Darlene looked at Mutt and lowered her voice. "It's insane to think the writer is one of us."

Who are you trying to convince? Kate thought. Out loud, she said, "I hope you're right. Let's find out."

Anne and Doug Gordaoff, sharing a room. Darlene Shelikof, a room to herself. Anne's son, Tom, a room to himself, although after what she'd seen in the bar Kate was sure he wouldn't be sleeping alone. Anne's daughter, Erin, a room to herself. Tracy Huffman. Kate herself. That made eight, nine if you counted Mutt, and Kate never made the mistake of not counting Mutt.

"And then there's Paula," Darlene said thoughtfully.

"Who's Paula?" Kate looked again at the list. "She's not on here."

"Paula Pawlowski. She's the researcher I told you about," Darlene said. "She's been in Fairbanks, looking up stuff in the library there. She just flew in today, but she's not staying in the hotel. She lives in Ahtna. You wanted everyone working for the campaign. That's it. I'm going to go talk to Anne."

"Wait," Kate said.

"No, Kate. We are not hammering on her door in the middle of the night with a uniformed cop in tow. She'll think somebody else died."

"Darlene, I don't want anyone to know about this until I can watch the expressions on their faces. Don't —"

Darlene made as if to go nose-to-nose with Kate, and Kate saw the moment in her eyes when she remembered what had happened the last time she had done that. Darlene made a visible effort, and this time when her voice came out, it was low and dead even. "No dogs or Natives allowed," she said.

Kate blinked. "I beg your pardon?"

"No dogs or Natives allowed," Darlene repeated. "That's what the signs said in the grocery store windows before and sometimes even after statehood, in the shop windows, on the door into bars, in towns all over the territory. No dogs or Natives allowed. Have you forgotten the stories your grandmother told you?" A fine edge of contempt sharpened Darlene's voice. "Or maybe you didn't bother listening when she told them."

Kate's eyes narrowed. "My grandmother has nothing whatever to do with you warning Anne Gordaoff before I have a chance to question her about this letter."

"The hell it doesn't!" Darlene's words caused another thump on the wall from the room next door, another protest from Mutt. "I have a good chance of seeing Anne Gordaoff elected to the state legislature, Kate. A woman. A Native woman. One of our own."

"Anne isn't exactly the second coming of Christ

here, Darlene. There are two Native women in the legislature now."

"Two out of sixty," Darlene said. "That's not enough. That's not near enough. Let me make myself plain: I will do anything, I will say anything, to get Anne to that swearing-in ceremony in Juneau in January. You —" she said, stabbing at Kate's chest with a forefinger "— you are not going to get in the way of my accomplishing that."

Kate made a massive effort and refrained from breaking Darlene's finger off at the knuckle.

Darlene glared at her. "Do you understand me?"

"Perfectly."

Darlene walked out, and Kate nearly followed her, but at that precise moment the name of Darlene's researcher sunk in.

Paula Pawlowski.

Paula.

The woman who had shared her table for dinner the previous evening. The writer doing the research. Her writing habit underwritten by a job researching a candidate for political office for that candidate's opposition, what could be more natural.

A knock at the door interrupted her thoughts. It was Kenny, with Darlene, her drying hair frizzing up to make her look like an ambulatory ball of steel wool, coming up behind him.

"Kate."

"Kenny. Kenny Hazen, Darlene Shelikof.

177

Kenny's the Ahtna chief of police, Darlene. Darlene's Anne Gordaoff's campaign manager, Kenny. She's the one who brought me on board to work security for the campaign."

"You have the letters?"

Kate handed them to him, along with the newest one, handling it carefully by the corners, not that that was going to do much good as it probably already had Anne and Darlene's prints all over it. Doug's too, no doubt.

The small upright chair in front of the tacky desk creaked when Kenny sat down in it. He turned on the desk lamp and read through the letters, frowning. "This last one's a little different. None of the others are asking, they're warning."

"Yeah."

"Where'd you say it was found?" He looked at Darlene.

"Anne found it shoved underneath the door of her hotel room. We'd been out late, at a dinner given by the local Native association's board of directors. She and her husband, Doug, say they were in bed and asleep by midnight." Darlene carefully did not look at Kate as she spoke. "She woke up after two and got up to go to the bathroom. On the way she stepped on the letter."

"So it was left sometime between twelve and two."

"Yes."

Kenny looked at Kate. "Bar doesn't close till two."

"No. I was in the restaurant until after eleven."

"See anyone?"

She'd been trying to remember that since Darlene had knocked at her door. "A few people were leaving the bar at the same time I was. There were three drunks trying to figure out how to get in their truck. I took their keys away from them and gave them to Tony."

"Good girl. Anybody else?"

She looked at Darlene, who was still avoiding her eye. "I saw Doug Gordaoff coming out of Darlene's room."

"Yes," Darlene said immediately. "Doug was dropping off the text of a speech Anne wanted me to run through."

Whatever Kenny thought of that he didn't say and nothing showed on his face. "I noticed the door to the outside gives one hell of a bang when it closes."

"Yeah, I noticed that, too," Kate said. "Shakes the whole building."

"Feel anything like that after you went to bed?"

She shook her head.

"Could mean nobody came in from outside to do the deed."

Before Darlene said anything, Kate said, "It could also mean that whoever did it is familiar with the door and held it so it wouldn't bang. That damn door has been banging shut for years, and I bet everybody in the Park has stayed here at least once."

He sighed. "You're right." He looked at her.

"How do you want to play this, Kate?"

"I want to question everybody in this trailer, and I want you to stand around looking mean while I do."

He grinned, a tight, hard grin. "I can do that."

First stop, Anne and Doug's room. Anne looked tense and exhausted, wrapped in a flannel robe, dark red with a black moose print. She was sitting beneath the covers of one bed, reading a book, or trying to. Kate got a look at the title. Stephen King. Doug was curled up motionless on the other bed, covers up to his chin, back to the door.

Clothes were hung neatly in the closet. Toiletries were laid out on the bathroom counter with almost military precision. Used towels were folded and hung over the shower rod.

Kate introduced Kenny and asked Anne to tell them what had happened. It didn't differ in any of the particulars from what Darlene had said. "No, I didn't see anyone. I didn't hear anyone, either. Whoever left the letter didn't make enough noise to wake me up. I got up to use the bathroom, which as you can see is right next to the door to the room. I stepped on the letter. When I turned on the light, I saw what it was, and I went to get Darlene." She looked at Kate. "What does this mean, Kate? I'm not in any danger. Am I?"

"I don't know," Kate said. She sensed Darlene stir in back of her, and repeated, "I don't know.

I don't think so, and that's not just a gut instinct. I've got reasons. I'm going to talk to the
rest of your people right now." She exchanged a
long, unsmiling look with Kenny. "For the moment, why don't you try to get some sleep?
We'll be going up and down the hall for a while,
see if we can find out if anyone in the building
saw something."

Anne's eyes went past Kate to Kenny Hazen.
"Hello, Chief Hazen."

"Hello, Ms. Gordaoff."

"Mrs.," came a voice from beneath the covers
of the second bed. "It's Mrs. Gordaoff."

"Mrs. Gordaoff," Kenny corrected himself
without a blink.

"Please, call me Anne." She gave him a wan
smile. "I expect Kate rousted you out of bed to
come down here. I'm sorry about that."

Kenny shook his head. "That's my job, Anne."

Doug condescended to roll over and confirm
that he'd dropped off a speech at Darlene's
room at a little after eleven, that he hadn't been
gone more than five minutes, and that he hadn't
seen anyone in the hallway except Kate. Anne
listened without expression.

The next room belonged to the son, Tom,
who either wasn't answering the door or wasn't
home. Kenny stepped up with a passkey. "I
stopped at the front desk on the way in," he said
in answer to Kate's look.

A nylon duffel bag sat open on one bed, clothes
were scattered everywhere but the closet, CDs

181

spilled out of a case, nearly burying a portable CD player with earphones. A laptop computer was open on the desk, not running. A bottle of shampoo, three different kinds of designer hair mousse, dental floss, toothpaste, a toothbrush, and a box of Trojans sat on the dresser. Towels sat in a damp heap on the floor.

"Hey, what the hell?"

They turned and saw Tom standing in the doorway.

"What the hell are you doing in my room?"

He was lean like his father and moved like a basketball player, putting his feet down lightly in anticipation of a midperiod shift of defense from zone to man-to-man.

"Where have you been?" Kate said.

"None of your goddamn business," Tom said, unintimidated by the uniformed police officer looming at her back. "I asked you what the hell are you doing in my room?"

He had a point. Kate explained. "I don't know anything about that," he said, when they showed him the most recent letter. "No, I didn't see anyone. All I did was shower and change after we got in from that dumb dinner Mom made us all go to. Me and a friend closed down the bar. Now, if you'll excuse me, I've got a date." He reached past Kate and picked up the box of Trojans. He grinned down at her, thirteen years her junior and at least a foot taller. Everybody was always a foot taller than her, and she found it irritating in the extreme. "Forgot these." He left.

"Well, now, he's real worried about the possible danger to his mother," Kenny said.

Darlene said nothing.

Tracy Huffman's room was empty. They went in with the passkey, found clothes hung in the closet, toiletries on the dresser, a briefcase jammed with schedules and flyers and posters, and a DayTimer in which every single day forward until November 7th had two or more entries. It made Kate tired just to look at it. "What do you know about this one?" Kenny said.

Aware of Darlene listening, Kate said, "She was at UAF with Darlene and me."

"She's probably in the sack with some guy," Darlene said.

Kenny cocked an eyebrow at Kate. Kate shrugged. "She, ah, does make friends fast."

"And you never introduced us. I may never forgive you."

The next door down opened before they knocked. "What's going on?" Erin stood there, rubbing sleep out of her eyes.

"I'm glad you're awake, Erin," Kate said, stepping forward so as to crowd the younger woman backward. "We need to talk to you."

Erin saw Kenny and her eyes widened. "What's wrong?"

"Nothing's wrong."

The young woman's face lit up and for a moment she looked almost pretty. "Did you catch who killed Jeff? Is that it?"

"No, Ms. Gordaoff," Kenny said, his voice

gentle. "We haven't caught the person who killed your fiancé yet. We just need to talk to you for a few minutes."

Erin's face crumpled. Kate hoped she wouldn't cry, and she didn't. "Can't it wait until morning?" Her voice, a high-pitched, sulky whine, was beginning to get on Kate's nerves.

"Can we come in, please?"

Erin gave way before her advance. "I suppose so. The dog can't come in, I'm allergic."

"Stay," Kate said, and Mutt made a face, sniffed suspiciously at the carpet outside the door, and sat down with her tail in a fastidious curl around her legs.

Erin sat primly on the edge of the one made-up bed. Kate showed her the letter. Erin's eyes widened. No, she hadn't seen anyone loitering outside Anne's room, or in the hallway of the trailer, or in the parking lot, or to and from the Ahtna high school gym. No, she had no idea who might be writing the letters. She couldn't imagine anyone doing anything so sick. Of course, now that she knew this crazy person was following Anne around, she would watch for anyone who looked suspicious. She was sorry she wasn't able to help this time. It was important to get her mother elected to office, but it was even more important to keep her safe. Erin understood that perfectly well.

They stood in the hallway, waiting for Erin's door to close. When it did, Kenny said softly, "Why didn't she just put in a tape?"

As they stood there, the three of them became aware of sounds coming from a room down the hall, a thumping of headboard against wall, at first gentle, then vigorous, then just plain loud. After a few moments it was accompanied by cries, female, and grunts, male. Everything got louder and speeded up.

"Let's get out of here," Kate said. They retreated down the hall and were about to go into Kate's room when Tracy appeared, a dreamy look in her eye and whisker burns on her face. The dreamy look vanished when they told her about the new letter, and she readily gave the name of the man she had spent the past few hours with. He was someone Kenny knew when she described him, which was fortunate, because Tracy didn't know either his last name or his phone number.

"Man, I'm beat," Tracy said, yawning. "Okay if I hit the sack?" Without waiting for a reply she winked at Kate and vanished into her room.

"I guess it's okay," Kate said. She turned to Darlene. "Who's next?"

"That's it."

"No, it isn't. What about you?"

"Me?"

"Yeah, where were you this evening?" Kate had to hold back a grin when Darlene's mouth fell open.

"Why, I was — I didn't — what do you mean, where was I? I was right here in my room, just like —" She halted.

"Just like everybody else," Kate finished for her, "one door away from where a ransom note was delivered to Anne Gordaoff."

A thundercloud descended over Darlene's face. "I — you — what are you — do you really think that I've worked this hard to get Anne elected that —"

"I'm merely saying that you had as much opportunity as anyone else to slip the letter under her door."

"I was in my room," Darlene snapped, "until Anne came to tell me about the letter."

"Okay," Kate said.

They knocked on the rest of the doors, and got a lot of bad-tempered people out of bed to no purpose that Kate could see. "Well, that was a big help," she said to Kenny as the last door slammed in their faces.

"We had to check," Kenny said. "Getting the door slammed in our face comes with the territory. I say we pack it in for now."

But Kate remembered someone else they had to talk to. "What about the researcher you were talking about?" she said to Darlene. "She's working on the campaign, where is she?"

"She's got her own place," Darlene said. "I told you, she doesn't stay at the hotel."

"You know where she lives?"

"Yeah. I had to find it when I wanted to hire her."

Kate looked at Kenny. "In the morning," he said.

186

"We're up," she said.

"In the morning," he repeated. "It's at least got to be light out. I'll be back around nine; we'll drive out in my rig. You'll go with us," he told Darlene.

"Oh, but I can't," she said, "Anne's got a breakfast with the local Guns-and-Ammo group, I have to . . ."

Her voice trailed away beneath Kenny's steady stare. Cops have their uses, Kate thought.

"I guess I could take an hour," Darlene said.

"Good," Kenny said. "See you both in the parking lot at nine."

Darlene vanished into her room with a flounce.

Kate, groggy now with fatigue, fumbled with the key to her door. It opened at last, but she stood for a moment on the threshold, glancing down the hall.

The sheet-beating they had heard earlier had been coming from Anne and Doug's room, she was almost sure of it. Darlene hadn't so much as turned a hair that fresh out of his lover's bed, he was giving it to his wife. Kate had to give him points for stamina, but if she'd been his wife, she would have been more careful. Who knew where that penis had been?

The covers were up to her chin when she thought, And why did Doug feel it so necessary to mark his territory so publicly?

9

Kenny Hazen didn't show up until ten. He had Jim Chopin with him.

Kate bristled, but Darlene walked around her and got in Kenny's pristine white Suburban with the discreet gold shield on the side. Jim looked at Kate with a raised eyebrow, and she motioned Mutt into the back, and got in behind Kenny.

"Good morning, everyone," Kenny said, sounding as cheerful as the recreational director on a cruise ship, and they were off.

Darlene's researcher lived five miles out of town in a little Airstream trailer that gleamed like a silver hot dog-shaped UFO. The trailer was parked by itself on a riverside acre of ground overgrown with white spruce and birch and alder and cottonwood and diamond willow and salmonberry and raspberry and blueberry bushes and pretty much any plant that produced leaves at that latitude. It looked as if the only thing that was holding it up out of the water rushing past was sheer force of will. A wooden rack of fifty-five gallon drums, much like the one in back of Kate's cabin, leaned against the wall near the door. A picnic table stood between the trailer and the river, in the only clear space in the tangled undergrowth other than the trail in. A wire leading from a pole on the road indicated that the trailer had electricity, but there were no lights on inside.

"Paula?" Darlene said, knocking.

There was no answer. Darlene knocked again, more firmly this time. The door's loose latch gave and it swung open. Mutt's ears went back about the same time it hit Kate's nose.

"What's that smell?" Darlene said, peering inside. "Paula?"

Kate pushed her back with no apology.

"Hey," Darlene started to say, sounding indignant, and then Kate was no longer there. Instead, Kenny said from behind her, "Don't touch the wall switch."

Kate found it and elbowed it on. For some reason the light made the smell stronger.

"Miss Pawlowski?" Kenny said, sidearm out, sliding inside with his back to the door. Jim was right behind him, also with his sidearm out. "Paula Pawlowski?"

"Kate, what's going on?"

"Wait out here, Darlene," Kate said, trying unsuccessfully to see around the not inconsiderable bulk of two Alaskan law enforcement officers. She heard the sound of a footstep squishing into a wet carpet.

189

"Goddamn it," Kenny said.

"Oh hell," Jim said.

Kate wormed her way past him to see.

"Kate? What's going on?" Darlene shoved in next to Kate. "Oh my god. Paula. Paula? Paula!"

In the awkward sprawl of the dead lay the woman with whom Kate had shared her dinner table at the Ahtna Lodge restaurant the night before.

"I got the body off to the ME in Anchorage on the noon plane," Kenny said, settling himself in his chair. "It's getting to be a habit."

It was about one o'clock. Anne and her entourage had been questioned, had denied seeing Paula the night before, except for Darlene, who said she had spent half an hour with the researcher before going to the VFW dinner with Anne and Co. None of them knew Paula other than professionally, and as she had spent most of her time working for them in one library or another around the state, even Anne had difficulty remembering what she looked like. No, they couldn't say if she had any enemies. No, they hadn't seen anyone suspicious lurking around. Hadn't they all been asked that question before? they wanted to know. Like about six hours before? In the middle of the friggin' night?

It wasn't long before Kenny ran out of questions to ask them, and Darlene was quick to pounce on the opportunity. Was that all? she wanted to know, and when Kenny said that was all, she shepherded everyone to Anne's next appearance, a performance of *The Mikado* by the Ahtna Junior High Dramatic Society.

Kate stayed with Kenny and Jim. Also, as Darlene pointed out, the campaign had lost its researcher, and she wanted Kate to get hold of Paula's notes and laptop, always assuming Kenny could be convinced to give them up, something Kate pointed out to Darlene and something Darlene of course blew off. "At least get him to let you take a look at them," she said, her voice impatient. "Do I have to do everything?"

"Whoever it was got close enough for her to grab the gun," Kenny said now, looking at Jim, "or it looks like it from the tears on the palms of her hands. Be a while before we get results from ballistics, but it looks like a twenty-two caliber pistol."

"Another twenty-two," Jim said. "What a coincidence."

"This one also firing at close range, another amazing coincidence. The bullet went into her chest, and there's no exit wound, so ballistics should tell us something if we ever find the weapon." His glum voice told them how likely an event he thought that. Kate thought of the river running past the Airstream and felt a little glum herself.

"Tears on her hands," Jim said. "You're thinking this one maybe wasn't meant to be murder?"

Without answering, Kenny brought out two

clear plastic bags. In one, there was a box of Expert brand typing/copy paper, letter size, not quite full. In the other, there were two Sharpie Fine Point Permanent Markers, one still half in the shrink wrap it had been sold in. "It's the same paper as the other letters, all right, same watermark, twenty-five percent cotton bond, eight and a half by eleven."

"Did the letter Anne got last night come from the paper in that box?" Kate said.

"I haven't seen it yet, by the way," Jim said.

Kenny tossed him the letter, encased in a clear plastic document protector. Jim read it. His eyebrows went up. "Hello. This one reads like blackmail."

Kate looked at Kenny. "So? Same paper?"

He shrugged. "I counted the pages left. There are four hundred and ninety-two. Eight letters sent. Eight pages missing."

"Envelopes?"

Kenny produced a third bag, filled with white envelopes. "No window, lined on the inside for security, gummed flap, you can buy them a hundred at a time. I've only seen copies of the previous letters." He tossed the bag to Jim.

Jim caught it. "Hell, I don't know, envelopes look pretty much the same to me. Doesn't look any different than the ones the other letters came in. Kate?"

She took the bag from him. "Yeah. Look the same. How about the handwriting?"

"Block printing. Pen strokes seem a little

longer on the previous letters, but that may be the copy effect. I'll send the new one off to the lab today. Were there fingerprints on any of the others?"

Jim shook his head.

"Hell."

Jim grinned. "If it was easy, everybody'd be doing it."

"I had dinner with her last night," Kate said.

Both men looked at her. She fixed her eyes on Kenny. "At the hotel. It was crowded; she had a seat at her table she didn't mind sharing."

"Why didn't you tell me this before?" Kenny said. He was every inch the cop now, unbullshitable eyes trained on Kate's face.

"Things started happening kind of fast after we found the body. I figured it would keep. I didn't know it was her," she said, before Kenny could say anything. "I mean, I didn't know I was having dinner with the researcher Darlene hired."

"You didn't talk?"

"Oh no, we talked. We talked until after ten." She saw the look the two men exchanged, and sighed. "She told me she was a writer. She told me about the book she was writing, some tale about a dance-hall queen during the gold rush and her daughter and granddaughter. Or that's what it was turning into. She'd been doing a lot of research, she said, but she never mentioned the campaign. Although Darlene did say later that Paula had just gotten off a plane from Fairbanks, where she'd been doing some research at the library. We only exchanged first names."

"Yeah, right," Jim said, with a quick, dismissive laugh. "Two women sit down at a table, five minutes later they know each other's favorite floors at Nordie's, their book club's most recent book selection, and how dumb their men are."

"No," Kate retorted, "that's only what we want you to think, Jim. Actually we're trading notes on how bad you are in the sack."

"If we could get back to the case?" Kenny said.

"Certainly," Kate said.

Jim jerked his head. The gesture caught Kate's eye and when she glanced over involuntarily she saw that his skin had reddened beneath its tan. The traitor Mutt, sitting between them, bumped his hand and he scratched behind her ears.

"Did you walk back to the trailer with her?"

Kate shook her head. "She said she wanted to stay on a while and watch what happened at the bar. Said she was going to have some bar scenes in her book and since she doesn't — didn't drink, she needed to put in some research."

"Any guys around?"

"Yeah. Couple of them asked us to dance, but we turned 'em down."

Kenny glared at Jim before he could say anything.

"Anybody making a pest of himself?"

"No. Pretty mellow crowd. I saw Tom Gordaoff

in there just before I left, putting the moves on a girl."

"Recognize her?"

"No."

"Would you know her again?"

"Kenny."

He waved a hand. "All right, all right, dumb question."

"Where are Pawlowski's personal effects?" Jim said.

"Jeannie's sitting on them outside." They followed him into the outer office.

Paula Pawlowski's possessions, or what they had found in her trailer, were pitifully few and carefully spaced out across a work table. There was a laptop computer, a black three-ring binder, half a dozen notebooks, and a Ziploc bag full of pens and pencils. There was a cheap carry-on stuffed with one change of clothes, worn, and a ditty bag, probably the bag she'd taken to Fairbanks with her. Kate pulled on the surgical gloves Kenny gave her and opened it up. "Shampoo, conditioner, toothbrush, toothpaste. No perfume, no eyeliner, no mascara."

"Like you would know a mascara wand if you saw one," Jim said.

She gave him her most dazzling smile, at the sight of which Mutt's ears went straight up. "Like you would have any idea what I would know or not know."

"Yeah, okay," Kenny said. "Jesus, you two,

you just get worse and worse. Anybody'd think you were shacking up."

There was a split second of silence. "No jewelry," Kate said. "Was she wearing a watch when we found her?"

"No."

"She wasn't wearing one at dinner, either."

Kate looked at the laptop. "Can we turn on the computer?"

"Why not?"

Kate pulled over a chair and opened the computer.

"Kenny," the woman at the desk behind them said, "Andy Anderson's calling, wants to know if you've seen Jerry Dial in town."

Kenny went to the phone.

A Windows 95 desktop popped up on the computer, no password necessary. One of the icons was Word for Windows. She clicked on it on the assumption that a researcher would use a text and not a graphics file, and she was right. Paula had organized her professional life into folders containing files. One file was labeled NOVEL and contained seven separate files labeled DRAFT1 through DRAFT7. Everyone of them had a different title, as if Paula had been unable to decide between the relative merits of "Pointing North," which brought an involuntary grin to Kate's face, and "Years of Gold," which made her want to gag. She was more interested in the folder marked DIRT, however. She clicked on it. There was one file called

HEIMAN and another called GORDAOFF.

"Click on Gordaoff first," Jim said, leaning over her shoulder.

"Uh-huh." Kate looked around. "Grab me one of those floppies, would you?" she said.

"Why?"

"Just do it, Chopin."

He did and she slipped it into the slot on the side of the laptop and copied both files.

Jim sighed. "Why didn't you just ask him if you could?"

"Because then he might have to say no to me. I don't like making my friends uncomfortable."

"Sure you don't," Jim said beneath his breath, as Kate slipped the floppy into a pocket.

"You aren't my friend," she said before she could stop herself.

There was another of those tense silences between the two of them that seemed to be popping up with uncomfortable regularity. "You got that right, if nothing else," Jim said, his voice cool and his words clipped.

Kenny came back and picked up the expanding file folder that was also part of Paula Pawlowski's effects.

"Anything in there?" Kate said.

"Notes about Peter Heiman, mostly. About his brother, his dad, his grandfather. Mostly history, starting back in Fairbanks right after the Klondike. That what she was supposed to be looking up?"

"I think she was supposed to be finding out

anything about Peter Heiman that would help Darlene beat him in the election."

"I thought Anne Gordaoff was running against Pete."

Kate smiled. "It's her face on the posters," she said, and left it at that. "Mind if I take a look?"

Paula's handwriting was large and sprawling, with a lot of marginal notes surrounded by balloons with arrows pointing to other balloons and paragraphs. There were a few doodles here and there, asterisks, five-pointed stars, a hand-drawn game of Dots the likes of which Kate hadn't seen since grade school. "Think I could have copies of what's in here?" she asked Kenny.

"Oh, like the copy you made of the files on the laptop?" Kenny asked.

Kate refused to blush. "I was thinking more of a Xerox machine for the paperwork."

"You might have asked."

"But then you might have had to say no."

"True." To Jim Chopin's immense and visible disgust, Kenny waved her to the copy machine.

"Thanks, Kenny," she said when she was done.

"I don't like this, Kate." He stood in the center of the outer office, arms folded, his large figure dominating the space and infusing it with a sense of purposeful menace. "I get paid to keep a peaceful, prosperous community peaceful and prosperous. The community doesn't like it when somebody gets killed here, and I don't like it when the community doesn't like it."

"I know."

"Now there have been two murders."

"Yes."

"And I don't have a suspect for either one."

"I know."

"I don't like that, either." Kenny spoke with deliberation, giving each word its due weight. He wouldn't be deflected and he wouldn't be rushed. Kate listened to him with a sober expression. Jim listened in without kibitzing, not something he would do for every other one of his brothers and sisters in arms. "I want this cleaned up, and quick. Okay, Billy Mike and the mayor and anybody who is anybody is telling me to low-key this, fine. But a man is dead, murdered. A woman's dead, murdered, and she lived here. I didn't know her, but that doesn't matter. She was one of mine."

He raised his eyes to Kate's. "You're working for the campaign, Pawlowski was working for the campaign, you've got the best shot at figuring this out. Figure it out. Meantime, I'll get on forensics in town. She fought. Maybe some of all that blood isn't hers. Call me, everyday; tell me what's going on."

"All right."

He gave her an envelope for the copies. "Thanks."

"I've got the Cessna." Jim Chopin said, staring into the air over her head. "Want a ride?"

After Gilbert and Sullivan, Anne and company had been scheduled to fly out to Niniltna, leaving Kate to follow how she could.

199

The best that Kate knew of Jim Chopin was that he was an excellent pilot, even of planes he'd never flown before and never would again, as witness their brief and, for lack of a better word, exhilarating flight together in a Lockheed C-130 the previous July. "I want to check out Paula's trailer again." She looked at Kenny for permission. He considered, nodded.

The Airstream was on a lonely stretch of riverbank, no neighbors around for two miles in any direction. "We've already gone through it."

"I know, but I want to look again."

"Fine. I'd have to change my flight plan anyway."

Kate left, followed by Mutt, who pasted a wet one on Jim in passing.

The two men watched them out of sight. She looked sad in repose, Jim thought, quieter, less irritable. He didn't like it.

Kenny looked at Jim and shook his head. "Boy, Chopin, you've got it bad."

"Shut the fuck up," Jim said.

10

"What do you drive?" she asked Tony.

"A Ford Escort, also known as a McCar," he said.

"Could I borrow it for a couple of hours?"

"Sure." He pitched her the keys. "Two door, dark blue, should be around back of the kitchen."

"Thanks, Tony. I'll fill her up before I bring her back."

At the Airstream, Kate ducked beneath the crime-scene tape and opened the door. Mutt looked at Kate pleadingly from the cement square that served as the trailer's front porch. "God knows you deserve it," Kate said. "Take the afternoon off, girl. Go." Mutt gave a joyous bark and in two leaps was in the underbrush. A spruce hen exploded upward, squawking indignantly. The hydraulic hinge pulled the door shut behind Kate and nudged her the rest of the way inside the tiny living room. She set the envelope containing the copies of Paula's notes down on the table and took a long, slow look around.

You had to train long and hard to see the rest of the room a body was laying in. Maybe Kate was out of practice, but she didn't remember the matching flowered print of the curtains and the sofa cushions on the two couches with the table between them. Poppies, it looked like, on a dense forest green background that gave the material the look of tapestry, and almost hid the bloodstain from view.

The corresponding bloodstain on the white linoleum-tile floor had dried a hard brown. She'd been shot once, had fallen to the couch, then to the floor. They'd found no evidence that she'd hit the table.

Bookcases, homemade but sturdily built and nicely finished with a natural stain and a light coating of varnish, filled every available inch of the wall space above the couch backs, between the windows, and below the ceiling. The books were alphabetized by author, all history, all about eras of Alaskan history, World War II, gold rush days, the Civil War. Some Kate recognized from her own library: *The Thousand Mile War* by Brian Garfield, *The Flying North* by Jean Potter, Pierre Berton's *The Klondike Rush*, his mother's *I Married the Klondike*, and Murray Morgan's *Confederate Raider*. Little yellow sticky notes festooned the pages, where passages had been marked in light pencil.

She saw an oversized book bound in leather

with fading letters on the spine, which proved to be a copy of the duke of Abruzzi's account of his expedition to climb Mount St. Elias in 1897, a book Kate had given up on acquiring when Rachel at Twice Told Tales in Anchorage had told her it was priced on the Internet at seven hundred and fifty dollars. There were photographs, and she sat down on the unstained couch and leafed through them, pausing to read a paragraph here and there.

She replaced the book on the shelf with due reverence, and wondered what other treasures Paula had hidden away in her little tin hot dog. There was no filing cabinet, no notes. Everything Paula had been working on must have been either in the notebooks or on the laptop.

The kitchen cupboards were neatly organized, the dishes melamine, the pots and pans Paul Revere, the glassware Wal-Mart, the flatware Costco. In the little refrigerator fitted beneath the counter there was an aging block of cheddar cheese, a half-empty carton of eggs, and a bunch of green onions that looked like they were melting. The remainder of a loaf of Wonder Bread on the counter was dried hard. There was a box of Walker shortbread rounds in the cupboard, the only evidence of sin. The sink, the tiny gas stove and oven, everything was spotlessly clean. The countertops looked new, some kind of fake wood. The cupboard below was stocked with dish soap, clothes soap, bleach, paper towels, and plastic trash bags, all in giant economy-size boxes. Paula hated to shop, and bought large when she did so she wouldn't have to do so again anytime soon. Kate's heart warmed to her, and hardened toward her killer.

Down the tiny hallway the bathroom was stocked with Ivory soap in hand-bar and bath-bar sizes, half-gallon jugs of generic shampoo and conditioner with pump handles, another half gallon of generic hand lotion on the sink. The single bed (more room for bookshelves) had two changes of sheets, one on and one in the clothes hamper, a quilt for summer and a down comforter for winter. Paula hadn't liked to shop, and she wasn't a prisoner of her possessions, and for no reason this realization made Kate's anger at Paula's killer run higher. Paula Pawlowski had refined living down to its essentials, so that she could concentrate on what mattered.

What mattered was books, if the bulk of the contents of the trailer was any indication. Shelves, built-in and freestanding, took up every available inch of floor space, were wedged between bed and wall, were mounted over all the windows. Everyone of them was lined with books. It took Kate a while to see that they were in alphabetical order, clockwise from the door, starting with the five-shelf bookshelf nailed to the divider between the kitchen/living room and the bedroom, and ending with the two shelves mounted on brackets over the toilet in the bathroom. She saw Jane Austen, L. Frank Baum, Lois McMasters Bujold, Bernard Cornwell by the door; Loren Estelman, Steven Gould, Robert Heinlein, Georgette Heyer (and now she was seriously angry), John D. MacDonald, L. M. Montgomery, Ellis Peters, J. K. Rowling, Sharon Shinn, Nevil Shute down one side of the little hallway, around and over the bed; Laura Ingalls Wilder and Don Winslow over the toilet.

There weren't that many people in the world who read for fun, who would rather read than watch television, who were physically incapable of walking past a bookstore. Kate had come to it late, a gift from a gifted English teacher at the University of Alaska in Fairbanks, which meant that she had a keen sense of time wasted, a reverence for the art, and deep respect for those who practiced it. She looked at all of Paula Pawlowski's books and realized that Paula had been a lifelong friend of hers before they'd ever met. She found herself growing very calm.

I will find out who did this to you, she said silently to the spine of *The Death and Life of Bobby Z*. I will find out, and I will make them pay.

A knock at the door startled her. She went back into the hallway, and could make out a shape through the translucent glass pane in the door. "Who's there?" she called.

"It's me, Paula, open the damn door." Another knock, impatient this time. "Look, I know you're mad at me, but —"

Kate opened the door and found a man

staring up at her in surprise. "Who the hell are you?"

"My name is Kate," she said. "What's yours?"

"Gordy Boothe, I — wait a minute. What are you doing in Paula's trailer? Where's Paula?" He craned his head to look around her. "Paula?"

She stepped outside and closed the door behind her. "How well did you know Paula Pawlowski, Mr. Boothe?"

"What?" Now he was staring down at her in bafflement and growing anger. "Look, what the hell is this? Where's Paula? Paula!" He banged on the door with his fist. "Paula, open this door!"

"Mr. Boothe. Mr. Boothe!" She put a hand on his arm. "She won't hear you. She's not here."

"What do you mean, she's not here? She just got home last night; I drove her home from the Lodge."

"Really," Kate said. "What time was that?"

"I don't know, eleven, eleven-thirty."

"Did you stay with her?"

"No." He hadn't been happy about it, either, and he still wasn't. "She wouldn't let me. She said she'd had this great idea, and she wanted to work on it before she lost it." He'd been watching Kate's expression. He was a pleasant-faced man in his mid-fifties, about five-ten, with a bald spot that made him look like he was tonsured and a body that looked like it had once played team sports in a desperate battle to stave off a middle-aged spread. "Look, Miss — what did you say your name was? — what's going on here? Who are you?"

"Were you and Paula close, Mr. Boothe?" Kate looked behind him and saw the picnic table with two benches on either side of it. She moved toward it, and he followed her.

"We had a relationship, sort of," he said. "We were good friends."

"Which was it, were you friends or lovers?"

He was starting to get angry. "Look, I don't know what business that is of yours. Look here, what's —" His face paled, and the stuffing went out of him so suddenly that he collapsed on the nearest picnic bench. "Did you say 'was'?"

"I'm sorry to tell you this, Mr. Boothe. Your friend met with an accident last night."

He uttered a low groan. "A bear? Was it a bear?"

"Why do you say that?"

"Because we heard one crashing through the bushes when I dropped her off last night. Is she okay? Where is she? Is she at the hospital?" He rose to his feet.

Kate pulled him back down. "Mr. Boothe, I'm sorry to have to tell you this, but I'm afraid Paula is dead."

He stared at her, his face very white. And then he burst into tears.

He was a history teacher at Ahtna High School and the coach for both the girls's and boys's volleyball teams. He'd met Paula three years before, when she came to him for help with some historical research for her novel, and they'd had an on-again, off-again relationship since. He was supposed to have met her at the airport when she flew in from Fairbanks the day before, with dinner at the Lodge to follow, and the rest of the night at his house, but their plans had gone awry when he'd been late getting back from a school trip to Kuik, and she had come up with her brilliant idea. "If I'd insisted she come home with me, she'd still be alive," he said, blowing his nose. Fresh tears started down his face. "I should have made her come with me. Damn it!" He thumped the picnic table in sudden rage. "Damn it, damn it, damn it!"

Paula hadn't had any enemies, he said. She had lived out here because the rent was a third of what it was in town. Her parents were dead, and she'd been an only child. Where had she come from originally? He thought Chicago. Or maybe it was Cincinnati, he wasn't sure. She'd moved up with her mother twelve years before, and supported herself by writing grant applications for nonprofit corporations and hiring herself out to do research.

"Mr. Boothe, did she say or do anything last night in any way out of the ordinary?"

He shook his head. "No. Nothing."

"What was this new idea she had that she wanted to work on?"

He blew his nose again. "She'd found a story about a murder back in, god, I don't know, 1919 or something. One of the girls in one of the hook shops in Niniltna, back when it was party town for the Kanuyaq Copper Mine. She was all excited about how she could work it into her novel. She couldn't wait to get started." He sat, knees splayed, hands dangling between them, chin sunk on his chest.

"Anything else?"

He stared at the ground, oblivious to the afternoon growing cooler around them, looking unutterably weary. "She was so nice. And so smart. And she read." He looked up. "Books," he said.

"I know."

"She liked to jitterbug. Did you know that?"

"No. I didn't know that."

"She was good at it, too. Danced me right off the floor more than once. When I had to chaperon a school dance, Paula would come and we would dance, and the kids would stand around in a circle and clap and yell and whistle." He smiled at the memory. It didn't last. "There'll never be anyone else for me. Paula was it. At my age, you just don't meet a lot of women you like." He raised his head, blinking away tears, and saw her watching him. "You're still young. You think you've got all the time in the world. Well, you don't." He got up and walked a few steps toward the battered Toyota Land Cruiser parked next to Tony's Escort. He stopped halfway there and wheeled around. "You're sure?" he said. "You're sure she's dead?"

"I'm sorry, Mr. Boothe."

His shoulders sagged. "Where is she?"

"An autopsy is required in every incidence of violent death in the state of Alaska."

"Can I have her back, afterward? I'd like to see her buried, if I may."

"I'll tell Chief Hazen."

"Thank you. Thank you for everything. You've been very kind." When the Toyota had backed halfway down the driveway, he stopped and rolled down the window. "She said she'd married well!"

"Who had?"

"The hooker! Paula said she'd married well! That's all I remember, though!"

"Thanks!"

He waved and rolled the window back up.

Kate sat where she was for a good ten minutes after the sound of the engine had faded away. Gordy Boothe must have walked into the restaurant the night before five minutes after Kate had walked out. Like him, she wished he'd talked Paula into staying with him, or that he had stayed at the trailer with her.

It was early afternoon, about four o'clock. She ought to go back into town and catch a ride of some kind to Niniltna. Mutt wasn't back from lunch yet. She thought of the grizzly Gordy Boothe had heard in the bushes the night before, and hoped Mutt didn't bring it back with her.

She could have called Mutt, but she didn't. She wasn't ready to go back to town yet, to be around people yet. She went back into the trailer and into the bedroom and took a second look at *Helm*. Kid puts on a weird helmet, acquires another personality; father beats him with a stick until he learns how to get out of its way: he goes to war at the head of an army and kicks serious enemy ass. She was immersed from the first page, and didn't hear the quiet purr of an approaching engine. She didn't even hear the door open. The Airstream, sitting on a solid foundation of cement blocks, didn't shift. The hydraulic hinge slammed the door closed though, and Kate looked up from where she was sitting on the floor, back to the bookshelf, startled but not quick enough. The tiny hallway was so short that the bedroom could be reached in one long step. There was a creak of wood over her head, and Kate looked up to see the five-shelf bookshelf and all its books come crashing down on her.

Kenny Hazen dropped Jim Chopin at the Ahtna airport, and Jim would have been in Tok by now if he hadn't discovered a minute trace of oil on the hose leading from the engine to the oil pan. So he had to track down a new hose, and that took time, but it wasn't like he was in a hurry. There wasn't a lot going on back at the ranch. Well, except for Steve Glatter trying to kill his wife Barbara and Terry Moon when he caught them parked on a very short dead-end road a mile away from the turnoff of the Glatter homestead, clearly visible from the highway. If somebody had to do the nasty, why couldn't they practice a little discretion? It would make his life a lot easier. As it was, Terry was in the hospital, Barbara had retained an attorney, and Steve was in jail on the charge of assault in the third degree with the handle off a meat grinder. Terry wasn't all that beat up, and the Glatters had three minor children. Assault in the third was only a Class-A felony. Jim would have downgraded it to assault in the fourth or even reckless endangerment if he'd thought he could have gotten away with it, but the magistrate on duty that day had been partying late the night before at the Do Drop and, as a consequence, had been in a severe mood the following morning.

It was six o'clock by the time he finished the job. It wasn't one a licensed A&P mechanic would have to sign off on, so all he had to do was wash his hands and he was halfway home.

Still. It wouldn't hurt to drive out to Paula Pawlowski's trailer, which he had visited with Kenny Hazen that morning, and see if Kate was done communing with her new best friend's spirit. Not that he owed her a ride home or anything, but it was the neighborly thing to do.

You've got it bad, boy.

"Yeah, and the horse you rode in on," he said out loud, alarming the young man who fueled planes for the local Chevron dealership.

He borrowed the airport manager's truck and drove out to the trailer, on the way nearly sideswiped by a dark green truck speeding in the other direction. He was sorry he didn't have lights and siren, sorrier still that he'd left the ticket book back in the plane, and sorriest of all that the truck he was driving had a shimmy in the front end and a distressing tendency on the part of the gearshift to resist going into and popping out of third gear, or it would have been his very great pleasure to haul this sorry excuse for transportation in a U-turn and give chase. He didn't catch the tag number, either.

It was in no very cheerful frame of mind that he pulled into the driveway. For one thing, he didn't know what the hell he was going to say. "Want a ride home?" wasn't quite going to cut it this time.

When he got out of the truck, he heard a dog barking. It got louder as he approached the trailer, and when he got to the door he saw Mutt hurling herself at the window in it. If there had been a little more glass, she would have broken through.

"Mutt!" he said. "Stop it! Kate, where are you? Kate!"

He barged inside, or he would have if Mutt hadn't hit him square in the chest on her way out. She hit the ground over his head and made for the road, barking all the way, sharp, urgent barks.

"*Mutt!*" he roared, and she skidded to a halt. "Stay! Stay right there, girl!" She took a few steps toward him and whined, a few steps toward the road, whined again, and was repeating this dance as he got up and made for the trailer door. The next thing he knew he was on the ground again, Mutt having caught the hem of his pants leg and yanked him off his feet. "What the hell?" he said, staring up at her. "Will you knock it off! Jesus!" He got to his feet again and made the trailer in one giant step. Mutt started barking again.

A hurricane appeared to have passed through the neat home he had seen that morning. Every dish, serving bowl, pot was out of the cupboards. The box of Tide had been emptied into the middle of the floor, along with the garbage and a box of Special K. The clothes had been torn off their hangars, the closet emptied.

There was no indication that this was an office as well as a home: no desk, no filing cabinet, no fax machine. There were books, though, and every single one of the books was on the floor, in heaps he had to step over. Those bookshelves not fastened to the walls had been overturned, as if the hurricane had wanted to look behind them.

A pocket door between the kitchen and living area had been locked from the other side. He kicked it out of its frame and found more chaos: the covers ripped from the bed, the mattress and springs tipped to the floor, and more books pulled from their shelves and more bookshelves pulled from the walls.

Kate was nowhere to be found.

Mutt's barks became louder and more frantic.

There was a second door, however, that had been hidden behind one of the bookshelves. It was slightly ajar, held so by a book that had fallen into the crack. There were more books on the ground outside.

He waded back to the front door, taking one last look around in a vain attempt to see if Kate had even been here. He damned her for not carrying a purse, standard issue for every other woman in the world, but oh no, not her. He gave a pile of books a savage kick and missed, and the toe of his boot hit the corner of the bookcase instead. He let out a yell and tried to hop up and down, but there wasn't any room. His good foot hit another pile of books and they tilted, and he lost his balance and fell heavily on another pile. Outside, Mutt's barks increased in frequency and intensity.

He damned the books loudly and with imagination, glaring down at the bookcase as if it were animate. It lay drunkenly on one side with a piece of rubber caught in a splinter on one corner.

He climbed to his feet and reached for the door. Mutt bounded over, alternately whining and barking, her attitude one of frantic urgency. "Hold on, girl, I think we're onto something here." There was a long, thick rubber band dangling from the doorknob on the inside, snapped in half, ends ragged. It matched the piece of rubber caught on the splinter on the corner of the bookcase. He let go of the knob and the door slammed shut, nearly catching Mutt's nose in it.

If the bookcase were raised to what he thought was its proper place, at right angles to the door, someone could wrap a long rubber band around the doorknob and, providing it were long and thick enough, stretch it to wrap around the corner of the bookcase. Thus keeping the door closed.

Why?

He opened the door again, let it slam shut again. Pretty efficient hydraulic hinge. Why bother with the rubber band?

He thought of how Mutt had been on the other side of that door.

Suppose Mutt was on the outside, Kate on the inside and in trouble.

Suppose whomever Kate was in trouble with was also on the inside.

That whoever would think three or four times before stepping into the teeth of a one hundred and forty pound dog who was half gray wolf and all fangs.

He turned and looked at the pocket door he'd kicked off its hinges.

Suppose whoever had come in, cold cocked Kate, searched the trailer, and had prepared to leave, to find Mutt at the front door. The back door was only a few feet away down the same wall, reachable by Mutt in a single bound.

Whoever was stuck.

Unless whoever rigged the door with the rubber band and then propped it open a crack — say with a paperback, perhaps? There were enough of them laying around. Whoever could be fairly certain that with even a little toehold, Mutt and her claws would be able to get the door open, just not right away, which might be the point. When the door opened, the book would fall out.

He looked outside. The paperback edition of *The Handmaid's Tale*, a book which had left him about as terrified upon reading it as he was now, lay on the concrete square in front of the door. He'd fallen on it when Mutt tackled him and hadn't noticed.

As the book fell out, the dog got in. The hydraulic hinge would close the door. Hydraulic hinges were common in the north, helped to keep the cold out when you had your arms full of groceries. The doorknob was a smooth metal. Even if a dog was smart enough to open a door, this one wouldn't open easy.

He turned and looked at the pocket door again. The rubber band would take even Mutt sometime to negotiate. Maybe just long enough for whoever to scoot to the back of the trailer and close the pocket door, and lock it behind them. Then all whoever had to do was wait for the front door to close behind Mutt, forming a neat little trap.

Whoever then exited the back door.

Why did whoever take Kate?

Maybe whoever didn't take Kate, maybe Kate followed.

But then there would have been no need for the neatest little animal trap Jim had seen in a long time.

"Son of a bitch," he said, and yanked at the door knob. Standing stiff-legged on the other side, Mutt growled at him, the first time she'd ever done so. She lunged forward and grabbed a fold of his blue uniform pants, and it wasn't her fault she didn't get a mouthful of thigh while she was at it. Jim almost overbalanced again. "Damn it, I'm coming, let go!"

She didn't believe him and backed out of the trailer, pulling him inexorably forward. "Damn it, Mutt, I said I was coming! Now let go, right now!" He glared down at her.

She let go long enough to bark at him. She trotted toward his truck, back toward him, toward the truck, and barked again.

A dark blue Ford Escort sat in front of his borrowed truck. He had thought it belonged to Paula Pawlowski, but now he remembered he hadn't seen it this morning. It was open, and empty but for a large box of dinner-size paper napkins in the trunk. The registration was in the glove box, in the name of Luiz Antonio Orozco y Elizondo, which name meant nothing to Jim. The keys were in it. He wiped a hand across the back seat, and it came up covered with a lot of stiff, gray hairs that exactly matched the coat of the dog who squeezed into the car, turned around on the size of a quarter and barked once, right in his face, and then growled again, as if to underline the bark. If Kate had borrowed this car, if she and Mutt had driven out to the Pawlowski trailer in it, then why had she left it behind?

More importantly, why — and how? — had she left Mutt behind?

She hadn't.

Suddenly he remembered the truck that had nearly sideswiped his borrowed truck on the way down the road to the trailer. "Mutt! Let's go!"

One sharp bark, easily translated as, About time! She was in the back of the pickup before he was in the cab.

Fairbanks

1907

"*Are you a lady or a whore?*"

It was only an inquiry, not an attack, and the young man with the bowler hat shoved to the back of his head, shirtsleeves rolled up, and a baggy tweed vest over even baggier tweed pants didn't look all that interested in the answer after his first speculative once-over, earmarking her for future reference: redhead, a little long in the tooth but still toothsome.

"*A whore,*" *she said, her voice steady. Her son looked at her, and she smiled at him.*

The young man saw the boy and had the grace to flush. "Your son?"

"*Yes.*"

"*You plan on keeping him with you on the Line?*"

"*No.*"

Her expression didn't change, but the young man shifted anyway. It was a simple, single-syllable word, but she managed to infuse a great deal of feeling into it. For reasons he could never explain, it moved him to say, "You might want to check with the MacGregors. Lily MacGregor has been known to

220

look after a child now and then. *Fine woman. Well-respected in the community.*"

"*Thank you.*"

"*Yes. Well.*" Uncomfortable with his unaccustomed shift into altruism, the young man hawked and spit, thereby reasserting his masculinity and erasing any notion that he might be turning soft, and said in his gruffest voice, "*There are rules on the Line.*"

"*I know.*"

"*It's my job to tell you what they are.*" He reeled them off with the habit of long practice. No soliciting in saloons or dance halls. There were special hours for going to the movies and visiting the shops, when she wouldn't be mingling with respectable society. Regular health inspections and a small monthly payment of something he called a "*fine*" but which sounded to her like a license to operate.

If she abided by these rules, she would have the backing of the community and no threat of legal reprisal. "*Do you have any capital?*" he said. "*Any money to invest?*" She gave a small nod, wary of admitting to the carrying of any cash.

"*Then you can buy your own house on the Line or, if you like, buy a lot and build.*" Seeing her expression, he added, "*It's not like that. The rents are reasonable. So are prices for the lots.*" He shrugged, losing interest. "*You'll see for yourself. Next!*"

She stepped to the gangway and paused. "*Sir?*"

He looked over his shoulder. "*What?*"

"*Thank you for your kindness. We are strangers here, and we appreciate it.*"

221

He grunted. "Are you a lady or are you a whore?" he said to the woman behind her, and she left the deck of the stern-wheeler Georgia Lee *behind and descended to the shore of the city of Fairbanks, on the banks of the Chena River, in the heart of interior Alaska.*

She hadn't taken the boat for Fairbanks that day in Nome seven years before. Alex Papadopolous, who had staggered away after she had shot him, hadn't looked dead enough to her, and she didn't think for a minute that if he survived that he would think she had gone to Seattle. She was a whore, it was her trade, and the most profitable place to practice it at present was Alaska. Alex would know that, and he would look for her, and he would find her. Outside, she had all the room in the world in which to disappear.

Gunshots attracted no attention in Nome in 1900, where they averaged one murder a day. She had put Matt, unconscious from the time she had shot Alex, into her own bed and bound the wound in his shoulder as best she could. She'd thrown some clothes in a valise, exchanged one of Matt's precious nuggets for a case of canned milk, and had smuggled herself and the boy down to the beach, where she found a ship's captain with an eye for a pretty woman willing to hide her away in his cabin for the duration of the voyage, and willing to be seduced out of the irritants supplied by the presence of a toddler. He had been kind, after his fashion, and mercifully normal in his attentions, and she had parted from him in Seattle with no bad feelings and no regrets.

Percy was so thin and so pale and so listless those first days at sea that she had been afraid she might lose him. When the captain was absent, she spent all her time with Percy cradled in her arms, holding him, covering his face with kisses, rocking him, talking to him, talking to herself. For a month, as the steamer wended its way slowly south and east, she had nothing to do but submit to the captain's demands and tend to Percy's needs. These duties left an uncomfortable amount of free time in which to think, and as the days passed and the relative peace of the voyage remained unbroken, she had time to reflect, to interpret, to determine, and, finally, to plan.

Her entire life to that point passed in review before eyes newly opened and bitterly critical of her actions to date. She had been so secure in her beauty that she had allowed herself to be sold at auction to the highest bidder, confident that she remained in control of her life and her destiny. She had promptly fallen in love with a man who gave no thought to their future, and had, folly of follies, actually married him and borne his child, and for what? To be widowed and sold into slavery, and this time into slavery not of her own making.

"Pride goeth before a fall." She remembered that verse from the Bible teachings her minister father had bellowed at them daily over the table at breakfast and dinner, if she remembered none other. She had been proud, and overconfident, and she had fallen, hard, right to the bottom.

There, at the bottom, she had allowed Alex Papadopolous literally to beat her into submission, to force her to sell herself over and over again. She hadn't fought him for her share of the money she earned, and she had allowed him to take her son away. She had let herself believe Alex when he said the boy was all right. It was easier, she thought now with a shudder of self-loathing, easier and less painful to believe Alex, not to challenge him to a conversation that would only end in his fists striking her body, carefully placed hits that would not show to the casual customer who usually cared little how much of her was covered so long as her skirts were up to her waist. He knew how to hit, Alex did. Even now there was lingering soreness on her back and shoulders.

"How did I put up with it for so long?" she asked herself now. "How could I? Matt was shot because I couldn't act for myself." Matt, who she saw with the wisdom of hindsight had cared for her all along, ever since Dawson. Matt, who had saved her and Percy both, had risked his life, and handed over his poke in a sacrifice all the more painful because it had been so willing.

The day before they reached Seattle, she had looked at the boy child in her arms, had seen the pinkness creeping back into his cheeks and the roundness creeping back into his limbs, and had felt a surge of terror at the prospect of ever losing him again.

She looked that terror full in the face for a long moment, acknowledging its presence, and then she spit squarely in its eye and made three vows.

Never again would she put her child in peril.

Never again would she put herself in peril.

Never again would she have to be rescued.

She sent a telegram to her parents in Missouri, telling them about their grandson for the first time and asking for money. They sent it to her with a terse request that she not return home. She sent a telegram to Sam's parents in Minneapolis. They, too, wired money, and when she went to collect it saw two policemen waiting outside the telegraph office, and remembered all that Sam had told her about the wealth and power of his father. She waited, watching, and two days later when the policemen had become bored and began to wander off, bribed a street urchin to fetch the bank draft for her. She cashed the check immediately, collected Percy, and took the first train to Denver.

She rented a small apartment, hired a nursemaid, and lived quietly and frugally while she looked for employment in the only profession she knew. She found it eventually in an establishment owned by a big, bluff woman with a nearly impenetrable Irish accent, shrewd eyes, haired dyed a defiant brassy blonde, and a raucous laugh that could be heard in Boulder. Mary Kelley looked the Dawson Darling over with a critical eye and said, "With that hair I could have won the West all by myself. You've got a trim figure, and you look clean. I like the name, too. So will the customers." She waved an all-inclusive hand and an enormous breast popped out of the low-cut bodice of the red velvet dress she wore. She

225

reached up to stuff it back in, pausing to scratch unself-consciously at the equally large brown nipple. "In my experience, nothing'll get a man up and off quicker than a hint of the exotic. When can you start?"

"How will I be paid?"

One outrageously blonde eyebrow went up. "Oh, so she's not all looks and no brain, now, is she?"

Both had a healthy respect for each other's financial acumen when negotiations were concluded. Mary showed her her room, large and well-appointed with fashionably heavy furniture and a rectangular mirror on the ceiling over the bed. "I've never seen such a thing," she said.

Mary cast a disparaging glance upward. "Yeah, well, it's all the rage now, lovey. The boyos seem to like it well enough."

Mary ran a quiet house and employed two large men to escort anyone who wasn't quiet enough outside to see how high he could bounce. Mary couldn't abide violence, and abusive customers were shown the door just as soon as they showed their stripes. She sold liquor on the premises, but she wouldn't put up with drunkenness in employees or in customers. She wouldn't tolerate thievery in any form, and one girl who was caught going through a customer's wallet was promptly thrown out and her belongings after her. She was a fanatic on the subject of cleanliness, and had had a large porcelain tub installed in the downstairs bathroom which she insisted employees use regularly. It was available to customers as well, and whether they used it alone or in com-

pany was a matter that affected only the price. A doctor was a regular customer, who bartered services for the privilege of Mary's company.

One room downstairs was reserved for the playing of games of chance, and winners were expected to tip the house ten percent of the night's winnings on their way out. There was a piano and a selection of ragtime sheet music. A burly member of the local constabulary named Kevin O'Leary dropped by every Wednesday evening for a drink and a tussle with Mary, who always emerged from these encounters with her eyes sparkling, her cheeks glowing, and her exuberant breasts threatening once more to leap the bounds of her dress. The house never had a problem with the Denver police.

The girls ranged in age from fifteen to thirty-five, in race from Swedish to Japanese. The roster remained remarkably steady but for the depredations of a series of piano players, who always seemed to fall fatally in love with one or the other of them. Mary Kelley finally threw up her hands and hired a piano teacher to instruct the girls, who took a night off upstairs in exchange for a night downstairs on the piano stool. The Darling came to love that piano, the feel of the ivory keys beneath her fingers, the way she could make music sound from beneath the polished wood of the upright.

Soon after she went to work for Mary, she bought a tiny house in a quiet, working-class neighborhood on the opposite side of Denver, and moved Percy and his nursemaid there. She had Thursday afternoon and all day Monday off, and she spent every free minute she had with her son, reading to him, playing with him, singing him to sleep. He was tall for a child, blue of eye and fair of hair like his father and with the promise of his father's long, lanky frame. He was intelligent and inquisitive and friendly to a fault to any passing stranger. He played with the neighbor children, but they didn't invite him home. Their parents watched when she left, and they watched when she came home, and they weren't fools.

So the Dawson Darling smiled, and one night a week played the piano, and the rest of those nights opened her legs for a succession of increasingly faceless men, some of whom would have been willing to love her if she'd given them half a chance. She saved her money, and dreamed of the day when she would have enough to support herself and her son for the rest of their lives.

The years slipped by and that day didn't seem to be any closer than it had been when she arrived. In 1906, Mary called the girls together and announced she was selling out. They stared at her, and she snorted her laughter. "You look as if you'd seen the Pope himself walk in the front door, the lot of you," she informed them. She patted her hair, this year a bright brown, and said, "The fact of the matter is this, that Kevin O'Leary, fine man that he is, has taken up a sheriffing job in Oregon, and he's had the great good sense of asking me to accompany him there as his wife, and I have accepted him." She sat, placid and satisfied, waiting for the cheering and the applause to die down.

But it did die down, when they came to realize that their safe haven was no more. The house would be closing at the end of the month, with one big party that last night for all the steady customers, at which Mary expected everyone's presence and the morning after which bonuses would be paid. They wouldn't be big bonuses, they knew that already, as Mary Kelley was tight with a dollar, but it was enough to keep them working for her until the end of the month and she knew it, and she knew the girls knew it. They dispersed in ones and twos, whispering, making plans, going upstairs to their rooms to look at their belongings and decide what to take and what to leave behind. Mary had given them names, people to contact, other houses to go, but Mary Kelley's had been a special place and veterans all, they knew it and were sorry to see it go.

The Dawson Darling sat at the piano after everyone else had gone, fingering the keys, drifting from one tune to another, and looked up suddenly to see Mary watching her from the doorway. "I'm sorry," she said, closing the lid of the piano and rising to her feet. "I'm late, I know. I'll go get into my working clothes and —"

Mary held up a hand. "Wait." She looked her over with the same critical eye she'd used the day the Darling had walked in her door for the first time. "That town you've taken your name from, Dawson. It's in Alaska, isn't it?"

"Almost," the Darling said, smiling. "Next door, anyway." Everybody Outside had very vague ideas about the north.

"Mmm," Mary said. She swished across the floor and sat down in an armchair, waving the Darling to one opposite her. "I've been hearing things, I have, about a different place in Alaska, good things for the working girl." She paused. "Have you heard how things used to go on in St. Louis for girls like us?"

The Darling's interest sharpened. Of course she had, they all had. St. Louis in the early seventies was a dream come true for the working girl, where pimps were outlawed, where there was a special district within the city where they could own their own homes, where medical checkups were held on a regular basis, where there was hospitalization for the diseased. The saloonkeepers and the cops on the take hadn't been happy with the result and it hadn't lasted long, a mere four years, but St. Louis continued to be a place where the working girl had a fighting chance of keeping what she earned, without being beaten, robbed, or murdered along the way.

"A fella passed through the house last night," Mary said reflectively. "Said he was down from the gold fields in the Klondike. Says there's a new mining town up along some river or other in the middle of the Alaska territory. Name of — what the hell was it now, Fairbanks, that's it. Says there was only seven working girls in the whole town the last time he passed through. Says they were plumb tuckered out. Says a new girl arrived on the same boat he left on, and the city fathers met her with a parade."

The Darling was silent.

Mary shrugged. "Thought you might be interested, seeing as you hail from those parts. And you might want to start thinking about providing for that boy of yours." Her breasts shook with silent laughter when she saw the expression on the Darling's face. "What, you thought none of us knew? Denver ain't that big a town, honey. You've about scandalized your neighborhood with your comings and goings and carryings on." She clicked her tongue reprovingly.

"I never — carried on at home!"

Mary shook her head pityingly. "Do you think that matters?" Serious now, she leaned forward and gripped the other woman's knee. "Go north. I know you left under a cloud, whatever it was, but it's been six, almost seven years. Whoever it is you're on the run from is long gone. They're pulling gold out of the ground by the fistful, and some of it has your name on it. And your boy's name." She sat up. "You've got a few good years left in you, Darling. Make them work for you."

She'd thought it over and concluded that Mary Kelley, hardheaded businesswoman turned sheriff's wife and Oregon rancher, was right. Alex Papadopolous was very probably long gone. If the ratio of men to women was even half of what she remembered, if the stories Mary had heard were even partially true, then she would be welcomed with open arms.

And paid better than she would ever be south of the fifty-three.

So she packed up and moved north again, and

231

now here she was, in Fairbanks, Alaska, a city of eight thousand on the edge of a narrow river an unattractive grayish-brown in color from the glacial silt in it, with thickly wooded hills rolling away in every direction. On a clear day, if you squinted north from the top of a high hill, you could see the icy peaks of the Brooks Range. Many days in summer, the air was blue with the wood smoke of forest fires blazing unchecked through the territory's interior.

The Line, as it was referred to, was all she had been led to believe. She had her own crib, a narrow building containing a sitting room with a large window, beneath which ran a boardwalk. Customers could stroll down the boardwalk as they window-shopped for a companion for an hour's entertainment. Customers were mostly miners, although businessmen and city fathers, some of whom were Line landlords, picked a partner for the long, juicy waltz often enough, too. She was afraid that at thirty-two she would be too old to attract attention, but there were women working the Line in their forties. The money was ten times what she had earned at Mary's in Denver, and soon she had a steady roster of regulars, which enabled her to work a six-hour shift in the evening.

Best of all, she had found wonderful care for Percy with Lily MacGregor, an Athabascan woman married to a Scotsman named James, who had invested heavily in Fairbanks real estate some years prior to the booming of the town and the creation of the Line, and subsequently had a great deal to lose when

232

he developed the habit of beating Lily when he came home of an evening. Lily waited until he passed out after one beating and then went to the judge who was running against James for mayor. The judge was delighted to grant Lily a divorce and the ownership of all her husband's real estate.

When it came time for the Dawson Darling to invest in her own crib on the Line, she went to Lily, a tiny woman with rosy brown skin, tilted brown eyes, and sleek black hair who held title to two lots on Cushman Street. Lily's home was full of strays, old, young, men, women, children of every age and race tumbling over one another in the house, in the yard, in the trees of the yard, in the stream running through the yard. They looked tanned and fit and happy. Percy joined them without a backward glance at his mother and was accepted without question, a tow-head among many darker ones.

Lily MacGregor not only sold the Darling the best of the two lots, she found her a contractor to put up a crib, two stories with a scalloped awning, a dainty porch, and the biggest sitting-room window on the street. It was a design much envied and quickly copied.

It took no time to settle into a routine, and she picked up a steady clientele with no trouble. Several of her clients fell in love with her and proposed.

Why not? she often thought. It wasn't as if it didn't happen on a regular basis, girls of the Line marrying into the first gentlemen of Alaska, retiring into a quieter life of housewifery and gardening, even motherhood for some of them not too old to bear children.

But *in the end she refused them all, wary of ever again ceding power over her life to anyone else, no matter how charming he seemed on the surface. In the meantime, the Dawson Darling plied her trade, saved her money, and raised her son. In 1910 he cel- ebrated his eleventh birthday, and no one looking at him that day, covered with dirt from playing hide- and-seek in Lily MacGregor's yard with Lily MacGregor's many and various children, would recognize him for the sickly child she had carried from Nome those long years ago.*

Tuesday of the week following Percy's eleventh birthday she looked up from the pink silk settee upon which she displayed her wares, and saw Matt staring back at her through the plate-glass window.

11

The truck tore down the road as the needle on the speedometer swung hard to the right and stayed there. How long had he dawdled at the trailer, trying to figure out what had happened? Five minutes? Ten? How fast had the green truck been traveling? Fifty, sixty miles an hour? Faster?

There was only one highway, but there were hundreds of roads, marked and unmarked, leading off it. How far? Which one? Mutt, her nose into the wind, barked encouragement. SuperMutt, his own personal DEW Line, his Early Kate Detector.

He didn't want to call what he felt panic. He didn't want the disappearance of one woman, of one person, to have this clutch on his gut. He was worried, of course he was. He would be worried about anyone he'd gone looking for and been unable to find. Leaving a Force 10 mess behind. Leaving her canine soul mate behind.

Get a grip, Chopin, he told himself, and made

a desperate effort to think rationally. Who had come on Kate at the trailer? Had they kidnapped her? If so, why? Had she seen them? Were they disposing of a witness? If that were the case, what possible reason could they have for keeping her alive?

An ancient Ford Ranchero pulled onto the highway a foolish three hundred yards in front of him, and Jim pulled into the left lane and slowed down to eighty miles an hour to pass. There was a white, frightened blur in the driver's side window and then it was gone.

His lights picked the letters of signs out of the dark as they flashed past. 14 MILES TO AHTNA. FOOD, PHONE, LODGING, RV DUMP, arrow pointing right.

The truck spit gravel in every direction as he wheeled into the parking lot of the Ernestine Creek Lodge. Two campers, one Winnebago, a pickup, and a van. No green truck. No road around the back. He pulled into a circle and roared back out to the highway.

Fluorescent snow guide on the left, marking an access road. He pulled in, drove a hundred feet over a series of rocky craters, saw nothing, heard nothing (Mutt was growling and snapping at the open driver's window, her teeth five inches from his ear), put the truck into reverse, and backed out onto the highway again.

REST STOP, ONE THOUSAND FEET. No cars in front of the toilets. He got out anyway and ran to open the doors, Mutt barking at him, she didn't smell Kate, had to check anyway, had to, great place to dump a body. Women's, empty. Men's, empty. Dumpster, a few empty cans and bottles, a few candy wrappers, an empty box of Kleenex, nothing else. Back in the truck, back on the highway.

Miles flashed past. He almost hit a cow moose and calf crossing the road. He left his foot on the gas. SCENIC VIEWPOINT, ONE MILE. No cars, no trucks, no one. When he slowed, Mutt barked once, sharp, admonitory. Don't stop here. He stepped on the gas.

AHTNA LANDFILL, NEXT RIGHT.

Mutt exploded, and when he hit the brakes she didn't wait. She went over the side and vanished down the access road. The truck skidded to a halt twenty feet past the turnoff.

Landfill. Dump. Mountains of discards of modern life. Great place to lose a body.

He cursed the truck into reverse and didn't bother turning around, just backed down the road to the Ahtna landfill with the gas pedal all the way down. He oversteered and almost hit a tree on one side of the road, overcorrected and almost hit another on the other side. He came into a clearing at full throttle. He hit something, bounced the ass end of the truck up in the air, came down again, hard. It sounded like something might have fallen off. Might not. He snapped off the engine without bothering to let out the clutch. It bucked and snorted, and he baled out before it dieseled to a halt. "Mutt?

Where are you, girl? Mutt? Kate? Are you here? Kate? Kate!"

The truck had highcentered on a pile of garbage that looked as if it had been pushed off the back of a pickup truck similar in size and height to the one he was driving. The driver's side rear tire was off the ground. Worry about that later. "Mutt? Mutt? Kate!"

The Ahtna Landfill was a hole in the ground, a natural one, falling off from a steep, crumbling wall of hard-packed dirt. The stench was strong and sour. He stood on the edge and squinted into the twilight. "Mutt?"

He heard a yelp, and cursed himself for leaving his flashlight in the Cessna. "Mutt?" A movement caught his eye, off to his right. "Mutt, is that you?"

She yelped, and he broke into a stumbling run, around the edge of the drop-off to where it degenerated into a steep, jumbled slide of debris. He scrambled down into the pit, grabbing at handholds wherever he found them, a tree root, a poushki bush that gave beneath his weight and sent him slipping into a mess of something that smelled like he didn't want to know what it was, a rusty old bedspring that cut his hand. Mutt barked encouragement, providing him with a beacon and he moved toward it, stepping from a mound of garbage bags to the top of an old gas range. He tripped on a floor lamp minus a shade and fell face forward, picked himself up, and went on.

Mutt sounded nearer. "Where is she, girl?" he said, panting. Mutt let loose with a flurry of barks and yips and yells, interspersed with worrying at a dark lump laying between two mountains of trash. She growled at him when he got to her finally. No gratitude.

"It's all right, girl," he said, praying it was, falling more than dropping to his knees. He touched the lump and felt plastic, and remembered the dark green trash bags strewn across the kitchen floor of the trailer. "Oh shit, no," he said and tore at it. She was curled inside in a fetal position, and she was wet, he thought with sweat. He found her throat, felt for a pulse.

There was one, strong and slow and steady, and the wave of relief that swept over him then made him feel like he was drowning. Immediately in its wake was anger, so powerful and so vicious that he wanted to kill her. How had she let herself be sandbagged like this? How could she have been so careless of her own safety? Anybody would think she had a death wish, last September at George Perry's hunting camp, now here in Ahtna. What the hell was wrong with the woman? Plenty, and he couldn't wait to tell her, in detail.

He struggled for control, for breath. Mutt licked at Kate's face, whining. When he thought he could lay hands on her without doing serious bodily injury, he managed to get Kate into a fireman's lift, how later he would never know. Then began the nightmare journey back, during which he found even more things to trip over and fall into than he had on the way there. Almost to the edge of the pit, he thought close to where he had climbed and slid down, he heard the sound of a engine. "Hey," he yelled. "Down here!"

He was answered by a thrown garbage bag, which exploded on contact four feet away and which sprayed all three of them with something liquid that smelled like sour milk.

"Hey!" he bellowed. "There's somebody down here!" but the vehicle was already leaving.

"You miserable —" Jim stood where he was and called the driver every name he could think of and some he made up on the spot. He threatened him with arrest for assaulting a police officer, fleeing the scene of an accident, and being a deaf motherfucker whose father's identity was in serious doubt. He promised him no bail and no parole. The driver didn't hear him, and didn't come back, on the whole a good thing for both of them.

When he ran out of steam, he felt better. Over his shoulder, Kate uttered a faint groan.

"Hang on, girl," he said, and began the grim climb up the steep bank, in the dark, with a hundred-pound sack of potatoes over his shoulder. When he got back to his truck, he set her down carefully in the cab and told her, "You have not been a fun date."

The potatoes stirred. "Jim?"

His heart leaped. "Kate? Can you hear me?"

"Of course I can hear you," she said, sounding fretful. "I can smell you, too."

His laugh was short but heartfelt. "You should talk."

"Where are we? What are you doing here? What — where's Mutt?"

Mutt wormed her way in between them and lavished Kate's face with her tongue. For once, Jim envied her.

"What happened?" Kate said, when Mutt finally calmed down. "Where are we?" She blinked at her surroundings. "Whose truck is this, and why am I laying in it?"

He told her.

She was silent.

"Was somebody in the trailer with you?"

"No, I — no."

"What is the last thing you remember?" A brief silence. "Kate?"

"I was reading a book, I think."

"Reading a book?"

"Well, she had a lot of them, and I didn't find anything else, and I was there and so were they, so . . ." Her voice trailed away.

"I see. You were reading a book," he said, his voice very calm. "Did you, while you were reading this book, notice if anyone joined you in the trailer?"

"I — no."

"No one did, or you didn't notice?"

"No one did."

"Right. You didn't notice. Either that, or you

241

stuffed yourself in a garbage sack and dumped yourself in the landfill." The rage was back. He tamped it down.

At every scene, your first act is to establish your authority. State Trooper 101, first day. For some reason, Kate Shugak could make him forget every rule he'd ever learned in class or on the job. For one brief, sweet moment he was tempted to finish the job whoever had started that afternoon. He mastered the impulse, and was proud of himself, and then was mad all over again.

In a level voice he said, "Did you find anything in the trailer?"

"I don't know. Let me think a minute. No, I — no. Nothing but books. That's what she had most of."

"Did you dump them on the floor?"

"What?"

"Pawlowski's books. Did you dump them on the floor?"

"No! I would never — she had some old books, one was . . . do you mean somebody pulled them off the shelves?"

"Yes. All of them."

"The same person who attacked me?"

"That would be my professional opinion, yes."

She grabbed the steering wheel and pulled herself erect. The dome light was burned out, and she couldn't see Jim's face. "Come on, we have to get back there."

"Like hell, we have to get you to a hospital."

"You don't understand, Jim. Some of those books were really valuable."

"I don't care if the covers were made of gold and the pages were made of silver! Your shoulder's messed up, something could be broken, you've got scrapes and bruises everywhere. When's the last time you had a tetanus shot?"

"Last year," she said, annoyed, her voice stronger now. With Jim bellowing on one side and Mutt yipping anxiously on the other, she was not feeling at the top of her game. "It's okay," she said to Mutt.

"Okay my ass! You —"

"Jim," she said. It was one word, his name, flat, devoid of emotion. It meant business.

It stopped him, mercifully, at least for the moment. "What?"

"Shut up. Please. I've got a hell of a headache, and you yelling and her yipping makes it worse."

He dropped his voice but he was still mad. "Why won't you go to the hospital? Give me one good goddamn reason!"

She felt an insane desire to laugh at the hissed whisper. That way lay a descent into hysteria, and she fought it back. "If you'd been stuffed into a trash bag and tossed into the city dump like last week's garbage, would you be in a hurry to tell anyone about it?"

They compromised, and went back to Ahtna. As Jim pointed out, they were all in need of a

243

change of clothes. Kate took a shower. Mutt took a bath. Jim borrowed jeans and a sweatshirt from Kenny Hazen, who dropped Jim's uniform off at the only dry cleaners in town the following morning. There was no ridding his boots of the smell, though; for months afterward he would look down and see flies buzzing around his ankles.

Kate checked on the whereabouts of the other campaign staffers, who were all present and accounted for at another basketball game at the gym. Halftime and Anne was working the bleachers, Darlene at her elbow, Erin in tow, Doug chasing some skirt on the opposite side of the room, Tom at the center of an admiring group of teenage girls, Tracy snapping pictures, getting names, keeping one eye on the schedule.

Darlene saw her first, and looked furious. "Where the hell have you been?" she said beneath her breath when Kate reached her side.

"I got tied up," Kate said without a smile.

"Yeah, well, you're supposed to be watching out for Anne, and you can't do that if you're not here!"

"You're right. Want to fire me? Oh wait, that's right, you can't, you don't pay me. Put a lid on it, Darlene," she added, when Darlene's face darkened and she opened her mouth to retort. "Where do you go after this?"

"Back to the hotel," Darlene said, putting on a false smile when Anne turned to give them a curious look.

"Fine, I'll see you back there."

"You're leaving again? What about Anne, damn it?"

"Don't let her wade too far into the crowd."

"Where are you going?"

"I'll be back to the hotel later."

With difficulty, Darlene bit back whatever she had been going to say, but Kate could feel the other woman's eyes boring into her back all the way to the door.

"Why don't the two of you just shoot it out at thirty paces and be done with it?" Kenny said. "What's going on there, anyway?"

Kate, feeling generous since she'd been the last to score, said, "Oh, I don't know. Personality conflict, I guess."

The four of them drove back out to Paula's trailer, carrying with them Paula's laptop and notes retrieved from the cop shop on the way. As Kate had expected, the manila envelope containing the copies of Paula's disk and notes were gone.

Seeing the picnic table triggered her memory, and she told them about Gordy Boothe. "So she was tucked in by midnight," Kenny said. "And she didn't own a car. And the letter to Anne was discovered at two-thirty. Well, hell, I don't know. I suppose she could have walked in."

"It's five miles, Kenny, and she didn't look like an athlete to me."

"Or someone could be trying to throw suspicion her way. Maybe it was supposed to look like suicide."

"She killed herself because she felt guilty she was trying to blackmail Anne Gordaoff? Come on, Kenny."

"Yeah, yeah." Disgruntled, Kenny squeezed behind the table, apparently not noticing that he was sitting on the stain left by Paula's blood.

"Think blackmail material was what they were looking for?" Kate said, more to be saying something than because she needed an answer.

"She was looking up stuff on Peter Heiman. Could be she found out something he doesn't want us to know, and told someone who told him."

"She was also looking up stuff on Anne," Kate said, picking books up, straightening bent pages, and slipping them back onto shelves. Jim leaned up against the sink, staring at nothing with a frown on his face. "Hey," Kate said. "Books. On shelves."

He looked at her. "What? Oh. Yeah, what the hell, okay."

"She had them arranged alphabetically by author, starting there." She pointed at the now righted shelf.

Jim muttered something under his breath, but he bent to the task. Like Kate, he rifled through each book before he put it back on the shelf, looking for anything the hurricane might have missed. He found nothing. Kate got the nonfiction section reshelved and sat down with Paula's handwritten notes. Kenny had plugged in Paula's computer and was calling up files and scrolling through them, lips pursed in concentration.

After fifteen minutes various aches and pains began to make themselves felt, and Kate put the kettle on for tea. Paula had Lipton and honey in the cupboard. She made three cups. "Thanks," Kenny said, reading through a file. "Did you know Peter Heiman lost his brother in Vietnam?"

"You didn't? It's part of the family legend. The Heimans have been around a while."

"I was in Anchorage then, and I never bothered with the news. Never do now, for that matter. Reporters are all a bunch of kids who've majored in anorexia and minored in big hair." He drank some tea. "Ever notice how they're always talking to each other instead of you? Start all their sound bites with 'Well, Maria'?"

"Well, no," Kate said. "I don't have television out on the homestead."

"Smart woman." He went back to the computer.

The bathroom had been tidied. The bedroom was still half in chaos. Jim had put the mattress and the springs back on the frame and was sitting down, immersed in *Most Secret*. She set the mug at his feet. "Finding any clues as to who killed Paula?" she said. He grunted something without looking up.

The tea was hot and sweet, and woke her up enough to go back to Paula's notes.

The three-subject spiral notebooks took her right back to college: shiny red cover, wide-ruled pages, rounded corners, stingy bits of paper caught in the wire spine from pages being torn out. Paula was not a very organized notetaker, sprawling across margins, crowding interpolations between graphs, adding a comment that related to a subject where there was no more room and so had to be jammed into the bottom of the page or written into the margin of the following page, connecting the two by a number or a letter or an asterisk or a pound sign. The notebook was liberally adorned with such signs, and Kate did a lot of paging back and forth trying to reconstruct Paula's train of thought. It was like playing connect the dots without the dots.

"Did you know that Peter Heiman is a shareholder in Last Frontier Bank?"

"What?" she said, not paying much attention.

Kenny peered at her over the lid of the laptop. "Peter Heiman's grandfather was a silent partner in Last Frontier Bank."

It took a minute for her to surface. "Last Frontier? Yeah, I think I knew that. You didn't know Abel Int-Hout, did you?"

In the bedroom Jim stirred.

"I've heard the name. Big spread on the road into the Park? Just down the road from your homestead? He's dead, isn't he?"

Kate didn't blink. "Yes. His son Ethan lives there now."

"Ethan's back in the Park?" Jim said. She

looked up and saw him standing in the doorway, finger marking his place in the book.

"Yes, he moved back last year." She looked back at Kenny. "Abel was sort of my guardian when I was growing up. Pete Heiman was one of his running buddies. I remember something —" Her brow creased. "Something about his grand-daddy being a silent partner with, who was it —"

"Margaret and the kids with him?" Jim said.

"They came with him," Kate said. Wasn't any of Jim's business if they weren't still there.

"No wonder his campaigns always run in the black," Kenny said.

Kate stood to walk around the table and read over his shoulder in silence. "Interesting. Paula was a good researcher."

"I'm glad she wasn't looking into my past," Kenny agreed.

"Why, what have you got?" Jim said.

"Paula must have taken notes by hand and then transferred them to the computer, because some of that stuff is in the notebook, too." Kate thumbed through it until she found the right page. She read out loud, "Last Frontier Bank. James Seese, Matthew Turner, Peter Heiman." Paula had drawn a balloon around them, and a connecting balloon around Last Frontier Bank. Below the balloons there was an arrow pointing down, and in the right-hand corner an arrow pointing into the corner. "Means turn the page," Kate said, and did so. On the reverse, Paula had written, "Peter and Anne. Hosford?"

"Peter being Peter Heiman?" Jim said.

"Yes."

"Anne meaning Anne Gordaoff?"

"I don't know," Kate said. "Let me think a minute."

"Meaning," Jim said, "Hosford was the link between the Heiman and Gordaoff campaigns. Like maybe Hosford was spying on Anne for Pete."

"I don't know," Kate said. "Just slow down here." She jerked her chin at the computer. "What else has Paula got on Peter Heiman and Last Frontier?"

"Reads like a history lesson." Kenny scrolled back up. "It's a Seese bank today, but a hundred years ago it was founded by two partners, James Seese and Matthew Turner, Paula says with Pete Heiman's grandfather as a silent partner. Matthew Turner was Elizabeth Turner's brother."

"Elizabeth Turner —" Kate said.

Kenny nodded. "Elizabeth Turner was married to Peter Heiman. The first Peter Heiman. The first Peter Heiman was a silent partner in Last Frontier. The second Peter Heiman inherited his father's interest. So did the third Peter Heiman, who remains a minority stockholder in the bank today." He sat back. "That's it."

"That's enough," Kate said, with the hint of a smile at the corners of her mouth.

"What?" Jim said.

She looked at him with no hint of awkwardness or challenge for the first time that day.

250

"Paula doesn't mean Anne Gordaoff. She means Anne Seese."

"Who the hell's Anne Seese?"

Jim caught on first. "Dischner, Seese, Christensen, and Kim. That Seese?"

"That Seese."

"And you think Paula's referring to Eddie P.'s law partner?"

"Yes."

"Why?"

"Because Peter Heiman and Anne Seese have had a long-term affair going on, oh, at least since Pete's last divorce, and I'd bet before."

"Holy shit," Kenny said, faint but pursuing. "Anne Seese is Pete Heiman's main squeeze, Eddie P.'s law partner, and one of the Last Frontier Seeses?"

"One and the same."

"So Jeff Hosford's real job, when he wasn't hustling bucks for Anne Gordaoff, was gophering for Peter Heiman's mistress?"

"Yes."

"And Paula Pawlowski found out," Jim said.

"Yes."

"Think he'd kill to keep it a secret that he's porking Anne Gordaoff's daughter on Peter Heiman's dime?"

"He might, if he were still alive," Kate said.

"So," Kenny said, "we've got the perfect motive to kill Paula Pawlowski, only the guy with the perfect motive was killed before she was. Great."

Kate had a flashback to being submersed in a dark, warm sea. Too warm, she was sweating, and the sea seemed to be clinging to her eyes, her nose, her mouth; she couldn't breathe. She clawed at it. It resisted, then gave, and she could breathe again, and she sank back down into the current and let it take her where it would.

"Kate?"

She blinked, and realized that that was the second time Jim had said her name.

"Are you all right?"

She shook herself. "Yeah. I just had a — yeah, I'm fine."

Kenny reached for his jacket. "Everybody with Gordaoff still at the Ahtna Lodge?"

"Until tomorrow morning. We're supposed to drive to Klutina."

"Both murders are about this campaign, Kate," Kenny said.

"I know."

He looked from her to Jim and back again. "Watch your back."

"You said that already."

"Somebody tried to kill you today."

"I hadn't forgotten."

Kenny was far from satisfied, but there wasn't much else he could do. "I want to talk to every member of the campaign before they go to Klutina in the morning."

"Darlene'll bitch about throwing off the schedule."

"I don't care if I ruin their whole day. I want

statements from all of them about what they were doing yesterday afternoon, and I want to reinterview them concerning the night of Hosford's murder."

"I'll tell her."

"Get them down to the station at eight A.M."

"All right."

12

What did Anne Gordaoff say when you told her that her chief fund-raiser's day job was working for the enemy?"

"She said Ronald Reagan used to be a Democrat."

Jim was surprised into a laugh. "She's pretty tolerant, for a politician."

"She's not a politician, yet. What's the ME say about Pawlowski's time of death?" Kenny asked.

"Somewhere between midnight and four A.M., but that from the temp we gave them from the trailer it could have been earlier."

"Midnight would have been just after Boothe dropped her off, so he was either waiting for her or right behind her."

"Or *she*."

"Or she."

"I told him she hadn't turned on the heat yet for the winter. Pretty chilly in that trailer."

"She wasn't laying there that long."

"What did you get from the statements?"

"Jack all," Kenny said, not sounding happy about it. "The whole bunch of them were at the basketball game, but there were about five hundred people there, and no one can voice for anyone of them being there the whole time."

"Even Anne?"

"Everybody remembers seeing her all over the place. Nobody can put a time to when they did, though, other than sometime between the jump ball and the buzzer sounding to end the last period. People are always coming and going at a game, you know how it is, going to the john, buying popcorn, sneaking out for a drink, fathering a child. It's just damn near impossible to know where everyone is at any given time, especially after the fact. Hell, Kate's one of the best eyeballers around, and even she couldn't place any one of them at any one place at any one time the night Hosford died."

"Turn up anything new when you asked them about that night again?"

"Not a goddamn thing. Unless you count the couple we turned up who'd been going at it in the front of his daddy's pickup. But they didn't see anything except his daddy coming and then they were too busy running in the other direction to pay attention to something like someone getting shot."

Silence.

"You know, Kenny," Jim said at last, "it occurs to me that the middle of a political campaign is a great time to commit a murder."

"Only one you wanted to get away with."

Jim said, on the phone from his office in Tok, "Where's Kate?"

On the phone from his office in Ahtna, Kenny said, "She's tracking down Peter Heiman."

Jim hung up and swiveled his chair to stare out the window. The grin, when it came, was slow and sneaky.

He wouldn't be in Peter Heiman's shoes right now for any amount of money you could name.

"Don't give me that crap, you old smoothie," Kate said furiously.

"Then don't interrogate me like I'm the suspect and you've got the rubber hose," Pete snapped. "Jesus, Kate, it's just politics we're talking about here, not nuclear secrets."

"So he was spying."

Pete shrugged and gave an unrepentant grin. "Rat-fucking, I think Nixon's guys used to call it."

"This time he fucked and fucked over the opposing candidate's daughter."

The grin vanished. "What?"

"You didn't know? Erin Gordaoff thought she was engaged to your rat fucker. So did her mother and the rest of her family and friends."

"That wasn't part of the plan," Pete said, frowning. "If that's true, I'm sorry for it, and for her. He was an opportunistic bastard, I'll give him that, but I didn't know he'd go that far."

They were sitting on stools in the Alaskan Bar

in Cordova, coffee in front of Kate and a Bloody Mary in front of Pete. It was ten-thirty on Monday morning, two weeks before the election. So far, all the media had hold of was Paula Pawlowski's death, and it was of more interest to them at present that she was a frequent contributor of articles to newspapers around the state than that she had been doing research for Anne Gordaoff's campaign. Kenny Hazen and Jim Chopin were stonewalling on the issue of suspects.

"Hey, Pete," someone said, and Kate looked around to see Kell Van Brocklin give Pete a hearty slap on the back. "Good to see you. How's it hanging?"

"All the way down to my knees," Pete said. "You know Kate Shugak?"

Kell nodded. "Kate."

"Kell," Kate said, and recalled that the last time she'd seen him it had been the Fourth of July and he'd been drunkenly trying to mate the *Joanna C.* with Tracy Steen's *Dawn* on Alaganik Bay. He looked sober today, but as he ordered a beer and a refill for Pete, odds were good he wouldn't be for long.

"How's the election looking?" Kell said, taking a long pull at his beer.

Pete took a token sip of his new drink. "It's in the bag, so long as you vote."

"No problem there," Kell said with a wink, and ordered another beer. "Although that little gal running against you has got a way with her.

If she wasn't married, you might be in trouble."

Pete grinned. "When did that ever stop you?"

Both men laughed, big-chested, hearty, good-old-boy laughs.

When Kate had left Anne that morning, she had asked, "Anything you'd like me to pass on to Pete Heiman?"

The two women stared at each other, until Anne said, speaking with slow deliberation, "Tell the old son of a bitch that I said thanks for the compliment."

Kate didn't work it out until she was in the air. Anne Gordaoff, challenger, was telling Peter Heiman, incumbent, that she knew that he regarded her challenge to his office with such alarm that he had gone to the length of planting a spy in her campaign.

It was the first time Kate had heard Anne say anything less than circumspect in speaking of her opponent, and she liked her the better for it, although she still wasn't sure it came from the love she bore her daughter or the anger she felt at having been so screwed over herself. Now, her daughter's heart was broken, her campaign was out a fund-raiser, and murder had been done.

Kate finished her coffee and stood up. "Hold on, I'll walk you out," Pete said and took his leave of Kell.

Outside the rain came down in a fine drizzle, as it almost always did in Cordova, when it wasn't hammering down like roofing nails. They both donned ball caps. Mutt got to her feet and shook all over them.

"Where you headed?" Pete said.

"Back to Niniltna."

"Need a ride?"

She shook her head. "George is waiting for me out at the airport. Oh, by the way —"

"What?"

"Anne says thanks."

She left him to figure it out.

Back in Niniltna, Kate checked her copy of the typewritten schedule. Anne was scheduled to be beat up on that afternoon by the Rude River chapter of the NRA for daring to suggest that you don't need an Uzzi to shoot a moose. The campaign was flying back into Niniltna the following day, to attend a cheerleader exhibition and basketball game at the high school, as well as consult with Billy Mike on a new fund-raiser.

Until then, Kate had the day off. When she started heading for the red Ford Ranger long-bed parked at the side of the airstrip, Mutt let out a joyous bark and raced ahead to leap into the back. They had left the rain behind in Cordova and here in the Park the sun glinted off the thin layer of snow that began on the peaks of the Quilaks and ended in the crunch beneath her feet. A light breeze, crisp and cold, ruffled the hair at the nape of her neck, and when she started the truck, she turned the heater on for the first time that year.

The first freeze followed by the first snow turned the twenty-five miles of gravel between Niniltna and her homestead into the Park equivalent of a superhighway, and she was home in less than an hour, which had to be some kind of record. She parked the truck in the pulloff at the head of the trail and shouldered her duffel. Beneath the trees the snow was a fine layer of powder, leaving clear imprints of her shoes as well as the tracks of all the most recent visitors to the homestead, which included several rabbits, a porcupine, a bunch of ptarmigan which Mutt immediately went chasing after, a moose cow and a calf, and a pair of grizzly cubs, probably the two whose mother had charged Kate at the creek breakup before last. The cubs would only be two years old, kind of early for them to be on their own. Kate wondered if anything had happened to the sow, and hoped the cubs would not become a nuisance.

When she came into the clearing, smoke was coming from the chimney of the cabin. She knew who was there; she had followed his footprints down from the road. She trod up the steps and opened the door.

Johnny looked up from pouring hot water into a mug of cocoa mix and jumped, spilling hot water from the kettle all over his shoes. "Damn it!" The kettle thumped down on the stove. Kate dumped the duffel on the floor and grabbed a dishcloth.

"I've got it," he said, snatching the dishcloth

from her. "I made the mess; I'll clean it up."

She stood for a moment, looking down at the bent head, and then Mutt hit the door and bowled him over with that exuberant and unreserved reception she reserved for people she liked. There weren't that many of them. Kate had an uncomfortable flash of the way Mutt greeted Jim Chopin.

Johnny's face was flushed, and he was laughing as he tried to squirm out of reach. "Come on, Mutt, cut it out, stop it, that tickles!"

Kate smiled. Johnny saw it, and stopped laughing. He gave Mutt's head a final pat and got to his feet. "I didn't hear the truck."

"I left it at the pulloff. I have to go back into Niniltna tomorrow. What are you doing here?"

She tried to make the question mild, but it was a wasted effort; he bristled anyway. "It snowed last night. I came over to light a fire and take the chill off the cabin."

"It's Monday. Why aren't you in school?"

"School gets out at three o'clock. I came here first."

Kate nodded. "The heat feels good. Thanks." She nodded at the cocoa. "Is there more of that?"

"What? Oh, yeah."

"I'll start some bread."

He watched her put flour, water, salt, and oil in a bowl. "How do you know how much of everything to put in?"

It was the first civil question she'd had out of

him since he'd showed up in the Park. She answered it in kind. "At first you use a recipe, you measure. When you've been doing it long enough, you just know." She kneaded the dough a few times, draped the damp dishcloth over the top, and set the bowl on the shelf over the oil stove. Johnny had lit the wood stove; now she lit the oil stove and set the temperature on high. She removed the cast-iron skillet and cast-iron Dutch oven from the oven and hung the thermometer in front, where she could read it without opening the oven door all the way. The Pyrex bread pans had also been in the oven, and she greased them and set them on the counter.

Johnny warmed up his cocoa and retired to the couch, Kate's copy of *Have Spacesuit, Will Travel* in his hands and Mutt's head on his feet. Kate looked through the mail she had picked up on the way home. There was a letter from Cindy Sovalik in Barrow, another from Olga Shapsnikoff in Unalaska. Cindy's was short and to the point, "Come when you want." Olga's was a little more subtle but not much: She began by telling Kate that Sasha was drawing stories on the beach sand with her story knife, stories that imagined various and wonderful adventures Sasha and Kate had together. Both letters made her smile.

The third letter was also an invitation, from her cousin Axenia in Anchorage. Actually the invitation was from a friend of Axenia's whom Kate had never met, to a baby shower. Axenia was pregnant.

Kate put the letter down and stared at the bookshelf above Johnny's head. Axenia and Lew Mathisen were having a baby.

"What?" Johnny said, and she lowered her eyes to see him staring at her. "Is something wrong?"

She stuffed the little yellow card, decorated with colorful birds carrying flowers tied with pink and blue ribbons in their beaks, back into its envelope. "No, nothing. My cousin's having a baby is all."

"Oh."

She looked out the window, where night was creeping down into the Park from between the cracks and crevices of the Quilaks. "Will Ethan be worried about where you are?"

Johnny's face closed up. "Why, don't you want me here?"

She looked at him. "Does Ethan know where you are?"

He ducked his head. "He knows I come over here," he muttered.

"Mmm." She got up and raised the dishcloth to poke the dough. The imprint of her finger smoothed out almost immediately. Nice to know she hadn't completely lost her touch. She divided the dough into two loaves and set them back on the shelf beneath the dishcloth to rise. "We'll take him a loaf when it's done."

"I was wondering when you'd wander in out of the snow," Ethan told Johnny when they walked in the door.

"I was over at Kate's."

263

"And you found her." Ethan smiled at Kate. He'd shaved and put on clean clothes since last month. His hair was brushed and pulled back into a stubby little ponytail. "How's life on the campaign trail?"

Kate set her daypack down next to the door. "You ever listen to NPR?"

He nodded. "Yeah."

"Some actor was on one morning, and he said, 'Keep us away from politicians. Lying is our business, and we know it when we see it.' He was right."

Ethan threw back his head and laughed, a big, robust laugh that filled up the room. "Yeah, well, let it be a lesson to you, Kate. Sometimes the job just isn't worth the salary."

Kate shrugged. "It'll be over soon."

"Come on in, I'll pour you some coffee."

Johnny vanished upstairs.

Kate spoke softly. "How often is Johnny over at the homestead?"

"I don't know, a couple of times a week, I'd guess. He likes his alone time, that boy." He smiled. "He's a lot like you. Probably why you don't get along."

"It's getting darker earlier."

"Yeah? And your point is?"

"My point is I left him here so he'd be safe."

He smiled at her over his shoulder. "That kid's safe wherever he goes, Shugak. Haven't you figured that out yet?" He got out two mugs. "He's just like you. For all practical purposes, you were autonomous from the age of four, when your dad started teaching you how to track game and how to shoot it. Johnny told me you got him that thirty-thirty of his. First grownup firearm he's owned, he says. He's pretty good with it, too, at least at a stationary target. Says he's looking to shoot his second moose. He doesn't belong in Arizona, Kate, any more than you did."

"Nobody ever offered me Arizona."

He snorted. "Yeah, like you would have taken it if they had." He poured coffee and sat down. "You going to Bobby's tonight?"

"Why, what's going on at Bobby's?"

"You got to slow down, Shugak, or you'll miss all the good stuff. Bobby's throwing a party for Peter Heiman."

"You're kidding me."

Ethan grinned. "Nope. Wanna go?"

13

The first person they saw was Billy Mike.
"Hello, Kate," he said without a trace of embarrassment, balancing a bag of tortilla chips on a casserole dish as he shut the door to his Honda Wagovan.

"Covering all your bases, Billy?"

He grinned, a white slash in his round face. "You should talk. Where's Anne?"

"In Ahtna until tomorrow, then here for two days. I caught a day off."

"And used it to come to a party for Peter Heiman." He grinned again. "Hi, Ethan."

"Hey, Billy. How you doing?"

"Same old, same old. How's Margaret?"

"I wouldn't know," Ethan said easily. "She split."

"Oh. Oh. I didn't know. I'm sorry, Ethan."

"Don't be."

"Couldn't take breakup in the Park?"

"I think it was more that she couldn't take me, anywhere."

Billy gave a short, surprised laugh. "You seem to be fine." He looked from Ethan to Kate, and then to Johnny. "Hey, Johnny."

"Hi, Mr. Mike."

"Call me Billy, Johnny. How do you like living in the Park?"

The two of them went ahead as Ethan and Kate brought up the rear. Ethan cocked an eyebrow at her. "What?" she said.

"Billy'll have us shacking up all over the Park by tomorrow morning at eight A.M.," he said.

She shrugged. "You got a problem with that?"

"Well," he said, drawling it out. "I'd prefer that it was true."

She stopped on the upslope to the A-frame and looked him straight in the eye. "I understand your need to reinvent your manhood after being deballed by Margaret, Ethan, but don't imagine for one moment that I'm going to help you. I had a man, a real one, a good one. He was all I needed."

"He's also dead," Ethan said. "It's been over a year. How long do you think you can go without?"

"A lot longer than you, evidently," she said, and was up the hill and into the A-frame before he could reply.

"Shugak!" somebody yelled, and she heard the whisk of rubber tires over hardwood floor a second before something hit her in the back of the knees, and she fell into Bobby Clark's lap. He gave her a smacking kiss. "Goddamn! About time you showed up!"

Mutt tried to jump on top of Kate, to the peril of all involved. "Goddamn!" Bobby roared again. "It's that goddamn wolf again!"

Kate shoved Mutt down, where she stood with her tail wagging furiously and an adoring gleam in her eye. "That chair ought to be a registered weapon," she said, struggling to her feet.

Bobby's grin was wide and lecherous. "The better to get you horizontal, my dear."

Dinah, flushed and laughing, was stirring a pot of something at the stove. Katya, perched on Old Sam's hip, saw Kate, held out her arms and launched. Kate caught her, just. "Hey," she said.

"What?" Dinah said.

"This kid needs a new diaper."

Dinah nodded at the corner the crib had taken over. "Have at it."

Grumbling, Kate did so, Katya laughing up at her from the crib and doing her level best to prolong the process as long as possible.

There was a hooraw at the door and they both turned to look as Peter Heiman walked in, shaking hands with Bobby and coming over to kiss Katya on his way.

"Give me my woman," Bobby said, snatching Katya.

For the first time, Kate noticed a big glass jar on the floor next to the door, filling slowly with bills of one denomination or another. She hadn't noticed a jar when Bobby and Dinah had hosted Anne.

"Come on, Pete," Bobby said, wheeling around

and heading for the pillar, Katya's wild giggle floating behind, as well as a pained cry when Bobby rolled over someone's toes. "Now everybody, listen up. I'm pirating a little radio air for Pete tonight. We're all warmed up and ready to roll. Be prepared to make noise!"

A roar rose from the very overcrowded room, and the loudest yell came from Mac Devlin, the gold miner whose toes Bobby had rolled over, which led Kate to wonder how much Bobby's aim was off.

Pete sat down next to Bobby, and they both squared up to the microphone. Bobby flicked a few switches; there was some kind of electronic whine and into the mike Bobby said, "Okay, folks, it's show time. Bobby's all talk, all the time, when it isn't all music all the time, one and only Park Air. Tonight my guest is Peter Heiman, who is running for reelection this year. Pete, how the hell are you?"

"Fine, Bobby, just fine."

"Running behind in the polls, are you?"

"More like neck and neck, Bobby. I have a fine opponent this year, and she's working hard at throwing the bum out of office."

"Well, if she's successful, at least you won't have to work with Ramona Halford anymore."

Pete was surprised into throwing his head back and laughing out loud, and the crowd joined in. "That is surely the truth, Bobby."

"So why do you want to be reelected? My god, man, you have to live in Juneau five months out of the year. You have to associate with politicians on a regular basis. You've always got to have your hand out so you'll have enough to run the next time. The media is breathing down your neck every minute, so you can't take a whizz without it showing up on film at eleven. That's no life for a decent human being, and yet you're sitting up and begging for it. Tell me why."

Pete leaned forward and looked Bobby straight in the eye. "Babes, Bobby. Politicians get all the best babes."

It was Bobby's turn to throw back his head and whoop with laughter.

Next to Kate, Dinah said, "Did I tell you about the new documentary I've got going?"

"No," Kate said. "What's it about?"

"Grab up a pop and I'll show you."

On the opposite side of the pillar from Bobby's radio station equipment, Dinah had carved out a small workspace. She commandeered a couple of chairs and put them in front of a television monitor hooked to a VCR. Her camera was tucked carefully into the top drawer of a filing cabinet beneath the counter, the bottom drawer having been reserved for exposed videotapes, all carefully labeled. Dinah selected one and inserted it into the VCR.

Kate, watching the monitor, said, "That's the mine ruins, isn't it?"

"Yeah."

"You doing a documentary on the Kanuyaq Copper Mine?"

"Yes, I am. See, here's the idea — everybody knows about the TransAlaska Pipeline, how long it took to get approval, the design, the construction; everybody always whoops and hollers about how it's the biggest manmade construction effort in the history of the world, gets compared to the pyramids and the Great Wall of China."

"Yeah. So?"

Dinah waved a hand at the screen. "What about Kanuyaq? The guys who built that puppy humped the parts over rivers and glaciers, on their backs until they got the railroad built. They had hot running water in the living quarters at the mine by 1907. In 1907 most of the rural areas of the South Forty-eight didn't even have cold running water. Here they had electricity and telephones." Her smile turned sly. "And then there was Niniltna."

"What about Niniltna?"

"Niniltna was party town for the miners. Niniltna was where the miners got drunk and got laid. Just four miles down the road, all the saloons and booze and gambling and hookers a man could want."

"I didn't know Niniltna was a party town. Not something Emaa or Auntie Vi ever told me."

"Yeah, well, there's a lot of that going around," Dinah said. "I took a drive up to Fairbanks last month, ran into someone at the library who quoted me a little poem about how California got started. It goes like this:

The miners came in '49,
The whores in '51.
And when they got together,
They produced the native son."

Kate laughed.

"Substitute '99 and '01 and that could have
been written about Alaska. She said that half the
first families, first white families anyway, were
made up of gamblers-turned-bankers and dance-
hall-girls-turned-respectable-matrons, only of
course none of their descendants want to admit
it today."

Kate sat up, a stray thought running loose
through the back of her mind. Trying to round
it up she almost missed Dinah's next words.

"You read up on that time, it wasn't the
greatest for women. The only jobs open to them
were housework or prostitution. No penicillin,
either, if it comes to that. You've got to admire
somebody willing to take on that job just to
make a better life for themselves." She thought.
"You forget, until you start on a project like
this."

"Forget what?" Kate said, still distracted.

"How much was going on here at the same time
it was going on everywhere else. The dance halls
in Dawson. Front Street in Nome. The Line in
Fairbanks. The hook shops in Cordova." She
smiled. "And the Northern Light in Niniltna."

"That was —"

Dinah nodded. "That's what they called the

272

whorehouse in Niniltna, or one of them."

The Northern Light. She'd heard that name before.

"Kate, are you okay?"

Kate refocused and saw Dinah staring at her with a puzzled expression. "Sure. Why?"

"I don't know, all of a sudden you looked way far away."

"You mentioned running into someone in Fairbanks," Kate said. "The one who told you the poem."

"What about her?"

"It was a woman?"

"Yes."

"Do you remember her name?"

"No. She was just someone who was looking up stuff the same place I was. The same newspapers, magazines, like that. We didn't talk that much."

"What did she look like?"

Dinah thought. "Heavyset. Curly gray hair. Big eyes, long curly eyelashes, made her look like a ten-year-old. She —" She saw Kate's expression. "What?"

"Have you got a working computer here?"

"Sure." Dinah scooted over one space, and Kate reached into the daypack and pulled out Paula's computer disk, a second copy of which Kenny had made for her.

Kate moved her chair in front of the keyboard. This time she ignored the DIRT file and clicked on NOVEL, the seventh draft. She scrolled down a few pages. Paula's typing was similar to her handwriting, chaotic, with a lot of ellipses, dashes, exclamation points, and pairs of brackets, every kind there was to be had on the keyboard, holding in inserted thoughts and comments that were straining to burst free and spill all over each page.

Kate found the FIND function and used it. Dinah, reading over her shoulder, said in a marveling voice, "Wow. Did you know?"

Kate shook her head and scrolled slowly down the page.

"Do you think it's true?"

"She was a researcher. She took notes on what she found. If it was written down right in the first place, then it's true."

"Wow," Dinah said again. "Do you think Anne would talk about it on camera? It'd make for a great segment in the documentary. The candidate's family history. And maybe soon the Senator's family history."

"The filmmaker raising her ugly head," Kate muttered.

"Hey, I resemble that remark."

There was laughter on the other side of the pillar. Dinah peered around the counter. "Bobby and Pete are signing off. Hey, who's the blonde stranger you rode in with?"

"Ethan Int-Hout. Abel's son."

"Oh yeah." Dinah sighed, a sigh of pure female appreciation. "My, doesn't he look just fine." She turned her head to look at Kate, one speculative eyebrow raised.

"Johnny's staying with him while I'm on the road."

"Huh. Johnny going to stay in the Park?"

"He says he is." Kate closed the file and pulled the disk. "Dinah?"

"What?"

"Hang on to this disk for me, okay?"

"Okay."

"And don't tell anyone what's on it."

Dinah's gaze sharpened. "Why not?"

Kate sat back in her chair, linked her hands behind her head, and stared at the ceiling, unmoved by the increasing sound of rising voices and loud music and clinking glasses from the other side of the pillar. "Did I ever tell you about Darlene?"

"Darlene? Darlene who?"

"Darlene Shelikof. She's Anne Gordaoff's cousin, and her campaign manager."

"Don't think I've had the pleasure."

"We went to school together."

"At UAF?"

"Yeah. Anne wasn't there. She was going to nursing school Outside somewhere, I think. But Darlene was there, and she was running elections even then."

Dinah was mystified. "And this concerns you how?"

"The student government elections. She was behind one of the candidates for student body president. What the hell was his name?" She

275

shrugged. "I can't remember, and it doesn't matter now. What does matter is that I was curled up in a chair in the Student Union Building late the night of election day, kind of in a corner back where no one could see me, and I saw Darlene go into the student-union office. That was where the ballot box was being kept until the official count the next morning. I got curious —"

"Always your problem."

"— and I followed her, and I watched through a crack in the blinds, and I saw her fill out a bunch of ballots and stuff the ballot box."

Dinah's eyes were round. "You're kidding me!"

"No. Darlene's been stealing elections for a long time."

"You think she's stealing this one?"

Kate thought it over. "Not stealing, no. A student election at a small college, sure, if she thought she could get away with it. But a statewide election, with all the lights on? No."

"What, then? Why are you telling me this story?"

"She told me after I hired on to Anne Gordaoff's campaign that there wasn't anything she wouldn't say or do to get Anne elected to office."

"But Anne's ahead," Dinah said.

"Yeah. And Darlene would do anything and say anything to keep it that way."

"But why would this matter?" Dinah picked up the disk. "Who could possibly care? It was seventy-five years and three generations ago, Kate. No one gives a damn about that stuff nowadays."

"You said it yourself, Dinah. It's hard to find a descendent of one of those girls who will admit to it today."

"You ready to hit the road, Kate?"

They looked up to see Ethan. "It's getting late, and Johnny has to go to school tomorrow."

"Yeah," Kate said, getting to her feet and shooting Dinah a warning look. "Yeah, I'm ready."

"Kate," Dinah said.

"I'll talk to her tomorrow," Kate said. "Don't worry, Dinah."

"Yeah, right," Dinah said, walking them to the door. Johnny, whose face showed evidence of massive chocolate consumption, with reluctance gave Katya up to her mother and followed them out the door.

"Kate?" Dinah said.

"Go ahead," Kate told the guys, "I'll catch up. What, Dinah?"

"Did Darlene see you watching her stuff that box?"

Kate grinned. "What do you think?"

"Kate?"

"You going into town for the game tomorrow?"

"Kate!"

"Fine, I'll see you there." She waved a hand in farewell.

"You're in a good mood," Ethan said.

Johnny had fallen asleep in five minutes, his head heavy against Kate's shoulder.

When she made no response to his remark, he said, "What's this I hear about you being tossed out with the trash?"

"Where'd you hear that?"

He shrugged, and downshifted through a series of potholes. "Word about you gets around, Shugak. I heard it from your Auntie Vi."

"Oh great," she said before she thought.

His teeth flashed white in the dark cab. "Yeah, she wasn't best pleased."

Johnny muttered something and burrowed his face deeper into her shoulder. She shifted so he'd be more comfortable.

"Listen, Kate."

"What?"

"I'm sorry about that crack I made a while back."

"What crack?"

"The one about how long you were going to do without."

A brief silence. "I hardly remember, Ethan. Forget it."

"It's just —" He took a breath.

"What?" she said, against her better judgment.

"Hell, I don't know." He sounded annoyed. "I don't know what's wrong with me. I guess it's partly the unfinished business between us. We never got to see where we could go together. Dad made sure of that."

"The only place we were going was the sack."

278

Ethan's grin was unrepentant. "True." The grin faded. "But only at first. I liked you a lot."

"You didn't even know I existed until that summer, Ethan."

"Yeah, but you have to admit, when I noticed, I noticed."

She had to smile. "That you did."

"It wasn't all one-sided."

"No."

"You noticed, too."

"Yes."

He sighed. "And then I screwed up."

With the hindsight of going on two decades, Kate said, "Yeah, you did. But what the hell, we were both kids, and what does anybody know at that age? All you are then is one big itch wanting to scratch." She looked at him in the dim light. "I'm past it, Ethan. It's all right."

"Is it too late to say I'm sorry?"

"No."

"Then I'm sorry. I'm sorry as hell I hurt you that way."

She smiled. "I accept your apology."

The rest of the drive was accomplished in amiable silence. Ethan stopped at the pullout next to the red Ford. Johnny woke up, yawning. "What's wrong?" He snapped awake. "Is it my mom? Did she come back?"

"No, she's not here, she hasn't come back," Ethan told him, and then said over his head, "I feel like we're taking up three of the FBI's top-ten-wanted spots."

Johnny laughed, as Ethan had meant him to.

Kate got out. "Thanks for the ride, Ethan."

"See you tomorrow at the game?"

"I'll be there working."

"How much longer you got on this job?"

"Until November seventh, when the polls close."

His grin flashed. "I'm looking forward to it."

Niniltna

1915

She reread her latest letter from Percy, smiling. He was doing well in school, and girls' names were beginning to creep into his prose. Lily's accompanying note said that Percy was growing a foot a day and turning into a very handsome young man. She missed him so much. She wondered if she ought to take some time off, turn the house over to Eleanor, and go north for a month.

She thought of Matt, and her smile faded. No. Best to stay away from Matt. She should never have married him, never have yielded to his importunings, never have weakened in her determination to provide for herself and her son.

But she had. From that first moment in Fairbanks when she'd looked up and seen him staring at her through the window, she had abandoned all the good sense she had beaten into herself from Dawson to Denver. He'd been her only customer for a week, day and night, and at the end of that week he took her to Livengood, and then Circle City, and then Dawson, where they visited the ruins of the Double

Eagle Saloon, burned down in 1903, and laughed over that day so long ago. In their hotel room that night, he produced a length of chiffon and wrapped her in it from neck to ankle, and produced shoes with very high heels. She minced across the floor, smiling at him. He snatched her up and smothered her face with kisses. The pins fell from her hair. It cascaded over his arm in a rich, red fall.

He raised his head and stared down at her. "This is what I should have done that night," he said, his face tense. "I knew it then."

She smiled back at him. "I'm here now."

Her flesh gleamed through the sheer fabric. "Yes, you are. Yes, by god, you are." He stood her back on her feet and took one end of the material, pulling at it, so that she rotated slowly before him, her arms raised over her head, revealing herself to him, surrendering to him. He pulled her to the bed and took her at once. He was rough and demanding, and to her great astonishment she felt the beginnings of physical pleasure, something she had not experienced in years, perhaps not since Arthur had used her so shamefully the winter of Sam's death.

He bought her a whole new wardrobe of silk and lace, poured her the finest of champagnes, kept all other men at arms' length. There were so many younger, prettier women upon whom he could bestow his attentions that she couldn't help but be flattered and, in the end, her good sense was overwhelmed.

They married upon their return to Fairbanks, and almost at once things began to go sour. Matt didn't like Percy, Percy being a reminder of another

282

man in another time and thus a remembrance of all the other men. He would not take her out in company for fear she would meet men who had been customers and be tempted. He forbade her to go into town, where she might meet with insult. When she went to visit Lily, he returned home, discovered her absence, and came to fetch her back. He wanted to send Percy Outside to a boarding school. He said it was to further the boy's education, but she knew it was so Matt could have her to himself in the big new house he'd had built on the river.

After a year, she'd had enough and left him. He came to Lily's to fetch her back. This time, when he got her home, he hit her, and then he raped her. He was horrified the next morning and apologized, again and again. He kept her in bed for three days, carrying delicacies to her on trays he had prepared himself, bathing her, brushing her hair, lying with her in spite of her protests of pain. He hung diamonds from her ears and draped pearls around her neck, and he begged her over and over to forgive him. He loved her so much; he would never do anything to hurt her when he was in his right mind, but she had to understand, she was driving him crazy; he couldn't be responsible for his actions. They were married, weren't they? Shouldn't she stay home like a good wife and wait for him? He knew she knew he was right. The next morning he kissed her with great tenderness, took all her clothes, locked her bedroom door from the outside, and went off to work.

She knotted a dress together from a sheet, broke the window, climbed down the drainpipe, and

283

walked the mile to Lily's house.

"You need a lawyer," Lily said.

"What lawyer is going to represent me?"

Lily smiled. "My lawyer."

And he had. Matt, made to see how ridiculous he would look in contesting a divorce action from the Dawson Darling, offered up a substantial bribe. He wouldn't give her a divorce, she was told, but providing she moved out of town and didn't use his name, he would not pursue her or harass her in any way. Since she had no wish to marry again, and since Percy, back now with Lily, had been upset enough already, she agreed.

She took the money to Niniltna, where a copper mine and a railroad to haul the copper out had come into production and where the miners were looking for a little relaxation after a hard day's work. She bought a house with Matt's money, taking a perverse pleasure in seeing to it that the mortgage was from his bank, hired four other girls, and opened for business.

Business had been very good, so good that now, in the year 1915, she was thinking of selling out. She was forty, and while she had kept her looks and could afford to pick and choose her customers these days, she was tired of enduring the sweat of faceless men, of the tears they wept into her shoulder when they came, of the seed they left on her thighs. She was tired of being called by the name of every sweetheart who had been left behind when her lover had felt the pull of the north country.

She was tired.

She looked down at *Percy's* letter. *A small house,* just outside of town, with enough room for a garden. She sat down at once and wrote to *Lily,* requesting her to find such a place. She stamped the envelope and had one of the girls take it to the post office before she could change her mind.

When a long-time customer appeared on the doorstep that evening, she turned him away with a regretful smile and a few words of explanation, and the word went out that the *Dawson Darling* was moving on.

That had been *March.* Now it was *April;* the snow turned to slush and men were tracking up the floors with mud. She moved through the days with a sense of lightness and well-being that she didn't remember ever having before in her life. She sang in her bath. She mediated difficulties between the girls of her house with tolerance for their foibles. She paid all her bills, and accepted an offer for the house. She began sleeping through uninterrupted nights for the first time since she had been a child in her parents' house. One day *Lily* wrote, saying she had found exactly what was wanted, and she began to pack.

In the late afternoon of *April* ninth, she heard a knock at the back door. The girls had gone on to other jobs in other houses, and she was alone in the house. If it was the milkman, he was early, and if he was early, he wasn't here just to deliver the milk.

Instead, when she opened the door, her husband stood there.

Her hand went to her breast.

"Hello, Angel."

285

"Matt," she whispered.

"I came to see you, I — I heard you were moving back to Fairbanks."

"Yes."

They had moved into the parlor. She had yet to light the lamps — while there was electricity at the mine there was none in Niniltna — and they sat facing each other in the dim light that filtered in through the vines. "What are you doing here, Matt?"

"I came — I wanted to tell you —"

"Tell me what?"

He traced the brim of his hat. "I just wanted to see you again."

"It's over, Matt," she said. She was overwhelmed by a sudden feeling of sympathy for this man who had followed her from Dawson to Nome to Fairbanks to Niniltna. If he hadn't truly loved her, he had cared for her as much as any one man ever had.

"I know. I — did you like the oranges?"

"It was you who sent them?"

"Yes."

"Oh. Yes. Yes, I liked them. I hadn't had an orange in a long time."

"A shipment came into Fairbanks, and I bought them and had them sent down."

"Thank you." She saw his expression and added, "They were delicious. Thank you very much for sending them, Matt."

They sat for a few moments in silence.

"I ruined it, didn't I, Angel?"

"Yes," she said. "You did."

A spark of anger lit his eyes. "I had help."

She didn't answer.

He rose and held out a hand. "And now I've made things worse. I'm sorry, Angel. I'm sorry for everything."

She found herself taking his hand and rising to her feet. They stood very close together, and she could feel the need radiating from him like heat. It stirred her. She didn't want it to, but it stirred her.

He leaned forward, slowly enough so that she could move out of the way if she wanted to. She stood where she was, even angling her mouth to meet his.

He drew back. "One more time, Angel? Please?"

She couldn't find it in her to resist his plea.

He undressed her, one article of clothing at a time, not hurrying, barely touching her, hanging her garments one by one on the coatrack inside the front door. A frisson of awareness danced over her skin, not entirely due to the chill spring air and the stove not yet being lit for the evening. It had been a long time.

When she was naked, except for the stockings held above her knees with satin garters and the high-heeled shoes with the rhinestone heels, he stood looking at her in silence.

When he spoke, she was startled out of her sensual absorption by the real despair in his voice. "You're still as beautiful as ever." He walked around her, and she could feel his eyes on her body like a caress. "Damn you," he whispered, and kissed her again, thrusting his knee between her legs and pressing up.

He took her hips in his hands and ground her against him.

In spite of his ungentle handling she began to respond, but the wool of his suit was rough against her breasts, and she whimpered in protest.

He broke away, panting. "Don't move," he whispered. "Let me look at you."

He walked around her again as she stood trembling.

When he walked behind her for the third time, he paused for so long she asked, "What? What is it, Matt?"

"God, how I loved you," he said, and something hit the back of her head, and the Dawson Darling knew no more.

14

They were waiting at the Niniltna airstrip the next morning when George Perry flew in with the Anne Gordaoff entourage. She got out of George's leased 206 first, and when she saw Kate she smiled with what looked like genuine friendliness. "Hello, Kate."

"Hello, Anne."

"How was your day off?"

"Educational," Kate said. "You know Jim Chopin."

"Of course, as who doesn't?" Anne smiled and held out her hand.

"Ms. Gordaoff. Some information has come to my attention about Paula Pawlowski. I wonder if I might speak with you for a few moments."

Darlene, at Anne's shoulder, said, "We've got a schedule to meet, Jim. We don't really have time for —"

He kept his eyes on Anne. "That's a shame. Let's go, then." He put his hand beneath Anne's elbow and urged her toward the blue-and-white

289

Cessna 180 with the state trooper logo on the fuselage parked to one side of the strip.

"What?" Darlene said. "Wait a minute, where are you taking her? Jim?"

He halted, looking down at Anne. "We can talk here," he told her, "or we can fly to Tok and talk at the post there."

It was all pure bluff, of course. He didn't have a warrant — yet — and she didn't have to go anywhere with him. Kate thought Anne probably knew that. Darlene didn't, and she was spluttering with rage. Tracy Huffman glanced at Kate and then buried her nose in her DayTimer. Tracy'd always been good at staying out of the line of fire, a talent Kate envied. Doug Gordaoff took one step forward and then halted, silent, watching. Erin was indifferent to anything but her own misery.

Tom, to his credit, said in a loud, angry voice, "Get your hands off my mother." His father put a hand on his shoulder and he shrugged it off. "Let her go," Tom said. It was the first time Kate had seen him exhibit anything remotely resembling familial feeling, and she was surprised.

"You want to stay out of this, son," Jim said.

Anne stared up at him. "You know, don't you."

"Know what, Anne?"

She looked over her shoulder at Kate. "You found out."

"Paula Pawlowski did," Kate said. "It was in her notes."

Anne's shoulders slumped a little. "Maybe Billy

Mike will let us use the conference room at the association." Her smile looked forced. "At least we'll be in out of the cold."

"Let's go," Jim said.

Tom managed to contain himself until they were seated at the table in the conference room before he burst out, "Is this about Paula Pawlowski? Because if it is, and if you're dumb enough to think Mom had anything to do with it, you're just plain crazy."

Jim frowned down at his notebook and made a minute correction to an entry. Kate, looking over his shoulder, saw that the notebook was open to a completely blank page.

"Besides, she was giving a speech at a dinner in Ahtna at the time."

"At what time, Tom?" Jim said without looking up.

"The evening Paula Pawlowski died. And after that she was in our hotel room, with Dad, all night."

Tom couldn't know that, but for the moment, Kate held her peace.

Jim looked up for the first time, straight at Anne. "Where were you the following afternoon, Anne?"

She looked startled. "Why, I don't know, I —" She looked at Darlene.

Tracy Huffman snapped open her DayTimer. "She was passing the talking stick at a healing circle for recovering alcoholics at the Ahtna

Medical Clinic at three P.M. That lasted until five P.M., when she joined the residents of the Ahtna Pioneer Home for dinner in their cafeteria. She was there until seven P.M., maybe a little longer because they had a lot of questions about the plan to phase out the longevity fund."

"And after that, we went to dinner with the Kegturyaq Native Association, and then to our rooms, where we read until we went to sleep," Doug said.

Doug Gordaoff seemed to have rediscovered his marriage. Interesting, Kate thought, given that she'd seen him hit on more women in a twenty-four-hour period than even Jim Chopin could manage.

"Thank you, Doug," Jim said, with a corresponding scribble. The notebook was all for show, a tool of intimidation. Most people who'd been called in to help the trooper with his investigation couldn't keep their eyes off it. Something in the act of someone taking down your words as you speak made people immediately wonder what they had said wrong, made them want to correct themselves, rationalize their behavior, contradict what they'd said before, or, fatally, attempt to explain themselves. It was a natural human reaction to try put the best light on one's actions, no matter how amoral, asocial, abusive, or bloody.

And that was when Jim nailed them in interrogation. He never actually wrote anything down in the notebook, though. When it came to write the official report, he wouldn't have forgotten a single detail. It would all go into the computer and be printed out in damning black and white that always stood up in court. Jim Chopin was a district attorney's wet dream.

A good cop and a good pilot, Kate thought. Two good qualities.

She shifted in her chair. Speaking of rationalization, what had happened between them in Bering in July or at the garbage dump in Ahtna was no reason for her to endow Jim Chopin with character. He'd been kind to her, yes, and she was grateful, but it stopped there. She concentrated on the conversation, like she should have been doing in the first place.

"And you were where during this period, Doug?"

Aha, Kate thought, repressing an unwilling smile. Jim was making it known that he was well aware that if Doug Gordaoff was Anne Gordaoff's unbreakable alibi, then Anne Gordaoff was Doug Gordaoff's alibi as well.

Doug stared. "I was with her, of course."

Kate didn't know it, but she and Jim were thinking exactly the same thing at that moment. How convenient.

Jim looked at Erin Gordaoff. "Where were you, Erin?"

"Who said you could call her by her first name?" Tom said, rising to his feet and leaning forward with his hands on the table. "Who said you could call my mother or my father by their first name? Show a little respect, and we might think about answering your questions."

"Where were you, Erin?" Jim said.

"I don't know," Erin said, her tone close to a whine, and Kate thought what a dreary young woman she was. Hard to believe she was Anne Gordaoff's daughter. Maybe fairies had pulled a switch in the crib.

"What's with all these questions?" Tom said. "You march us in here like we're under arrest, and now you're interrogating my family like we know something about Paula Pawlowski's death. We don't."

"Someone killed her, Tom."

"Well, that somebody isn't sitting around this table."

Jim consulted his nonexistent notes. "Where were you that night?"

"Now, just a damn minute," Anne said, an unaccustomed flush rising up into her face. It was the first time Kate had seen her upset.

Jim looked up for the first time, meeting her eyes squarely. "Tell us about your great-grandmother, Anne."

There was a silence that stretched out like a rubber band pulled to its breaking point. No one moved. For a while it seemed like no one breathed.

"What do you mean, tell you about my great-grandmother?" Anne said, but it was a poor attempt, and she had waited far too long to make it.

"The Northern Light," Jim said.

There was another silence.

"She's dead," Anne said. "She's been dead since 1915. I never knew her."

"That's not what I asked you, Anne."

"What's going on, Mom?" Tom said. "Which great-grandmother?"

Jim waited for Anne to answer. She didn't. He said, "The last threatening letter you received, Anne, the one telling you to pay up or they'd tell."

Anne was pale but composed. "Yes?"

"I just got the report from the crime lab in Anchorage. It was written by someone else other than the writer of the original letters."

"Oh. I don't understand. I — have two people been writing me hate mail?"

"No," Jim said, "one person has been writing you hate mail, and a second person, a completely different person, has been trying to blackmail you."

"That's ridiculous," Anne said. "That's just — that's silly. I don't have anything to be blackmailed for." She looked around the table. "My family —"

"Yes, let's talk about your family," Jim said. "Your family's got legs in Alaska, both literally and figuratively, starting with the Dawson Darling, who danced for her supper at the Double Eagle Saloon in Dawson City, who worked the Fairbanks Line, and who later moved to Niniltna to open the establishment known as the Northern Light." He sat back, very much at

his ease, and waited, blues eyes steady in an un-
nerving stare. It was said that Jim Chopin could
look at you with that stare and make you con-
fess to murdering your own mother, even if
you'd been on Maui at the time.

"That was a long time ago," Anne said, almost
sullen.

"Yes, it was, and I couldn't give a damn, but
you might not agree."

Anne shifted in her chair. "It's not something
we talk about a lot in my family."

Jim agreed. "Some families are little more uptight than others."

"Uptight?" Anne said. "She was a prostitute.
She sold her body for money. It's not something
to be proud of."

"What?" Tom said.

"What?" Doug said.

"What?" Erin said.

Tracy's eyebrows flew up into her hairline.

Darlene's expression didn't change.

"Not something to be proud of," Jim repeated. "Is it a secret you'd kill to keep, Anne?"

"That's enough," Darlene said. "This conversation is over." She looked at Jim with a pointed expression. "Unless you want to arrest someone?"

Jim let them wait while he thought about it.
"No," he said at last, and let the room relax before he ratcheted up the tension again. "Not at
the moment."

Darlene didn't move a muscle. "Fine."

"I would like a list of Anne's activities for the

296

rest of the day, however."

"Fine," Darlene said again, giving Tracy a curt nod before she swept out the door, herding the Gordaoffs in front of her.

Tracy sighed. "Just once I'd like to be on a winning team."

Kate spoke for the first time. "You think the fact that Anne's great-grandmother was a hooker during the Gold Rush will lose her the election?"

Tracy shook her head. "Not the fact that her great-grandmother was a hooker, Kate. The fact that Anne kept it a secret." She opened her DayTimer. "Anne's having lunch at the Roadhouse in an hour. She'll probably be there until three, when we come back for the start of the cheerleader tournament."

"You overnighting here?" Jim said.

Tracy nodded and picked up her bag. "Well, hell, Kate. It was fun while it lasted."

They grinned at each other. "You sticking with the campaign?"

Tracy shrugged. "They're still paying me, so far as I know." She shook her head and said mournfully, "This was such a slam dunk a month ago. What the hell happened?"

When she was gone Jim looked at Kate and said, "Good question."

She sighed. "Yeah."

The door opened and they looked up. It was Dinah, flushed and breathing hard, as if she'd been running. "Finally," she said, trying to catch her breath.

"What's up?" Kate said, Dinah's urgency pulling her to her feet. "What's wrong?"

Dinah looked at Jim Chopin. "Good-bye, Jim."

He stood behind Kate. "What's going on?"

"It's personal," Dinah said. "Good-bye."

"I guess I can take a hint." He reached out a hand and chucked Dinah beneath the chin. "So long, gorgeous." He adjusted the ball cap over his eyes. "Kate."

When the door closed behind him, Dinah said, "Somebody told Jane how to get to your homestead."

"She came back? Where'd she stay last night?"

"I don't know. All I know is she went out to the Roadhouse and six-packed Frank Scully, and he loaned her his truck. Bernie drove in to tell Bobby she's on her way. Where's Johnny?"

Kate was already out the door. "With Ethan."

"Is your truck here?"

"Parked next to the airstrip."

"I'm coming with you."

"Like hell."

"Auntie Vi's got Katya, Bobby's already on his way, I'm coming with you." She was in the cab of Kate's truck before Kate was. "Kate?"

"What?" The truck scattered gravel and snow twenty feet as Kate pulled a broty on the way to the road.

"There's something else. Not about Johnny, about Anne."

"One thing at a time," Kate said, and floored it.

Bobby's pickup was pulled neatly to one side of the road, the offside wheels pulled to the extreme edge of the very narrow shoulder. Jane had left the end of Frank Scully's pea green Dodge Ramcharger sticking out into the road; Kate gave it an ungentle nudge with the Chevy, and it turned out Jane had left the Dodge in neutral. It rolled forward until the two front tires ran off the side of the turnaround and got itself well and truly high-centered on the edge. "Shit," Kate said.

"Serves Frank right," Dinah said.

"Yeah, but I'll have to pull it out." Kate bailed out of the truck, barely pausing to close the door as Mutt launched herself out of the back and hit the trail running. "Mutt! Don't kill her!"

Dinah's laugh petered out at the expression on Kate's face. "She wouldn't," she said. "Would she?"

Kate pounded past her without answering.

"Goddamn!" she heard Bobby yell when she was halfway down the trail. "It's the goddamn First Division of the goddamn Lupine Cavalry! You go, girl!"

Kate's worst fears were confirmed when she stumbled into the clearing, lungs burning, eyes tearing, to find Jane standing in the open door to the cabin, faced down by a Mutt standing on tiptoe, hackles stiff and straight up, head down between hunched shoulders, ears flattened, teeth bared, a steady, rumbling growl issuing promises of the most alarming kind. Kate almost felt sorry for Jane, frozen and white-faced, too terrified even to attempt to slam the door in Mutt's face.

"Mutt," Kate said.

Mutt snapped. The sound of teeth meeting was audible to everyone in the clearing. The growl changed to a snarl and escalated in volume.

"Whoa," Bobby said, grin fading.

"Kate, do something," Dinah said.

"Mutt!" Kate said. She made a large circle, coming around to where Mutt could see her before she approached. She didn't make the mistake of reaching out a hand. "Off," she said.

The snarl abated a fraction.

Kate put more whip into her voice. "Off!" she said. "Now, Mutt."

The snarl deteriorated into a low, throaty rumble, and then ceased.

Everyone relaxed except Jane. "Well," Bobby said, grinning at Kate, "she sure knows who she doesn't like."

Kate looked at Jane. "What are you doing here, Jane? Jane?"

Jane tore her gaze away from Mutt and blinked at them. "I — I'm — I'm looking for Johnny." Her voice sounded much higher and less certain than it had the last time Kate had heard it. When was that? One month ago? Two? She seemed to realize it, and pulled herself together. "I'm looking for my son. Where is he?"

"He isn't here," Kate said with exact truth.

Jane's eyes were deep blue and had thick,

straight white-blonde lashes, but they were marred by being too close together and by the expression of sheer malice they displayed every time she was in Kate's presence. "I know you know where he is. You give him back to me now!"

"He isn't here," Kate repeated. "I assume you looked through the cabin."

"Someone's hiding him for you, then!"

The best defense is a good offense, and Kate was a bad liar anyway. "So he's missing, your son," she said. "For how long?"

Thrown off her stride, Jane said, "That's none of your business. You —"

"I agree, it's yours," Kate said, "and you don't appear to be minding it. Did he run away, Jane?"

Jane stared at her.

"Has he done it more than once?" Kate said. "Like he did in Anchorage? I remember one time you took his shoes away so he wouldn't run away to his dad, and he did anyway. Barefoot. In March."

Jane flushed a deep red. Her mouth opened and closed without any sound coming out. Kate pursued her advantage. "Has he come back the other times? Does he usually run to the same place?"

"He didn't get this far last time," Jane said without thinking. "But that —"

"So he's done it more than once," Kate said, anger simmering under her skin. "If he's making a career out of running away then he's obviously unhappy. What have you done about that?"

"He's a kid; he does what I tell him!"

"Not noticeably," Kate said.

Bobby choked.

Jane's eyes narrowed. "You know where he is. I'm going to have you arrested for kidnapping."

"Fine," Kate said, "but in the meantime, you're trespassing. Get off my land."

"You —"

"Mutt," Kate said, and next to her Mutt went back up on tiptoe and kick-started the growl.

Jane looked furious and frustrated, but she stepped out of the doorway and sidled around the edge of the clearing, never once presenting her back to Mutt. When she reached the trail, she said, "I'll be back."

"We'll be here," Kate said.

As Jane vanished up the trail, she remembered Frank's Dodge, high-centered on the edge of the turnaround. Dinah remembered at the same moment, and touched Kate's arm. "I'll take care of it," she said, and followed Jane.

"Mutt," Kate said, and Mutt arrowed away from her side.

"Kate," Bobby said, sounding nervous for what might have been the first time in Kate's memory.

"It's okay," she said. "She's all right now. Besides, Jane can use a little reminder of why it's not a good idea to wander off into the woods by herself. Especially private property in those woods."

"I thought Mutt was going to eat her alive. Remind me never to piss her off."

Kate shrugged, stretching a little to ease the tension between her shoulder blades. "I could use some tea. How about you?"

"I could use a goddamn fifth of Scotch," he said.

Kate got the ramp from where it leaned next to the door and set it over the doorstep. When Bobby rolled to the top, he found Kate standing in the middle of the mess Jane had left behind. Books and tapes had been pulled from the shelves, the cushions had been tumbled from the built-in couch, canned goods shoved to the floor.

"What, she thought Johnny had hidden behind the *Selected Poems of Robert Frost*, or maybe the baked beans?" he said.

The look on Kate's face could be best described as unpleasant, and truth to tell, it scared him more than Mutt's growl. He hoped Jane had had the good sense to move herself out of range.

"I should have turned Mutt loose," Kate said in a very soft voice.

Bobby shook his head. "Nah. She would have fallen backward, and there would have been blood and guts all over the cabin. Blood's hell on books." He gave the wheels of his chair a brisk roll into the kitchen. "I'll start the tea; you start on the living room."

Kate had the couch back together and some of the books and tapes replaced by the time Dinah showed up, but there was still enough

303

disorder left for Dinah to purse her lips in a soundless whistle. Bobby sent her one of those meaningful looks reserved for the married of the species, and she closed her mouth on whatever she had been about to say and went to restore the canned goods to their cupboards. By the time the kettle whistled, the room looked almost normal, and Kate was restored to at least the semblance of her customary calm, until they sat down around the table, and she discovered that Jane had dumped the contents of the one-pound Darigold butter can and had taken off with two of the five twenty-dollar bills that had been in it.

"A petty thief," Bobby said, not without pleasure.

"Might have known it," Dinah agreed.

They both watched Kate from the corners of their eyes, like home canners watching as the steam built up beneath the lid of an old pressure cooker that might or might not be still working at optimum capacity.

It took a while, but the color eventually faded from her face. She looked around at Mutt, draped across the threshold of the open door, dappled with afternoon sun, and told her, "Next time, she's lunch."

Mutt flopped a lazy tail in agreement.

Relieved, Bobby squirted honey into his mug. "That's my girls."

"I have to say that I hate it that she knows the way here," Kate said, taking the honey in turn.

"Yeah, well, wait till Frank gets a load of what she did to his truck. It'll be a while before he rents it out again for a six-pack of beer."

Bobby raised an eyebrow. Dinah told him. When he stopped laughing, he said, "What is it about you that drives her so nuts, Kate?"

"Her son doesn't like her," Kate said.

"And he does like you?"

She thought of Johnny since he'd arrived in the Park. "He used to."

"Where is he, anyway?" Bobby said.

"Either in school or with Ethan."

Bobby started to laugh all over again. "You mean all she had to do was go up to the school?"

Kate shrugged. "She doesn't give a shit about the kid. She wants to get in my face."

Dinah was more practical. "What are you going to do about her?"

Kate sipped her tea. It was hot and sweet and burned all the way down, soothing nerves rubbed raw over the past few days. "I don't know yet."

"You're not going to let her take him."

Kate looked up and gave a short, unhumorous laugh. "She's got to find him first."

"How many times has he run off?" Bobby said.

"He won't say. I think he's been trying to ever since she shipped him out to Arizona to stay with her mother last fall after his father died."

Bobby winced. "Arizona. Jesus. A hundred and ten in the shade."

"Yeah," Dinah said, deadpan, "but it's a dry heat."

305

"Yeah, right." Bobby looked at Kate. "He going to stay here?"

Kate chose to answer in the oblique. "Jane won't give up. She'll be back, and next time she'll bring the cops."

"Not Chopper Jim she won't," Bobby said.

"Why not?" Kate said. "He's the law; the law's on her side."

"Kate."

She tried not to feel ashamed, and didn't succeed very well. "Whatever. But she will be back, Bobby. She hates my guts. She wants to do me dirt, as much as possible. It's not about the kid at all."

Unsmiling, Dinah said, "Then you make it be."

Kate, arrested, stared at her for a moment. "You're absolutely right," she said. "Of course you're right. It's not about her, it's not about me, it's about Johnny."

"Parents," Bobby said with an exaggerated shudder. "I don't know why anybody has them. I hope that kid is nothing like his mom."

Again Kate thought of Johnny's bitter anger. "In some things, he is."

"That's learned, Kate," Dinah said.

Kate's face was bleak. "Who are you if you can't be proud of your parents? Of your family?"

Bobby snorted. "Don't ask me," he said, and too late Kate remembered the right-wing couple in the conservative backwoods town in Tennessee whose rigid belief system had driven their only son out of the house, the town, and the country, to fight in a war in which he didn't believe, to suffer wounds beyond all repair, and to relocate in a place as far from the land of his birth as he could get.

He was lucky. He was alive. His girlfriend, instead of running with him, had climbed into the bathtub and cut her wrists.

"I forgot," Kate told him. "I'm sorry."

"It's okay," he said, shaking his head. "The expectations people place on their offspring can be truly horrendous. Too bad there's no school parents have to go to before they have kids."

"What about the expectations people place on their ancestors?" Dinah said, studying the surface of her tea.

They both looked at her. "What?"

She looked at Kate. "Your parents."

Kate stiffened. "What about them?"

"See? You look like Mutt did facing down Jane. You ever try to badmouth Jane to Johnny?"

"No," Kate said immediately, and then had to think about her answer. "No," she said again, more slowly this time. *She's your mother, Johnny. You will speak of her with respect.* "You can't do that," she told Dinah. "It doesn't matter how bad a kid is treated, there is still some part of them that loves their parents, some part that needs to believe they are loved in return." She paused, reflecting back on the five and a half years she had spent in Anchorage trying to protect underage victims of abuse. "That five and a half years I worked in sex crimes, I saw every imaginable evil inflicted on kids, from newborn babies to teenagers. Not one of whom ever wanted to leave home. Hardly any of the ones who were old enough to talk would admit to the abuse in the first place."

Bobby and Dinah exchanged glances. Kate never spoke of her work in Anchorage. She'd had had nightmares about it on Bobby's couch a time or two, and Bobby had made mention of it to Dinah. They both had imagination enough to know that they would never know just how awful it had been.

"That wasn't exactly what I meant," Dinah said with caution. "But I guess it works."

Kate looked up. "Oh?"

"If kids whose parents beat up on them are that protective of their parents, how protective are they going to be of their grandparents? Their great-grandparents?"

"I'm not tracking here," Kate said.

"Makes two of us," Bobby said.

Dinah reached into the capacious pocket of the rusty black duster that made her look like the trail driver out of a Zane Grey novel and pulled out a sheaf of paper. "I printed it out."

"Printed what out?" Kate accepted the bundle of paper and leafed through it.

"From the disk you left last night."

"Oh." Kate sat up and shoved her mug to one side. "What is this?"

"It's the report of an inquest."

"Whose?"

"Anne Gordaoff's great-grandmother."

"You're kidding."

"No. And get this." Dinah paused for dramatic effect.

"What," Kate said, in no mood.

"She was murdered," Dinah said, trying her best not to sound absolutely thrilled at the very idea.

"No shit," Bobby said. "Cool."

Kate was less impressed. "One of her tricks, I suppose."

"What?" Bobby said. "Anne Gordaoff's great-grandma was a hooker?"

"A dance-hall girl," Kate said, "down at the Northern Light."

"Goddamn," Bobby said, a slow grin breaking across his face. "Goodie Anne Gordaoff's great-grandma made 'em pay for the privilege. Who'd a thunk it?"

Niniltna

April 1915

Testimony taken at the inquest on the body of Mrs. Angel Beecham, also know as the Dawson Darling, April 9, 1915, before Joseph D. Brittain, U.S. Commissioner for the Fairbanks Precinct, Fourth Judicial Division, Territory of Alaska.

When **THEODORE OLDS**, being first duly sworn, testified as follows:

Q. Where do you reside, Mr. Olds?

A. The town of Niniltna, sir.

Q. What is your occupation?

A. I am a dairyman, sir.

Q. Relax, Mr. Olds, I don't bite.

A. Sorry, sir.

Q. Do you deliver milk in Niniltna?

A. Yes, sir. Twice a day, sir.

Q. Did you know a woman by the name of Mrs. Angel Beecham, who resided at Number 3 Front Street?

A. Yes, sir.

Q. Also known, I believe, as the Dawson Darling?

A. Yes, sir. I delivered a quart of milk there every evening at about half past five, sir. Well, it used to be six quarts, but when the other girls moved out, Mrs. Beecham told me to deliver only one. Sir.

Q. When did you last see her alive?

A. About half past four on Thursday evening, sir.

Q. That would be Thursday evening, April 1, 1915?

A. I guess so, sir. I saw her every Thursday evening at that time, sir, when I delivered the milk, sir. I saw her every Monday evening, too, at half past four, too, sir. Every Monday evening and every Thursday evening, twice a week, every week at the same time, sir —

Q. Did you see her at any other time?

A. Well, I, well, sir, I guess I saw her on the street in town sometimes.

Q. Did you see her in town last week?

A. I don't know. I guess so.

Q. Be more specific, Mr. Olds, if you please.

A. Maybe on Friday around the shoe store?

Q. So you saw Mrs. Beecham in town on Friday, the day after you delivered her milk, downtown in front of the shoe store.

A. Or maybe it was Lavery's store, sir.

Q. That would be Friday, April 2?

A. Yes, sir, I guess so, sir.

Q. What time of the day would that have been? Mr. Olds?

A. I'm sorry, sir, I don't remember.

Q. Was it light or dark outside?

A. Oh. It was almost dark.

Q. So between seven or eight in the evening, would you say?

A. I'd say so, sir.

Q. Was she alone?

A. I guess so, sir.

Q. Did you see anyone with her?

A. No, sir.

Q. She was entirely unaccompanied?

A. She had a lot of packages, sir.

Q. Did you offer to carry them for her?

A. How did you know that, sir?

Q. Did you carry Mrs. Beecham's packages home for her, Mr. Olds?

A. Yes, sir.

Q. When did you leave her house on Friday evening, Mr. Olds?

A. Uh, I don't know. However long it took to walk her home, sir, and carry her packages into the house, sir.

Q. You didn't stay to chat? She didn't offer you any refreshment by way of gratitude for carrying her packages home for her?

A. Oh, no sir. I'm a married man, sir. I only saw her when I delivered the milk.

Q. Yes, I see. So you saw Mrs. Beecham on Friday in town, alone, escorted her home, and then didn't see her again until Thursday evening when you delivered the milk.

A. Yes, sir. I didn't see her at all on Monday.

Q. What time was this?

A. About half past four, sir. I leave home at four,

sir, and it usually takes me about half an hour to get to her house.

Q. What did the house look like as you approached it? Was anything out of the ordinary?

A. Well, sir, the first thing was that the blinds were down.

Q. They weren't, usually?

A. Well, no, sir. Could I have a drink of water?

Q. Certainly. Bailiff . . . thank you. Now, then, Mr. Olds. You have testified that the blinds were drawn on Mrs. Beecham's house as you approached it. This was out of the ordinary, was it?

A. Well, yes, sir. On that street, sir, the windows and the blinds are always open, especially at that time of day.

Q. Why is that, Mr. Olds?

A. Well, sir, I, uh, I don't, I . . .

Q. Perhaps so that the ladies who reside on that street can take some air?

A. Yes, sir, that's it, that's exactly right, sir.

Q. So the blinds on Mrs. Beecham's house were down. What else did you notice about the house that was out of the ordinary, Mr. Olds?

A. Well, sir, when I went to set down the full bottles on the porch and take away the empty ones, I noticed that the door was open.

Q. This was the back door?

A. Yes, sir, I always delivered the milk to the back door, and so I went around to the back of the house and put my milk down with the ticket on top.

Q. When you noticed the kitchen door was open.

A. Yes, sir.

Q. Did you go into the kitchen?

A. No, sir.

Q. Take your time, Mr. Olds.

A. Yes, sir, thank you, sir. It's just that it was . . . that she was . . .

Q. Now then. You noticed that the kitchen door was open. You didn't go inside. What happened then?

A. I looked through the door and saw the body. It was real dark with the blinds drawn, and I said, "Angel, what's the matter?" and she didn't say anything, and it was dark but I could see she didn't hardly have any clothes on and that she was dead.

Q. How did you know she was dead?

A. When I went in, I walked in her blood. And she didn't say anything. And she was cold when I touched her.

Q. What did you do after you discovered the body?

A. I went to the nearest place anybody could call home and told them Angel was dead.

Q. Did you notify the officials?

A. Yes, sir, Mrs. Croxton called the police.

Q. How long after you had discovered the body?

A. Well, sir, as long as it took me to walk to Mrs. Croxton's house, and as long after that to when they came.

Q. To whom did Mrs. Croxton telephone, Mr. Olds?

A. I guess the chief of police, sir, because that's who came.

Q. Now, Mr. Olds, how wide open was Mrs.

314

Beecham's door when you discovered the body?

A. Well, sir, you might say it was practically wide open. Something I had never seen before.

Q. Was anybody else in Mrs. Beecham's house between the time you discovered the body and the time the chief of police got there?

A. Oh no, sir. Well, I don't think so. I was up at Mrs. Croxton's house, you see.

Q. Did she go into the house?

A. No, sir. We went back down to wait for the chief of police, and we waited outside, sir.

Q. Who was next to arrive?

A. I believe Mr. Brittain, the coroner, sir. That would be you, sir.

Q. And after that?

A. Well, I guess that would be the United States Marshall and the district attorney, oh, and Dr. Davidson, sir.

Q. How long have you known Mrs. Beecham, Mr. Olds?

A. Oh, sir, since she became a customer, sir, I think.

Q. When was that, Mr. Olds?

A. Uh, last July, I think, sir.

Q. She moved into the house in July?

A. I don't know, sir, that was when I first met her. She has been a milk customer of mine for about four months.

Q. I see. Mr. Olds, this is now April.

A. Yes, sir.

Q. And you first met Mrs. Beecham in July.

A. Yes, sir.

315

Q. And she has been a milk customer of yours for four months.

A. Yes, sir. Oh.

Q. You see my difficulty, Mr. Olds. You claim to have known Mrs. Beecham only as a milk customer, and that for only the last four months, and yet you say you first met Mrs. Beecham in July. Mr. Olds?

A. Yes, sir?

Q. Can you explain this discrepancy?

A. No, sir. I guess I must have been introduced to her before then.

Q. Before when?

A. Before she became a milk customer, sir.

Q. When would that have been, exactly?

A. I don't know, sir. I'm a married man, sir.

Q. Yes, I see. Well, Mr. Olds, you may be excused for now, but please hold yourself in readiness to return should I need to speak to you again.

A. Yes, sir. Thank you, sir.

JOE FORTSON, being first duly sworn, testified as follows:

Q. What official position do you hold, Mr. Fortson?

A. Chief of police.

Q. Did you hold that position on the sixth day of April 1915?

A. Yes, sir.

Q. Were you acquainted with Mrs. Angel Beecham during her lifetime?

A. Yes, sir.

Q. When did you last see her alive?

A. I couldn't say. About Monday, I believe I saw her on the street.

316

Q. *Monday, that would be the fifth?*

A. *Yes, sir.*

Q. *Did you see her body on the evening of the eighth of April 1915?*

A. *Yes, sir.*

Q. *Where?*

A. *In the residence she occupied on Main Street, down on the river.*

Q. *How did you come to go there?*

A. *I received a phone call from Mrs. Elizabeth Croxton that she was dead.*

Q. *State what you found when you arrived at her residence.*

A. *There was a crowd of girls and a few men outside of her house, being held back from going in by Mr. Olds and Mrs. Croxton. I went into the house and turned on the light and found Mrs. Beecham's body on the floor.*

Q. *What did you do then?*

A. *When I saw that she was dead, I went out of the house and closed the back door and waited until the coroner got there.*

Q. *Did you make any examination of the body or the scene at that time?*

A. *No, sir, I could see the gash in her neck, and I could see that she was dead, but I did not examine the body.*

Q. *Who came after that?*

A. *Yourself [Judge Brittain], and then the U.S. Marshal.*

Q. *Any doctors?*

A. *Yes. Dr. Davidson came.*

317

Q. Who else came, in an official capacity?

A. The district attorney.

Q. Was there an examination of the body made at that time?

A. Yes, sir. And we searched the house.

Q. Who engaged in the search?

A. Yourself [Judge Brittain], Marshall Kelsey, and myself were the principal ones, I think.

Q. What did you find?

A. The house had been ransacked. The trunk was overturned, the drawers were pulled out and dumped on the floor, two valises had the sides cut out and were on the floor, too.

Q. Did you make a careful search of the home for the purpose of finding money?

A. Yes.

Q. Did you find any money in the house?

A. Yes. There was a little box with some change in it, and that was all the actual money that we found.

Q. What clothing did you find on the body?

A. A pair of stockings and a pair of shoes.

Q. What jewelry did you find?

A. She had on diamond earrings and a bracelet watch on her left wrist, and a gold bracelet on her right wrist, and a gold chain around her neck. She had one ring on her left hand and three rings on her right hand.

Q. Did those rings contain jewels?

A. Yes, sir, diamonds.

Q. Was her hair done up or loose?

A. Done up.

Q. Did you find the rest of the clothes she had been wearing immediately before her death?

A. Yes, sir, they were hung up on the coatrack inside the front door.

Q. All of them?

A. I should imagine so.

Q. Was there anything about the body that would indicate a struggle on her part immediately before her throat was cut?

A. No, sir.

Q. What was the appearance of the wound on her neck?

A. It started on the left side of her neck and extended over under the right ear, a very large, deep cut. Her head was almost severed from her body.

Q. Did you discover any articles in the house that did not seem to belong there?

A. I discovered a glove with a rock in it.

Q. Have you that glove and rock?

A. Yes, sir.

Witness exhibits rock, which is examined by judge and district attorney.

Q. These are the identical articles you found?

A. Yes, sir.

The glove and rock are admitted as evidence, marked Exhibit 1.

Q. The court notes that the glove is a man's glove, made of brown leather, lined, well-made, and almost new. Chief Fortson, where was the glove, containing the rock, when you found it?

A. It was by her right foot.

Q. Did you see a washbasin there?

319

A. Yes, sir, near the washstand, close to the body, about a foot from the body.

Q. What did it contain?

A. Bloody water, it seemed to me.

Q. Was there a towel?

A. Yes, sir, on the washstand. It was damp.

Q. Was it blood-stained?

A. Not that I could see.

Q. Other than the glove and the rock, did you find any other weapon of any kind in the house?

A. No, sir.

Q. Did you discover a knife that had the appearance of having been used by anyone to inflict the wound upon the person of Mrs. Beecham?

A. No, sir.

Q. You made a thorough search of the house and didn't find any money?

A. No, sir. I mean, yes, sir. No money other than the box of change, and the jewelry. Mostly just a lot of little trinkets.

Q. Of any value?

A. Not of any great value.

Q. Evidently the person who rifled the drawers and grips was not looking for jewelry?

A. Didn't seem to be. If he did, he overlooked a lot of it.

Q. Did you know Mrs. Angel Beecham in her lifetime?

A. Yes, sir.

Q. You knew her to be known as the Dawson Darling?

A. Yes, sir.

Q. Also that she resided at Number 3 Front Street in Niniltna?

A. Yes, sir.

Q. Did you know her personally or professionally?

A. I — I'm a married man, judge.

Q. Answer the question, please, chief.

A. I knew Mrs. Beecham to say hello to on the street.

Q. I see. Thank you, chief, you may step down.

J. R. STEWARD, being first duly sworn, testified as follows:

Q. What is your name?

A. J. R. Steward.

Q. What official position do you hold?

A. Chief deputy marshal.

Q. Did you hold that position on the eighth day of April 1915?

A. Yes, sir.

Q. Did you know Mrs. Angel Beecham during her lifetime?

A. I did. I knew her when I saw her.

Q. To say hello to on the street?

A. Yes, sir.

Q. Did you see her body on the evening of the eigth of April?

A. Yes, sir.

Q. Where?

A. In her house on Main Street, in the town of Niniltna, Alaska.

Q. What officials were there when you arrived?

A. Uh, yourself, Judge Brittain, and Chief Fortson,

and myself. Oh, and District Attorney Turner.

Q. Anyone else?

A. Oh, Doctor Davidson was also there. When I arrived, he was examining the wound in the neck.

Q. Where was the body at that time?

A. In the room called the kitchen.

Q. What was the position of the body?

A. Lying on her back in a pool of blood, with her feet, one under the washstand and the other right near the middle door.

Q. Was the body clothed?

A. Partially. Both legs from just above the knee downwards were clad in red silk stockings with reinforced tops and feet. These were held up by a pair of garters with the tops of the stockings rolled over the garters. The right stocking was torn. Both feet wore high-heeled shoes with rhinestone heels.

These garments as enumerated are admitted as evidence, marked Exhibit 2.

Q. Did you assist in making a thorough search of the house?

A. I did, yes, sir.

Q. How many times have you searched it?

A. Two times thoroughly, and two or three times I have been over there since to verify certain things.

Q. Chief Fortson testified that you found two valises, both cut open.

A. Yes, sir.

Q. Describe the cuts.

A. They were similar cuts, rectangular in shape. It looked as if a knife had been driven in at one end and pulled lengthwise across the grip, down and back again.

Q. What would be the purpose of such cuts, Marshal?

A. To see if anything of value had been hidden in the lining.

Q. What, if anything, was found that might be construed to be a weapon?

A. Well, nothing in my search. I was there when the glove and the stone were picked up, but there was nothing besides that found that I have ever seen that would be used as a weapon.

Q. No knife, or ax or anything of that kind at all?

A. No, sir.

Q. In your searches of that house did you find any money?

A. The only money we found was some miscellaneous change in a little tin box.

Q. Besides the knife, money was the next thing you were looking for?

A. Yes, sir.

Q. Did you make a thorough search?

A. We looked everywhere, into receptacles of all kinds, and even in the water in the basin, and the ashes in the stove, and everywhere. We made a very thorough search.

WILLIAM WOOD, being first duly sworn, testified as follows:

Q. Mr. Wood, where do you reside?

A. Here in Niniltna, Judge.

Q. What is your occupation?

A. Messenger.

Q. *Were you acquainted with Mrs. Angel Beecham?*

A. *Yes, sir.*

Q. *When did you last see her alive?*

A. *Right in her own house, between twelve and twelve-thirty at night.*

Q. *What night?*

A. *The night before they found her dead.*

Q. *So Wednesday after midnight, as she was found dead Thursday night. Where did you see her?*

A. *She was standing under an electric light, reading a paper or looking at something. She had on a pair of glasses.*

Q. *Do you know what kind of glasses?*

A. *No.*

Q. *Were they colored glasses or just clear white glasses?*

A. *Clear glasses.*

Q. *Was she alone when you saw her?*

A. *Yes, so far as I could see.*

Q. *Did you hear any sound in the house at all?*

A. *No, sir.*

Q. *Everything seemed to be quiet there then?*

A. *Yes, sir.*

Q. *Did you take a good look at her then?*

A. *Why, I looked in through the glass as I passed. I was on my way home from work, sir. My wife was waiting up for me.*

Q. *But you saw Mrs. Beecham in passing?*

A. *I looked in through the glass as I passed. There's a little square door with a thin screen curtain on the door, and the blind was up, and I saw her through the thin curtain.*

Q. Did she appear to be excited or nervous or anything of that kind?

A. No.

Q. Had you been there before that night?

A. Oh no, sir. That is, only in passing.

Q. Did you see any person in that house that night before that time?

A. No.

Q. Do you know of any person having been there that night?

A. No.

Q. Do you know from her whether or not she had been having any trouble with anyone?

A. No, sir.

Q. Do you know whether or not she was expecting any trouble?

A. No, sir.

Q. She never told you anything of the sort?

A. No, sir.

Q. Did you as messenger carry her anything to eat?

A. The night before I took her over a dozen oranges.

Q. What night would that be?

A. Tuesday evening.

Q. Did she order the oranges?

A. Well, she was surprised to get them, so I would have to say no.

Q. Someone else ordered them for her?

A. Yes, sir.

Q. Did she say who that someone was?

A. No, sir.

Q. How did you know to pick up the oranges?

A. It was included with other deliveries I picked up at the grocer's. She didn't order them, but they were sent to her direction, and the grocer had me bring them along.

Q. Which grocer is that?

A. Riverview Mercantile.

Q. Did you see anybody in the vicinity of the house at the time you saw Mrs. Beecham through the window between twelve and twelve-thirty?

A. I didn't see anyone near her house. I passed two or three fellows up around the Moose Hall, but it was too dark to tell who they were.

Q. Did you see any person there acting suspiciously at all?

A. No, sir.

Q. No unusual actions?

A. No, sir. Just like you see every night, fellows walking up and down by there.

DR. DAVIDSON, being first duly sworn, testified as follows:

Q. What is your name?

A. Henry Louis Davidson.

Q. What is your profession?

A. Physician and surgeon in the employ of the Kanuyaq Copper Mine.

Q. Were you called to the house of Mrs. Angel Beecham on the evening of the eighth of April of this year?

A. My wife was called, and she found me at the Red Cross Drug Store and sent me down.

Q. Did you recognize the body?

326

A. Yes, it was that of Mrs. Angel Beecham.

Q. Did you make an examination of the body?

A. I did.

Q. What did you find as a result of that examination?

A. I found that the body was cold. Rigor mortis had set in. There was a large gash in the front of the neck, and there was blood on the floor around the head of the victim. It had congealed by that time, of course.

Q. Was there any evidence of a struggle on the part of the woman just before the gash was made in the neck?

A. None that I could see.

Q. Was there any blood spatter over the body?

A. None except around the neighborhood of the wound on the front of the neck.

Q. Would the facial expression of the victim show an awareness of eminent danger?

A. Not necessarily. It did not in this case. The pupils of the eyes were not more than normally dilated.

Q. Now, Doctor, I will ask you to state just what you found as a result of the autopsy.

A. On the neck was a large wound, beginning at the posterior border of the right sterno-cleidomastoid muscle, that is the muscle that is attached here to the edge of the sternum and runs up back of the arm. This muscle on the right side was cut practically through, and the wound extended across the next to the anterior part of the left sterno-cleidomastoid muscle, which muscle on the left side was cut into but not severed on the right side. The length of the wound was five and three-quarter inches.

Q. Was there any way of ascertaining whether the wound was made from left to right or right to left?

A. I think if you will allow me to describe the wound more fully it will answer that question. The sterno-cleido-mastoid muscle, the vagus nerve, common carotid artery, internal jugular vein, external jugular vein, and the small muscles of the anterior part of the neck, in fact all of the structures in front of the sterno-cleido-mastoid muscle are cut, and the spinal cord is partly severed. On the left side of the center line the carotid artery, vagus nerve, internal jugular vein, are cut, the incision extending into the border of the sterno-cleido-mastoid muscle, which is not cut entirely through on this side. The trachea and esophagus are severed, the cartilage of the lower end of the third cervical vertebra had a piece cut off it. It was cut clear and clean as though it had been cut with a very sharp instrument. The muscular tissue lying in front of the fourth cervical vertebra is cut one-half inch below the cut between the third and fourth cervical vertebra. Passing to the right this cut diverges downward.

Q. Diverges downward from what?

A. From the first cut. Mrs. Beecham's throat was cut twice. The blow or blows must have been struck from the right side of the body. The instrument of death must have entered on the right side. The deeper injuries are on that side, and the knife passed through, and when it hit the vertebrae, it gradually edged out from it. The left edge of the wound is not as deep as the right, but tapers off. The second blow starts with the nick in the upper border of the wound.

Q. So you are saying the killer is left-handed?

A. That inference may be drawn, yes, sir.

Q. What else did the autopsy discover?

A. On removing the scalp, a contusion is found in the fascia over the left parietal bone. There was no fracture of the skull that we could see, either of the base of the skull or of the skull cap. In removing the top of skull, the surface of the brain just back of the frontal portion shows a congealed condition of the blood vessels.

Q. What inference may be drawn from this finding, Dr. Davidson?

A. That there had been some blow on the top of the head sufficient to cause insensibility, the blow on the head indicating that it must have been with a blunt instrument, such a wound as could have been inflicted with this stone in the glove.

Q. From your examination of the body what would you say caused her death?

A. The cutting of her throat.

Q. What is your best opinion as to whether the wound in the throat was inflicted after or before she had been struck with the rock in the glove?

A. I should say after.

Q. Why?

A. Because there was still circulation at the time the blow on the skull was struck, to cause the contusions on the fascia and the hemorrhagic spots in the brain matter.

Q. In your opinion, what was the position of the

body when the blow was struck that cut the throat?

A. I think the body was lying on the floor.

Q. Why?

A. There is no staining of the body in front, and no splashing of blood apparent; it evidently just flowed out on the floor. If the body had been elevated, it would have run down, and there would have been stains on the front of the body.

Q. You found no evidence of a struggle?

A. No. The blow on the head must have been struck from behind.

Q. Thank you, Dr. Davidson.

A. I should judge Mrs. Beecham to have been struck down over twelve hours prior to the discovery of her body. Rigor mortis —

Q. Thank you, Dr. Davidson.

A. Rigor mortis was well established. The house was cold and the blood had congealed around the head. Of course a body will cool a little more rapidly when there is no clothing or covering.

Q. Thank you, Dr. Davidson.

[Here the manuscript ends. Nothing further to be found in the Beauchamp inquest file.] Seal of the Archives of the State of Alaska, Juneau, Alaska.

15

The gym was packed when they got there. Nothing draws out a crowd in Bush Alaska like a basketball game. Attention was focused on the floor, where the Kanuyaq Kings were battling out the first half with the Cordova Wolverines. When the buzzer rang, both teams hit the locker rooms bloody but unbowed, a bare five points' difference in the lead. Everyone else got in line for popcorn at the Pep Club booth. Not much had changed since Kate had gone to school here, although her school had been brand-new and this one was more than a little scuffed around the edges.

Somebody got on a microphone. "Ladies and gentlemen, it is my very great privilege to announce that we have both candidates running for the Park senate seat in the house this evening. Pete Heiman, take a bow!" Pete grinned and waved from where he was already working the crowd, shaking hands with elders, winking at every pretty girl, admiring if not actually kissing every baby. There was a wave of polite applause, Kate thought more indicative of the mood Niniltna's five-point lead had given the crowd than of any general approval of the incumbent. "And his challenger, the lovely and talented Miss Anne Gordaoff!"

Anne rose to her feet from the third row of bleachers on the Kanuyaq side, her tight smile indicating she had not missed this relegation to the ranks of beauty-pageant contestant. The applause for her was a little louder but not much. Park rats by definition were cynical when it came to politicians. They would be polite to both candidates and no more. Kate wondered how many of them were registered to vote. She guessed maybe fifty percent, and knew she was being generous.

Jim Chopin was there, standing next to Dandy Mike. For someone who drank most of his meals, Dandy Mike was one good-looking man, muscular, graceful, thick dark hair falling over smiling brown eyes, and a grin with two adorable dimples. He was grinning at her. Her eyes passed over him to Jim, who gave her a cool nod and answered a question asked by Cheryl Jeppsen, one of six or eight women loitering with intent near the two men.

"They'll be here through the half," the voice boomed, which Kate thought was Billy Mike's, "ready to answer any questions you might have. Don't be shy, that's what they're here for." Whoever it was got off the mike, and there were modest surges toward both candidates. Anne made her way down the bleachers and stepped onto the floor. Something further up the bleachers caught Kate's eye, a thin, older man with a Chevron cap tugged low over his eyes. She stared, trying to figure out what seemed odd about him, and then realized he still had his jacket on, a down jacket that should have been far too hot for sitting through an entire basketball game. She started moving toward the bleachers without knowing it.

"Kate?" Dinah said, close behind her. She heard the squeak of tires.

"Stay here, guys," she said, not taking her eyes off the man. She'd seen him before. Where the hell had it been, Ahtna, Cordova? The NRA dinner in Valdez?

She cast a quick look at Jim, who looked up from Cheryl to catch her eye. She jerked her head toward the bleachers and kept going. The gun show in Nabesna?

She came up to the crowd surrounding Anne. "Excuse me," she muttered, twisting between two bodies.

"Well, excuse the hell out of me, too, girl," Old Sam Dementieff drawled, bright eyes curious in his wizened-up face. His nasty grin faded when he took in the expression on her face. "What's wrong?"

"Nothing, probably, but get back, Uncle, okay?" For maybe the millionth time in her life she cursed her height. All she had ever wanted to be was six feet tall, so she could wear three-inch heels and tower over everyone and intimidate the hell out of them. And see over the top of a crowd. She might have made a mistake wading into this one.

The crowd parted for a moment, and she caught sight of the man, descending the bleachers, almost to the floor, his hand pulling out of his pocket. "Gun!" she shouted, and rammed her way forward into the center of the circle, catching a very surprised Anne Gordaoff around the waist and bringing her down to the floor.

There were yells and screams. Jim went past in a streak of blue and gold, nine-millimeter Smith & Wesson drawn and ready. Dandy was right behind him with a .357 in his hand. Old Sam pulled out a Colt .45 that Kate knew for a fact had come over the Chilkoot Trail in 1898 and waved it around and from the floor it looked like someone had rolled out a cannon. Auntie Vi had a .38 and Auntie Balasha a palm-sized automatic that looked like it should have been tucked into a bra. Other weapons were flourished, although nobody seemed to be all that sure which way to point them. Every second person in the crowd was armed, which on a night when everyone would be going home late at a time of year when the bears were still up, in a state where a permit for carrying a concealed weapon was easy to come by, was not very surprising. Kate picked herself up to see

Jim disarming the man she had spotted, who was carrying a handgun she didn't recognize.

"Are you okay?" Jim said to Kate.

"Yeah. What is that?"

He looked down at the gun. "A Glock. Automatic, ten rounds in the clip. Good thing you spotted him. He could have done some damage."

"Who is he?"

"No ID."

"I told you to stay home," Parka Man said to Anne. "But you wouldn't listen, you godless whore."

"Anybody got any duct tape?" Jim said, snapping on the cuffs.

"In my truck," Old Sam said, "on my way."

"Anne!" Darlene cried, and pushed Kate out of the way so roughly that she lost her balance and came down hard on her right elbow. Kate bit back a curse.

Darlene didn't notice, helping Anne to her feet. "Are you okay?"

"Yes, I — yes, I'm fine, Darlene, don't fuss." She winced.

"What? Where are you hurt? Show me!"

"I'm just a little bruised, I think."

Darlene rounded furiously on Kate. "I hired you to protect Anne. You failed. You're fired."

"That's okay," Kate said, "you're under arrest."

"Don't try to change the subject, Kate! I said you're fired and I meant it!"

"Kate," Jim said.

"For the murders of Jeff Hosford and Paula Pawlowski," Kate said. "Not to mention intent to murder me."

"Kate," Jim said again.

"Darlene's maiden name is Turner. Darlene Turner Shelikof."

The name meant nothing to him. It did to Pete Heiman, who had come up to stand behind Jim. "Turner like the bank?"

"Yeah. And Turner like the dance hall girl down to the Northern Light, who got murdered back in April 1915."

There was an electric silence. Darlene's face turned an ugly red and without warning she launched herself at Kate, shrieking, "No! Don't — no, it's not true, it's not true!" She came kicking and punching and caught Kate a good clip on her right elbow. Kate saw a little red herself and snapped out a hand to hook a finger in Darlene's mouth, twisting her cheek hard between finger and thumb. Darlene screamed. Kate pulled her to her knees, and she went down without hesitation. Kate, elbow smarting, kept her there until Old Sam got back with the duct tape.

"No, Darlene!" Anne cried as they taped her wrists together. "Not you, no, you couldn't have done it!"

Darlene smiled, or at least tried to, all the fight gone out of her. "It seems I may have, Anne."

"Don't hurt her," Anne said, sagging against

the wall. "Please don't hurt her."

Jim muscled Darlene and Parka Man out of the gym, which was now filled with the wondering murmur of the crowd. Pete Heiman looked around at the avidly listening crowd and said, "Gee, thanks, Kate."

At that moment two sets of cheerleaders cartwheeled out into the middle of the floor, followed by two teams of basketball players, and the crowd moved on to more important things.

"Explain yourself," Jim said.

They were back in the conference room of the Niniltna Native Association. Darlene was huddled in a chair. Billy Mike and Anne Gordaoff were also present, Billy by virtue of having loaned them the room and Anne because she had insisted. Jim, no fool, knew he was facing down a woman who might one day be voting on the budget for the Alaska Department of Public Safety, so he let her.

Parka Man was handcuffed to the toilet in the men's room. He had displayed a tendency to drool when he yelled, so Jim hadn't gagged him with duct tape for fear he might drown in his own spit. Now and then they could hear him through the air vent, bellowing something about being a tool of God and how the spawn of Satan were interfering with his mission.

Kate folded her hands on the table in front of her, and forbore to look at Darlene, at the red fading to a bruise where Kate had snagged her like a spawning salmon. She didn't like Darlene, she never had, but she'd known her a long time and they'd gone to school together, and, well, there was just something indecent about a strong woman being brought low. That Kate had been the one to bring her low didn't help.

On the other hand, Darlene had committed murder. She had committed grievous bodily harm upon Kate's own person. Kate began to feel better, and took a moment to collect her thoughts.

A Styrofoam cup full of coffee, heavily creamed, appeared at her elbow. She looked up, surprised. "Thanks, Jim."

He served Billy, too; Anne, pale and tight-lipped, waved him aside.

"Darlene Shelikof hired Paula Pawlowski to do research for Anne Gordaoff's campaign." She sipped the coffee; it went down hot and strong and sweet. "What she didn't know was that Paula Pawlowski was a writer as well as a researcher. Darlene told her to look up things about Peter Heiman that Anne Gordaoff could use in her campaign for Pete's office. Moreover, she told Paula to research Anne's family history, too, in case Pete had somebody doing the same thing, so the Gordaoff campaign wouldn't be blindsided by any dirt the other side dug up."

Anne looked at Darlene, who looked at no one.

"I had dinner with Paula Pawlowski in Ahtna before she died. She loved research. She said it was addictive; you couldn't stop once you'd started. Plus she was writing a novel about Alaska, part of which took place during the Gold Rush, and both Anne's and Peter's families have roots in the Gold Rush."

She looked at Jim. "Along the way she found out other stuff, too, like Jeff Hosford was working for a law firm connected to Pete Heiman's campaign, and on instruction from Anne Seese, a partner in that firm who has been sleeping with Pete Heiman since before statehood, he had wooed Erin Gordaoff with a view toward getting a toehold with Anne. That succeeded beyond everyone's wildest dreams; he took up the post of fund-raiser." She looked at Anne. "How'd he do, Anne?"

Anne, looking sick and angry, said, "My daughter's fiancé was good enough for me."

Kate shook her head. "So okay, at first we didn't know who the hell killed Jeff Hosford. We knew anyone working with Eddie P. had to be bent, but there was no evidence and no witnesses.

"His murder probably would never have been solved if Paula Pawlowski hadn't been killed, with the same caliber bullet as Hosford. Although the ME didn't recover enough bullet to make a solid match, I was pretty sure the same gun had done both killings. What I couldn't figure out was, why the hell would anyone want to kill Paula? Jeff Hosford worked for Eddie P. and by definition anyone who works for Eddie P.

is bent like a paper clip, but Paula Pawlowski?"

Kate drank coffee. "Paula was a researcher, for crying out loud. And a grant writer. She dated a history teacher, who was heartbroken to hear of her death. She didn't have any money or any possessions worth stealing, other than a laptop and some notebooks." She looked at Darlene. "It was an accident, wasn't it, Darlene? When she came in from Fairbanks, she told you what she'd found when you saw her at the dinner. You didn't let on how dangerous you thought it was until you went out there in the middle of the night and tried to take the evidence from her at gunpoint. She fought you, though, didn't she? And the gun went off and either you got scared and ran, or the bear Gordy Boothe heard when he brought Paula home showed up and ran you off, and you didn't have enough presence of mind to grab up the laptop on the way."

Kate looked at Jim. "The jails aren't filled with smart people, are they, Jim?"

"We found the laptop hidden on a shelf behind some books," Jim said. "Looked like that was where she always put it when she wasn't working on it. The notes were one shelf down."

Kate looked back at Darlene. "So the following day I go out to Paula's trailer looking for something that could have got her killed. You came, too, still looking for that laptop, and you coldcocked me."

She dared Jim with a glare to add anything to

340

her story. Mutt was sitting next to him, head on his knee, and she whined a little when his hand tightened in her ruff, but he kept his mouth shut.

"So what could be so important that someone would be willing to kill for, not once but twice?" Kate looked back at Anne. "Paula was working for you, Anne. She told me she didn't have any family, and her life was mostly her work. It had to be either the book, or you." She drank coffee. "It turned out to be both."

Anne cast another anxious glance at Darlene, who had curled into as near a fetal position as she could get in her chair. "Look, Kate, I know you want to help, and I appreciate the work you've done, but —"

Kate sliced her right hand in a sideways gesture, and there was something in it that made Anne shut up.

This was what Kate hated most about politicians, the inability to recognize things as they really were instead of how they wanted them to be. "Let's start with the book," she said. She sat back and put her feet up on the shining red-gold surface of the teak table, ignoring Billy's scowl.

"It's a pretty good book. I've read it, what she got done before she was murdered, in a file we recovered from Paula's computer. Well, the most recent draft anyway. It's all about a woman born in France in 1875 who is basically sold into slavery when she is fourteen because her parents are too poor to feed her. She falls into

341

the hands of a gambler and a pimp in Paris, and he brings her to Seattle in 1897 when news of the Klondike strike gets out. There he has the bad judgment to try to win passage money by cheating at five-card draw, and is shot dead at the table."

Jim watched her, blue eyes steady and unwavering. Everyone else was silent, even Darlene, although Kate with a swift glance from beneath her lashes saw that she was still curled up, staring at nothing.

"Our heroine decides that the only way she can make a living is by practicing the only trade she was ever taught, and at that time there was no better place to practice it than the Klondike. So she works the saloons and the dance halls of Seattle for her passage, sails for Dyea, hikes the Chilkoot Trail, and winds up in Dawson City, where on Christmas Eve of 1897 she auctions herself off to the highest-bidding miner from the stage of the Double Eagle Saloon for thirty thousand dollars."

Darlene began moaning again. Kate looked at her and said, "Jesus Christ, Darlene. It was a hundred years ago. She hiked up over the goddamn Chilkoot Trail, she rode the Bennett Rapids, she could have been killed half a dozen times over, all in search of a better life for herself. What is wrong with that? So what if she earned a living on her back. What else was there available to her? She'd been sold into slavery when she was barely into adolescence."

"Wait a minute," Jim said. "We talking about a character in a book, here, or we talking about a real person?"

Kate looked at Anne Gordaoff, and waited.

It was Anne's turn to fold her hands on the table and look fixedly at them. "I think we're talking about my great-grandmother. Aren't we?" She glanced at Kate.

"You tell us."

"I don't know that much about her. She died before I was born."

"She was murdered before you were born, you mean."

Anne nodded.

"Murdered?" Jim said.

"Murdered," Kate said. "Back in April 1915. I've read the inquest, or that part of it that Paula managed to unearth and scan into her computer. She used it as a model for the inquest in her book."

"This is all very interesting," Jim said, "but what has any of this got to do with the murder of Paula Pawlowski?"

"Everything," Kate said, and looked again at Anne. "I thought you did it at first," she said.

"What!" Anne raised a white face.

"I've heard you talk interminably on the stump about the importance of family. I've seen you ignore your husband's constant infidelities, even with your own campaign manager. I watched Hosford with your daughter for one day. He just wasn't that good an actor, and since he was really working for Pete Heiman anyway I'm betting he was equally lousy at raising campaign funds, but you kept him on staff anyway, because he was Erin's fiancé and that made him family. I've heard you say that discipline was the most important gift we can give our children, and then I run a make on your boy Tom, and I see he's wrecked a car once a year for every year he's been driving, and I discover you're still buying his cars and paying his insurance. Your family's a mess, Anne, but they are your family, and you've stuck by them no matter what." Kate paused.

"So when Paula was found murdered, and when I found out that she was writing a novel loosely based on the life of your great-grandmother, one of the all-time great good-time girls, I wondered what you would do to keep that a secret. How far would you go? Would you murder?"

"No!" Anne said, red-faced, angry.

"Sometimes you go too far, Kate," Billy said.

"No," Kate agreed, "but I had help in thinking so. Didn't I, Darlene?"

Darlene, laying the groundwork for a plea of not guilty by reason of insanity, remained curled in her chair staring at nothing.

"What do you mean by that, Kate?" Jim said.

"That last threatening letter. PAY UP OR ILL TELL. And then the discovery of the ream of paper and the envelopes in Paula Pawlowski's trailer. Darlene was trying to make it look like

344

Paula was blackmailing Anne."

"Thus presenting us with a motive for murder," Jim said. "Very neat."

"Very."

There was silence in the room.

"But why?" Anne burst out. She got up and went to kneel in front of Darlene. "Why, Darlene? Did you think my great-grandmother working down to the Northern Light would kill my chance to win?"

Darlene didn't answer.

"It's not your great-grandmother she was worrying about," Kate said.

"Who then?" Anne demanded.

Kate looked at Darlene. "Her great-grandfather. I think he killed your great-grandmother."

"What!"

Kate watched Darlene, who had winced and shuddered. "No no no," she muttered in a constant murmur, "no no no, it's not true, it's not, no no no."

"Did you know your grandmother was murdered?"

Anne shook her head. "Nobody's ever talked about it one way or the other. I found out she worked at the Northern Light from some old health records I found up at the clinic, ones left over from when Kanuyaq Copper was still in operation. They had a whole ledger keeping records of the treatments they prescribed to the good-time girls down at the Light. My great-grandmother's name was one of them."

"Where is it? The ledger?"

Anne flushed. "I burned it."

"That's a shame," Kate said. "Not a crime, I don't think, but a shame to burn something so representative of a time and place. Niniltna was the good-time town for the miners up at the Kanuyaq Copper Mine and Mill. Four miles down the road, they could spend a few hours a week away from the noise and the rock dust, with all the booze and broads they could want. Paula's research turned up records of more than a hundred working girls in Niniltna at one time."

"Darlene?" Anne said.

Darlene didn't move.

"So yes," Kate said, "your great-grandmother was murdered. I think she was very, very good at her profession. I think her clientele was varied and ranged up and down the social scale, to include some of the more prominent movers and shakers of Niniltna in 1915. Remember, it was a town of fifteen hundred then, a positive metropolis by Alaskan Bush standards. They had hot and cold running water, a telephone system, central heating, all the modern conveniences. And of course a court system, with a resident judge, and a federal marshal, and a chief of police. And a district attorney." She looked at Jim. "And they were all buddies with a banker from Fairbanks named Matthew Turner."

"Turner of the Last Frontier Bank Turners?"

"The same."

"You're kidding," Billy said.

"The very same. According to Paula's notes, Matthew Turner owned a bank in Dawson for a while, and then followed the stampeders to Nome, where he opened up a saloon. Angel Beecham worked for him there, so they had something of a history."

"What makes you think he killed her?"

"Okay, a lot of this is guesswork on my part, pieced together from Paula's notes, and I admit filled in with other bits from her book. But the one really damning piece of evidence Paula dug up was a marriage certificate. In 1907, Matthew Turner married one Leonie Angelique Josephine Beauchamp Halvorsen. Angelique Beauchamp. Angel Beecham."

"He married her?"

"It says so in the Fairbanks city records. Celebrated the twenty-second of September 1910. Said ceremony performed by Judge Joseph D. Brittain. Two years before Brittain was transferred to Niniltna, and five years before Brittain conducted the inquest into Angel Beecham's murder."

"A Turner married a prostitute?" Billy Mike couldn't get over it.

"Those gals married up a lot. And into some of Alaska's finest families, too, didn't they, Anne?" Her smile was thin, and Billy and Jim, both listening with varying degrees of reluctant fascination, winced at it. "Handy, having a judge in your pocket."

"When was she killed?"

"April 1915."

"Why kill her?"

"Wait a minute," Anne said. "Matthew Turner married Cecily Doogan."

Kate nodded. "He sure did. And with Peter Heiman and James Seese he went on to found a bank, which looks after my money today." Such as it is, Kate thought. She looked at Billy Mike. Well, she'd probably saved Anne from getting shot by a neo-Nazi Park rat. Maybe her ten grand wasn't totally in the toilet after all.

"But he married Cecily Doogan in 1914," Anne said. "January 1914."

Kate sat up. "What? Are you sure about the dates?"

"Yes. Darlene has all the family marriage certificates in an album. She's very proud of the family, you know."

The irony inherent in Anne's words struck her the same time it did the rest of them, and she flushed.

"Did they have a child?" Kate said. "Does Darlene keep the birth certificates, too?"

"No no no, no no no, don't believe her, none of it's true."

"What?" Anne said.

"Darlene's grandfather, when was he born?"

Anne looked shaken. "Nine months after the marriage. I remember because I heard Darlene's mom laughing about how they just made it under the wire." She tried to smile. "She says she doesn't think the old folks were as prim and proper as the Victorian writers like to make out they were."

"How's that for motive?" Kate said to Jim.

"He was a bigamist," Jim said.

"Indeed he was."

"And if his marriage to Angel Beecham in 1910 was valid, then his marriage to Cecily Doogan wasn't, and that means his children were illegitimate. Unless he married her again, after Angel Beecham was killed."

"I'd like to have heard him explain that to Cecily," Kate said. "And I'd have to look up the state statutes on inheritance, but I would imagine that the children, who inherited Matthew Turner's shares in the Last Frontier, would be very much concerned with maintaining their legitimacy in the eyes of the law, or those shares could go to the real heirs."

"Who would they have been?" Billy Mike said.

"I have no idea," Kate said.

They turned to look at Darlene, who had ceased her mournful lament and had uncurled enough to lay her head on the back of her chair. As they watched, a tear trickled down her cheek. "My father told me, his father told him, his grandfather told his father. I wished he never told me. I didn't want to know, but he said someone had to know so we could be sure it never came out. He said it should have been his son, but he never had a son so it had to be me. I didn't want to know. I didn't want to know."

"What did Paula tell you?" Kate said.

"She came back all excited from Fairbanks, where she was doing some research for the campaign in the library. She said she'd stumbled across the darndest story of the murder of a prostitute in Niniltna. She had a good idea who'd done it, she said, even though the murder was unsolved. She was going to rewrite her book around it, she said. She had to quit, she said, because she had to write her stupid little book!" She sat bolt upright, bellowing out the words.

"I took my pistol out there, and I asked her to turn over her research. She grabbed the gun. I never meant to shoot her. It was her fault. I had my finger on the trigger, and she pulled the gun toward her, and it just went off. I don't know anything about Jeff Hosford; I don't know what you're talking about as far as he's concerned."

Kate remembered something. "Your hair was wet."

Everyone turned to stare at her.

"When you came and got me out of bed to show me the letter, your hair was wet. You'd just gotten out of the shower you took to wash off Paula Pawlowski's blood."

Darlene stared at her, mute.

"And you wrote that last letter, didn't you. Didn't you!"

Darlene flinched.

"You wanted Anne to think that Paula had found out about Angel Beecham, and that she was going to blackmail her to keep that information quiet. That way, it would look like Anne had a motive. Wouldn't it? Wouldn't it!"

"Darlene?" Anne said. "Darlene, say something!"

"Two murders with the same weapon, you knew we'd be looking at the campaign and everybody working on it hard. Anything to diffuse suspicion, even if it fell upon the candidate you had already murdered for in order to keep her in the race. What did you do with the pistol? Toss it in the Kanuyaq?"

"I don't know what you're talking about," Darlene said through stiff lips. "I want a lawyer before I say anything else. You're all out to get me."

Anne, shocked, drew back. "Darlene?"

"Yeah, you're right," Kate said. "I hit myself over the head."

"I don't know anything about that," Darlene repeated.

Yeah, and you don't know anything about how Jeff Hosford died, either, I heard you the first time, Kate thought. "That night in Ahtna when I came to work for Anne, you saw me with Peter Heiman and confronted me in the lobby of the Lodge. Doug broke it up when he came to get you. What was it he said?"

"I don't remember."

Kate's eyes narrowed in thought. "Anne wanted you —" She snapped her fingers. "Of course. Paula had called and wanted you to call her back. What did she want, Darlene?"

"I don't remember. I don't know what you're talking about."

Kate looked at Jim. "Remember Paula's notes?"

"Sure."

"Remember where she scribbled down Pete's and Anne's names and put a circle around them, and connected the circle to Hosford's name?"

"What?" Anne said.

"Yeah?" Jim said, knowing where she was going and willing to play straight man.

"And how we decided it wasn't Anne Gordaoff Paula meant, but Anne Seese, Pete Heiman's sometime girlfriend? And how maybe Anne Seese had loaned Jeff Hosford to Pete Heiman as a spy?"

"I remember that," Jim said.

Kate turned back to Darlene. "I don't suppose that's what Paula's phone call was about, that evening? She found out somehow that Hosford worked for Seese, and that Seese was sleeping with Heiman, and that as a result the Gordaoff campaign might hold no secrets from the Heiman campaign?"

"I don't know what you're talking about," Darlene said.

"And you lured Jeff Hosford out to the van, not a difficult thing to do, and you rode him shotgun, to coin a phrase, and you shot him when his attention was, shall we say, otherwise engaged. Because, like you told me, you'd say or do anything to get Anne elected."

"I don't know what you're talking about,"

Darlene said. "And I said I wanted a lawyer. I get a phone call. It's my right."

"Speaking of phone calls." Kate looked at Jim. "Cell-phone records can be subpoenaed, can't they?"

"They sure can."

"And we'll find a witness, Darlene. We always do. The month I spent watching you work, you were constantly on the move. One minute at Anne's elbow, the next halfway across town buttering up some elder. You had plenty of opportunity to slip away. To murder. We'll find someone. It's just a matter of time."

It seemed that everything had been said, and that it was time to go. They got to their feet, Jim with a firm hand on Darlene's elbow as he urged her forward.

"One more thing, Darlene," Kate said. Everyone stopped and looked at her. Kate looked only at Darlene. "She didn't know."

"What?"

Darlene looked exhausted and wholly unattractive sniffing the snot back into her nose, but Kate had no mercy. "There was nothing in her notes to indicate that Paula Pawlowski knew that Matthew Turner was your great-grandfather. I don't think she even knew that Angel Beecham was Anne's great-grandmother. She was interested in what happened to the people who lived then. She didn't give a damn who their kids were or who their grandkids were. She never bothered to trace the descendants. She didn't know Matthew Turner was your great-grandfather."

Darlene stared up at her.

"You did it all for nothing," Kate told her. "All of it, for nothing. You killed, you committed murder in the first degree, for no reason. Paula didn't know." She turned to the door and added over her shoulder, "I really liked her, Darlene. Paula Pawlowski. I only talked to her once, but it was a long talk, and an interesting one, and I considered her a friend. Just so you know. I'll be Jim's first witness up on the stand."

Darlene's curses followed her out into the night.

16

"There are holes in Angel's inquest you could drive a truck through," Jim said.

Kate nodded. They were at Bobby and Dinah's, sitting over the remains of a moose roast *avec sauce sauvage,* a little recipe Bobby had picked up from a French friend in Vietnam. Kate had never asked about the French friend, if it was *ami* or *amie,* and he never volunteered, but whatever the sex, the French friend had been one hell of a cook. She mopped up the last of the sauce with a piece of bread and let it dissolve on her tongue in sheer delight. Tony's partner, Stanislav, would kill for this recipe.

Jim nodded at the inquest into the death of Angel Beecham, which a week later they'd all had a chance to read. "They never call the husband. Can you believe that? Not only is he a material witness to the scene of the crime, the judge knows he's the deceased's husband because the judge is the guy who married them in Fairbanks, and he never calls him to the stand."

"How about the glove?" Dinah said. "Anybody ever look for its mate? Anybody ever try fitting it on Turner's hand?"

They were all calling her Angel now. Truth to tell, she was more real to them than Paula Pawlowski, something the writer in Paula would have rejoiced at. It was one kind of epitaph, Kate thought.

"What I liked best," she said, swallowing the last of her dinner with reluctance, "was when the judge asked all the witnesses if they knew Angel Beecham, how they all said, 'Oh no, sir, I'm a married man.' " She snorted. "Like the messenger guy who was walking along shopping for a girl, just like they all were, and he says he was on his way home to dinner. And the judge doesn't even question dinner at thirty minutes after midnight."

Ethan, next to Johnny, "I liked the doc best, especially his way of saying, 'The instrument of death' and 'That inference may be drawn, yes, sir.' "

"Yeah, but he's the only one really trying to do his job," Jim said. "I mean, Jesus, Brittain doesn't even ask for a time of death. All that stuff Davidson tries to get in about rigor mortis, the coldness of the house, the congealed blood, and Brittain doesn't ask for a lousy time of death, something any moron in magistrate's robes knows to do before he signs his first warrant."

"Probably because he knows Turner doesn't

356

have an alibi for that time," Ethan said.

"He's covering for one of his own," Bobby said, not without relish. "Feels like the Five O'Clock Follies in Saigon all over again."

Kate noticed that they were speaking of the inquest in the present tense, as if Brittain had taken testimony that day. Jim in particular seemed to be most exercised by the incompetence displayed on the part of the investigating officers. "Brittain cross-examines the milkman and the messenger about who they saw in the street; he makes them, insofar as you were able to in that time and place, admit to being customers of Angel Beecham. The police chief, the federal marshal, nothing like that."

Kate had not known that Jim could get this upset, in particular about a cover-up that had been contrived almost a hundred years before. He was someone she regarded as rather relaxed in his judgments of those who went wrong, at least for a practicing member of law enforcement. He was a good cop, though, and there is nothing a good cop hates more than a bad cop, even if he has been dead for seventy years.

She remembered, some years back, when Roger McAniff had shot all those people, only it turned out he hadn't shot one of them after all. Jim Chopin had had an affair with the odd victim out, who had then dumped him. Following her death he had flown to Anchorage to lay that fact out in front of the investigating officers, one of whom was Jack Morgan. No, if Jim

Chopin had been in Judge Brittain's place, or in Chief Fortson's place, or in Marshal Steward's place, or even in Doctor Davidson's place, he would have forced the truth into the open and slapped the cuffs on Matthew Turner himself.

"Why did he do it?" Dinah said, pushing her plate to one side. "Why did he kill her? Why not just divorce her before he married Cecily?"

"I don't think anyone who does something like that thinks it through rationally," Jim said. "That coshing, as they called it then, the almost ritualistic slitting of the throat. It's totally out of step with making it look like an assault in the middle of a robbery. A robber clobbers, grabs, and runs. This was — this was a ceremony."

"A leave-taking," Dinah suggested.

"Possibly."

"Brittain never asks if she was raped," Kate said. "She was undressed down to her shoes and stockings, with the rest of her clothes neatly hung. The blinds were drawn so no one could see in. She's flat on her back on the floor. And Brittain never asks if there was sexual activity prior to the death."

"Or after," Ethan said with a shudder.

"Maybe he'd stopped by to rip off a piece for old time's sake, or that's what he told her," Kate said.

"Maybe it wasn't the first time he'd done it, either," Bobby said, whisking around the table to pile empty plates in his lap and ferry them to the sink. Katya mumbled something fretful from her crib, and he was there in an instant. Mutt trotted over to stand next to him, head poked over the railing next to his, nose sniffing. Her ruff expanded, she backed up and gave a violent sneeze. "Yeah, I know," Bobby told her, reaching for a clean diaper. "It's a dirty job, but somebody's gotta do it."

Not me. Mutt didn't speak the words out loud but the back of her head going rapidly away in the other direction was very eloquent.

"Bobby's right," Dinah said. "Turner probably visited Angel regularly. He paid for her fancy house."

" 'Fancy house?' " Ethan cocked an eyebrow.

Dinah looked over at the couch, where Johnny, after inhaling his dinner, had ensconced himself with Kate's copy of *The Lost Wagon*. "Fancy woman, fancy house," she said in disapproving accents. Ethan grinned, unabashed. Kate tried to ignore the jolt the grin gave her. Leftover feelings from adolescence could and would be ignored. And then she thought of Jack, and of the last time they had all foregathered in this place, of the day of Bobby and Dinah's wedding and Katya's birth, and she thought her heart would break beneath the pain.

It didn't, of course. Men have died, and worms have eaten them, but not for love. Kate kept breathing in and breathing out; she kept waking early every morning and moving like she had a purpose through every day; she'd even taken on a job in her own field again, and sometimes, if a good-looking man twanged the heart that had once been the personal property of Jack Morgan, why, Jack Morgan himself would be the first to say, "Forward motion, girl, that's all that counts."

Warm hands settled on her shoulders and squeezed once. She looked up, and then had to look down, because the hands belonged to Bobby, seated in his chair, not the ghost whose blue eyes she had for a foolish moment expected to meet.

"Okay?" Bobby said.

She blinked away tears she hadn't known were there. "Okay," she said, and she pretty much was, except for crying in public, a thing she would rather die than do.

He bought her some time by asking Jim Chopin, "What happened to the guy at the gym?"

"Parka Man? He's in jail, where I'm probably going to be able to keep him forever, since he refuses to lawyer up. Says the justice system in this country is a sham and a joke run by niggers and kikes and spics and slopes who look out for their own by putting the screws to all those pure-as-the-driven-snow white folks out there, and he'll go to jail as a martyr before he allows it to make a mockery of his cause."

"Speaking as one of the niggers, albeit one who stays as far away as possible from the justice system," Bobby said, "what is his cause, exactly?"

"Exactly? I'm not sure," Jim said, creasing his brow in an elaborate and failed attempt to act like he really cared. "White supremacy seems a little conservative for the brand of separatism he's preaching. I think you're supposed swim back to Africa, just for starters."

"I've got news for him, I'm not even gonna roll back to Tennessee." Bobby grinned at Dinah, who laughed.

"Anyway, he took it upon himself as an upstanding white folk to discourage Anne's candidacy. He's not entirely stupid; he could read the polls, like all of us he knew she had a good chance to get in."

"So he started writing her letters," Ethan said.

Jim nodded. "Yeah, we found the stationery and the envelopes and the pens up to his cabin."

"What about the last letter?" Kate said.

"Like we figured," Jim said. "The lab came back today with the results. Darlene wrote it."

"She admit it?"

"No. Unlike Mr. Duane Mason, who is eschewing the American legal system in all its forms, Darlene Turner Shelikof has engaged herself an attorney, who has advised her to say nuffin to nobody."

"Who's her attorney?" Kate said.

Jim cocked an eyebrow, and the grin came out, cutting a finned and sinuous wake. "Guess."

She sat back, all thought of Jack and tears forgotten for the moment. "Oh man, tell me you're kidding!"

"What?" Ethan said, looking from one to the other, his expression indicating to anyone who was looking that he didn't particularly care for the fact that Jim and Kate understood each other so well. Dinah smiled down at the table.

Jim was nodding. "None other than good old Eddie P. himself."

Kate shook her head, marveling. "Man, I don't hardly believe this."

"I don't know," Dinah said. "It's all a part of the same story, isn't it? Turner and Seese — and Heiman, the not-so-silent partner — start a bank a hundred years ago. They marry — and murder — and have children and flourish, and their families grow along with the territory and then the state. One of Seese's descendants becomes a lawyer, one of Turner's becomes a political operator, one of Heiman's becomes a legislator. One of them becomes a murderer herself. Full circle. It's Oedipus. It's Hamlet. It's the Duchess of doggone Malfi." She stared off into space with dreamy eyes. "It's going to make for a great documentary, though. I figure two hours, or maybe even a miniseries."

"I knew the call to momhood wouldn't last long," Bobby said, heaving a sigh. Katya mumbled again, and he was at her side like a shot.

"The inquest on Angel Beecham was adjourned with a verdict of foul play by a perpetrator or perpetrators unknown," Kate said. "Matthew Turner's name is never mentioned. This case is still open, Jim."

"Not now, it's not."

"We don't have any evidence. Everybody's

362

dead, and you better believe Eddie P. won't let Darlene do any talking."

He shrugged. Wasn't his case. He'd closed his case.

"I suppose the cover-up was inevitable," Kate said, "given the good-old-boy mentality of the time and Matthew Turner's standing in the community. His bank was the one that stepped in after Barnette's failed and pretty much saved everyone's financial bacon. Cecily Turner hosted President Harding to tea. They named a town after him, for god's sake." She added, "Of course his son blew it by marrying a Native, but what the hell, you can't have everything."

Jim laughed out loud.

"Where is she?" Dinah said. "Angel, I mean. Where is she buried?"

"From what Paula's research shows, she was buried here at first, but later her son had her body moved to Fairbanks. He lived there; I guess he wanted her nearby." She shook her head, marveling. "What a waste. What a god-damned waste. I mean, who cares? Who cares what the founding mothers of our fair state did to get here, to stay here? What else was there to do for a woman back then? Wife, mother, maid, that was it. You were born, you got married, you had a bunch of kids first because there wasn't any way not to and second because the kids were your social security, and then you died, usually way too young, most of the time in childbirth. What did you do if you were a

363

woman and you didn't want that?

"Jesus!" she said in sudden realization. "They couldn't even vote!"

She looked at Dinah, at Bobby, cradling Katya, at Jim and Ethan. "And what is there in one woman's stepping outside that mold and making a living the best way she knew how, what is there in that to be ashamed of today? It wasn't like Lily MacGregor's hands were lily white. She was Angel's landlord. If I had a good-time girl in my family history, I'd shout it from the rooftops."

Jim's smile was slow, warm, understanding. It made her uncomfortable. "Yeah," he said. "You would at that. And you're right. Today is all that matters."

"What? What are you talking about?"

"Today is all that matters," he repeated. "Yesterday's gone, it's history. Who knows what shows up tomorrow."

He looked across the table at her, unsmiling, no attitude, almost a stranger. "Today, here, now. That's all that counts."

Ethan frowned.

Later, when Katya had been fed and rocked back to sleep, when the table had been cleared, the leftovers put away, and the dishes washed, they gathered on couches and chairs in front of the big stone fireplace. It was snowing outside, big fat flakes drifting down to pile themselves into broad, deep drifts. It was a sight Kate saw at the beginning of every new season, but was always astonished by the complete and total change achieved in utter, perfect silence. Trucks would be put away and snow machines brought out. Rakes would be hung up in favor of shovels. Moose and caribou would replace salmon on tables. Drift nets would go into net lofts, and traps would come out to be mended. People would sleep late, and eat too much, and read more, and in many cases drink more, and quarrel more often with their roommates, lovers, and wives, and mark days off on their calendars, counting down to the winter solstice, when once again the sun would begin its six-month climb back into the sky.

"I saw Anne in Ahtna," Jim said, over coffee and Kahlua. "She's still campaigning."

"Think she's got any kind of a chance?" Dinah said.

Kate shrugged. "This is Alaska. We've got legislators who use state funds to screw their mistresses in Denver, and get reelected by a landslide."

"What's a little murder here and there on the campaign trail?" Bobby agreed. "Pete Heiman shouldn't get cocky."

Kate thought back to the last speech she had heard Anne give.

"The buzz phrase for the Nineties was 'taking responsibility,' " Anne Gordaoff had said in a strong voice that was clear to everyone in the senior citizens' center in Ahtna, even those leaning up against the back wall to gossip in low tones.

"We were all supposed to take responsibility for our actions, stop passing the buck." Her voice carried well.

"So then when Alaska Natives try to take responsibility, to assume sovereign rights over their tribal lands and villages and homes, what does the legislature do but appropriate five hundred thousand of our state monies to fight us in the courts? What does the governor of the state do?" She waited a beat for what was becoming the chorus of this campaign tour.

"Tell us!"

"Say it, Anne!"

"Yeah, tell us!"

Anne smiled. "He directs the attorney general of the state of Alaska to sue us all the way to the Supreme Court!"

"Boo!"

"Hiss!"

"Aw, screw'm!"

"I ask you, what are these people so afraid of?" She paused. "And what about subsistence?"

Into the gathering silence the candidate had lowered her voice, causing people to lean forward in their seats, straining to catch her words. Even the gossips in the back stopped to listen.

"The sportsmen's fishing groups, the commercial fishing companies, what do they want? State control of the fisheries. Why? Because they're for-profit operations. We —" she thumped her chest "— we fish to feed our families!" She pointed over their heads to the two doors, propped open to let in the breeze blowing off the Kanuyaq River, a tributary rich with salmon, twisting and turning hundreds of miles from its delta on Prince William Sound to its source deep in the heart of the Quilak Mountains.

"We use the river in customary and traditional ways," she said, more loudly this time, and loud was the roar that acknowledged recognition of those two hot-button words incorporated into Title VIII of the Alaska National Interest Lands Conservation Act of 1980. "We are Natives! We have been fishing these waters for thousands of years! And what does the Alaska legislature say about that?" She dropped her voice again, commanding instant silence.

"They won't let us vote!"

Another roar.

"You know why?" Anne said, managing to be heard without shouting, a neat trick. "I'll tell you why, because they know the vote will go against them! Those white men in Juneau, they know the state wants rural preference! Those white men in Juneau, they know we'll vote to let us fish! Those white men in Juneau, they've taken too much money from those white men in Seattle to back down now!"

Anne Gordaoff had stood, hands folded in demure contrast to her rabble-rousing words, translator at the right edge of the stage, microphone and face in shadow, quick to fill Gordaoff's pauses with the Athabascan and Aleut equivalents, her consonants and gutturals swift and precise and timed to be out of the way when Gordaoff spoke again.

"It's our basic human right to control our own affairs," she told them. "It's our basic civil right to hunt and fish as our grandfathers and grandmothers hunted and fished.

"It's two weeks till the election," Gordaoff said. "When the time comes, I ask you to go to the polls, right here in the Ahtna High School gym, and cast your vote for me. Your interests, your concerns, will be my interests and my concerns in Juneau." She had smiled, raising her chin and giving them the full wattage.

"They already are," Gordaoff said in a softer voice. "I am your daughter. I am your sister. I am your auntie. I am your mother. I will go to Juneau, and I will speak with your voice."

She bowed her head, and a whisper of applause grew to a rumble and then another roar, and she smiled again and bowed herself off the stage. A woman who had been standing stage left beat her hands together, encouraging the audience to keep it up until Gordaoff was down on the floor among them, shaking hands and accepting hugs and greeting nearly everyone by name. They didn't know that her campaign manager was presently a guest of the state of Alaska, and if they did know, they didn't care. She was one of their own.

No, Kate thought now, Pete Heimen had best not rest on his laurels, not yet.

A log cracked and broke in the fireplace,

breaking the silence. Kate looked at Johnny.

He was sitting on the couch between Bobby and Dinah, holding Katya in his lap. She seemed to have fallen in love with him at first sight, and when she woke up, demanded his attention. She got it, too; Johnny was either one of those rare young men who liked babies or who had just taken a liking to this baby in particular. They talked to each other, Johnny in English and Katya in baby talk, appearing to understand each other with no difficulty. It made Kate dread all the more the coming council of war.

She looked at Jim. "You're here in an advisory capacity only."

"Understood," he said.

"It would be better if you weren't here, but we need you, so you are."

"Consider me invisible."

She took a deep breath. "You've met Johnny Morgan."

"I have."

"You've met his mother."

His face didn't change but his voice did. "I have." Johnny looked at him and grinned.

"Johnny Morgan is fourteen. His parents were divorced when he was twelve. His father had custody. When his father died, custody reverted to his mother, and his mother took him to live with her mother in Arizona. As you know, Johnny, Jim is a state trooper. Tell him what you told me."

The grin vanished, and his grip on Katya must have tightened because she uttered an inarticulate protest. "Sorry, Katya," he said, horrified, and resettled her. With an heroic effort Bobby managed to restrain himself from snatching his child to his bosom.

Johnny looked at Jim, making an obvious effort to stay calm, to keep his voice level, above all to present the appearance of someone who was old enough to determine his own destiny. Kate was glad he was holding Katya.

"Like Kate says, my mother took me to Arizona. I went along at first because I was —" his eyes flicked at Kate and away again "— well, because I was upset about Dad." His lips thinned. "Mom went back to Alaska as soon as she dumped me off. Grandma's okay, but she lives in a retirement community, and they're all mad because she's got a kid living with her. She didn't want me with her, and I didn't want to be there. I toughed it out as long as I could. I tried, I really did, Mr. Chopin, but I didn't like her, I hated Arizona, and I missed Alaska, and I just wanted to come home. So I left."

"You ran away from home," Jim said.

"I left," Johnny said stubbornly. "I left to come home." He looked at first surprised and then pleased at his own words. "She caught me the first two times, but the third time I made it all the way back. I came to the Park, to Kate's, and I'm not leaving. I don't care what she says or does or what the law says I have to do, I'm not going back to Arizona!" His voice rose in spite of himself.

"Uh — huh," Jim said thoughtfully. "You can't stick it out till you're sixteen? That's, what, two more years?"

Johnny shook his head, a mulish and mutinous expression on his face. "Can't and won't."

Jim looked at Kate. "So you been hiding him?"

"Yeah."

He looked at Ethan. "And you been helping."

Ethan grinned at Johnny. "Yeah."

"Shit, Jim," Bobby said, "if it comes to that, the whole Park's in on it."

They waited.

"As a matter of law," Jim said, "and as an officer of the court, I am required to return Johnny to his mother, who is his legal guardian."

Johnny flushed red up to the roots of his hair, opened his mouth, encountered Kate's level gaze, and shut it again.

"Are you thinking of pursuing legal guardianship?" Jim asked Kate.

"Yes," she said.

"Don't," he said. "All that does is tell his mother where he is. You'll have to produce him in any court battle, and you'll lose."

"I won't go," Johnny said.

"She already knows he's here," Dinah said.

"Yeah, but she didn't find him."

"And she'll be back," Bobby said. "That bitch has got teeth if I ever saw them; she's got them sunk into this."

"She doesn't care about me," Johnny said

fiercely. "She doesn't care where I live. She just doesn't want me anywhere near Kate. Not even in the same state."

That pretty much summed up Kate's feeling on the matter.

"My dad loved Kate," Johnny said, looking at Kate. She met his eyes. "My dad loved Kate, and my mom hated her for it. She wants me away from her."

Kate couldn't speak. Jim looked at the expression on her face and away again, quickly.

"I'm sorry, Kate," Johnny said.

"I know," she said. "It's all right, Johnny."

He opened his mouth as if to say more, and she shook her head, trying to smile. "It's all right," she said again. "It's okay. I understand."

There was a brief silence. Kate thought of the copy machine she had found when she had burgled Jane's residence in Muldoon, what was it, two years ago now. She'd figured then that Jane, who worked for the federal government in a department that allocated bids, had secretly been bringing bids home, copying them, and selling them to competitors. She could go to Anchorage, investigate, prove it.

She looked at Johnny, sitting on Bobby and Dinah's couch with a lapful of Katya.

No, she couldn't.

"It's a big Park," Bobby said. "We'll keep an eye out, make George watch for incoming moms. For the moment, best he stay with Ethan. She knows where Kate lives now."

"Works for me," Ethan said. "Okay with you, kid?"

Johnny nodded, face taut with hope.

"If George spots her coming, we'll shuttle Johnny around some. He can stay here, at Auntie Vi's; Bernie'll be glad to take him in for a while. Old Sam. Demetri. Billy and Annie Mike are running a boarding house for every stray kid in the Park now as it is, one more and Annie's cup runneth over." Bobby looked around and demanded, "I mean, how long can Jane Morgan keep this up? I'm assuming she's not independently wealthy; she's got a job she has to go to. She can't be out here all the time, and in two years Johnny will be sixteen and on his own, if he so chooses."

"I do," Johnny said.

"What if Jane shows up at the school?" Kate said.

"I don't have to go to school," Johnny said.

"Dream on, kid," Dinah said.

Johnny, who Kate had only just discovered had an enormous crush on Dinah, blushed at being directly addressed by his dream woman.

"Same thing," Ethan said. "If George spots her coming, he gets to the school himself or sends someone ahead to get Johnny out and gone." He added, "Who's teaching up to the school nowadays?"

"It's a pretty good group," Dinah said. "There's even one local, Billy Mike's oldest girl, who brought her degree home. She's teaching fourth and fifth grades."

"And Bernie's up there all the time coaching," Bobby said.

Kate looked at Jim. "What happens if she gets through us?"

"I give her the slip and get back the fastest way I can," Johnny said promptly.

Jim looked from Kate to Johnny and back again.

"Don't let her get through you," he said.

They were snowed in but nobody minded, and there were enough sleeping bags to go around. Bobby built up the fire and retired to the big bed in the back, where he could be heard making lecherous noises in Dinah's direction. She giggled and told him to behave, and he did, mostly. Johnny, sleeping the untroubled and dreamless sleep of those who have absolute faith in their friends, lay curled in a corner with his head on Mutt's flank.

Kate went out on the porch to breathe deeply of cold, fresh air. She moved to the top step, out from under the eaves. Snow melted beneath her bare feet, searing her soles with cold fire. It fell on her upturned face, cool, melting kisses that seemed to sink beneath her skin and become part of the blood moving slowly and steadily through her veins.

The door opened, and she looked up to meet Ethan's eyes. He pulled the door shut behind him and walked forward. In silence, he took her hand and pulled her up to the porch. In silence, he took her place on the top step, which put his head on a level with hers. They were so close that she could feel the heat of his body.

"So the kid stays with me?"

Asked and answered, she thought, but replied, "For now."

"Fine by me." He raised a hand to smooth her eyebrows, tuck a strand of hair behind her ear, trace the line of her lips. She watched him through lashes heavy with snow. "At school, that thing with Darlene."

She waited.

"It didn't mean anything. She saw that you wanted me, so she wanted me, too. That was Darlene all over."

"So it was all Darlene's fault?"

"Oh hell," Ethan said, disgusted. "You just won't let me lie, will you."

It was a rhetorical question, and Kate's only answer was the tiny smile at the corners of her mouth.

He grinned. "The truth was, I was hornier than a bull moose in rut," he said, "and I wasn't having any luck with you. She came to my room and offered it up, and I wasn't about to turn it down."

"That's more like it."

His grin faded. "Okay, that was then. Seventeen years ago, I was just a kid being led around by my dick. Today I'm older, and maybe a little smarter. You want to give this another shot?"

It was his turn to wait. "Kate?"

She opened her mouth, and closed it again. "I don't — Jack was — I'm not —" She gave her head a tiny shake, annoyed with her inability to say what she felt, to give him an answer.

"I admit," he said, "this whole Kate-and-Jack thing. It's intimidating as hell. I only saw you guys together a couple of times, but when I did it was like you were reading each other's minds. Margaret and I — well, it was nothing like that with Margaret. Maybe I'm jealous."

He watched her for a long moment, and she waited for him to go back inside the house. Instead he bent his head, taking his time, giving her a chance to step away.

She didn't.

On the other side of the window, Jim Chopin stood, watching, as his hands clenched into slow, heavy fists.

Epitaph

Fairbanks

Unkempt, neglected, forgotten, abandoned to the privations of elements and time. Markers made from rounds of wood sliced from a downed tree, splitting with age and decay so that the words carved upon them are hardly legible.

Each successive autumn another untended drift of leaf and bracken falls; the white picket fence has long disintegrated; a clump of diamond willow suffers from the attention of every wandering moose; the mounds of the dead have been overtaken by the wild rose and the devil's club. Black hairs from a passing bear stick in the sap of a living spruce tree's trunk where he has rubbed against it, more than once. The sunshine caresses equally the golden leaves of the aspen and the deep red stalks of the fireweed, as both stir slightly in the merest breath of a wind that as yet carries no hint of the winter soon to come.

The sound of an engine is heard, stops, a door opens, closes, footsteps approach. Grass yellow from age and a dry summer crackles underfoot. The chickadees cease their song, and wait, and watch.

A woman picks her way through the trees, a beast with yellow eyes and silver fur pacing at her side. They stop at the edge of what is no longer a clearing. The woman's shoulders slump in momentary defeat as she looks around at the crowded trees, the thickness of the brush, the height of the grass that obscures what lies beneath.

Her shoulders straighten. Stepping with care, she seeks out each remaining marker, one by one, pulling the foliage away so as to see what there is left to read. Her short cap of hair gleams raven's wing black in the light; the rich nut brown of her skin takes on an added glow of exertion from the warmth of the day, a deeper color from the heat of the sun. Her companion sits, motionless and silent at the edge of the clearing, ears flickering to follow each sound, alert, vigilant, patient. A magpie comes scolding into the clearing and, seeing them, departs at once. The three ravens roosting high above in the cottonwood keep their own counsel.

The edges of the words have been eaten away by weather and insects, but some may still be read by those who take the trouble to seek them out. "Valentine Carlyle, Faithful Servant and Friend, born Glasgow, Scotland, 1882, died Fairbanks, Alaska . . ." year illegible. "John O'Henry," or is it O'Malley, "Bachelor, Miner, born 1893, died 1920, Jeremiah 17:17," or it might be 19:19. "George Washington Smith, born Savannah, Georgia 1837, died Fairbanks, Alaska 1917, The Secret of Freedom a Brave Heart."

The sun travels across the circle of blue sky and into the tops of the trees, and the shadows they cast outline a marker unnoticed before, a marker placed beneath a rose bush that has flourished to command its corner of this undisciplined garden. It is different from the other, wilder roses, as a last bloom testifies in hanging its heavy head to shed blood-red petals on the upturned faces of tiny blue flowers carpeting the mound beneath. The sweet perfume is a caress of the skin, a lure to the senses.

The woman kneels before the marker, a round slice of spruce trunk with bits of bark still clinging to its sides; the face planed and sanded smooth once, warped now, split; the letters and numbers rotted through almost to the other side, but they were well executed to begin with, and the slab is by comparison to its fellows easy to decipher. Many words, of this life much to say. "Here lies Leonie Angelique Josephine Beauchamp Halvorsen, born Melun, France 1875, died Niniltna, Alaska 1915."

And nothing else, except — yes, lower down on the slab there are more words, hidden where the stiff dry grass has grown so thick. The woman pulls the marker from the ground with great care, for fear it will break in her hands.

The tenacious roots cling, and the marker falls to pieces anyway and must be put together like the puzzle it is.

She carries them one at a time to where a last ray of sunlight illuminates a small patch of grass, still green and cropped close by the Arctic hare peering at her from beneath a hemlock. The light disappears into the letters shaped long ago by a loving hand. The remnants of white paint help draw them forth from the shade into the bold statement of a life.

Here lies
Leonie Angelique Josephine
Beauchamp Halvorsen
Born Melun, France 1875
Died Niniltna, Alaska 1915
Beloved wife of Sam Halvorsen
Beloved mother of Percy Halvorsen
Beloved grandmother of
Leonie Halvorsen Gordaoff
and Angelique Halvorsen Shugak

And in letters smallest of all, placed where they are least likely to be noticed once the slab is in the ground, unless you know they are there and look for them, are the words

A Darling Girl

High up in the bough of a tree a bird, smaller than all the rest, trills out three pure, clear notes on a descending scale.

The woman raises her face into the last rays of the setting sun, and she smiles.